Friends at
Thrush Green

* * *

Miss Read

Illustrated by J. S. Goodall

An Orion paperback

First published in Great Britain in 1990
by Michael Joseph Ltd
This paperback edition published in 2009
by Orion Books Ltd
Orion House, 5 Upper St Martin's Lane,
London WC2H 9EA

An Hachette UK company

1 3 5 7 9 10 8 6 4 2

A CIP catalogue record for this book is available
from the British Library.

ISBN 978 0 7528 8425 7

Typeset at the Spartan Press Ltd,
Lymington, Hants

Printed and bound in Great Britain by
Clays Ltd, St Ives plc

The Orion Publishing Group's policy is to use papers that
are natural, renewable and recyclable products and
made from wood grown in sustainable forests. The logging
and manufacturing processes are expected to conform to
the environmental regulations of the country of origin.

www.orionbooks.co.uk

To Chris
with love

CONTENTS

* * *

1. Friends Return

'It is an extraordinary thing,' said Harold Shoosmith one breakfast time, 'but I seem to have lost my reading glasses.'

'I shouldn't call that "an extraordinary thing",' replied his wife Isobel. 'You lose your glasses six times a day on average.'

There was a commotion at the front door.

'Ah! That's Willie Marchant with the post,' said Harold, hurrying into the hall to escape his wife's censure. He returned with a handful of envelopes and began to sort them at the table, holding each at arm's length the better to see.

'Yours, mine, junk. Junk, junk, yours, mine, junk, yours.'

'Junk always gets the biggest pile,' commented Isobel, beginning to slit open her own three envelopes. 'When you think of all the trees that are cut down to end up as junk mail which nobody bothers to open, it really makes one livid.'

She glanced at her husband who was now peering with screwed-up eyes at a lengthy form.

'Do go and get your glasses. Try the bathroom window-sill.'

'Why on earth should they be there?'

'Because I saw you put on your glasses in the bedroom to see the time, and you then went straight to the bathroom, and I haven't seen you wearing them since.'

'Want to bet on it?' said Harold smiling.

'No. I'd hate to see you lose.'

She heard him overhead, and he soon reappeared wearing his spectacles.

'You were spot on, my love. Bathroom window-sill it was.'

They applied themselves to their respective letters, and coffee cups, in silence.

It was broken by Isobel's cry of delight.

'Now here's some good news. Dorothy and Agnes hope to visit Thrush Green next month. "We can easily put up in Lulling or at The Two Pheasants, and we shouldn't dream of imposing ourselves on you and Harold as you so kindly suggest, but of course we hope to see a great deal of you both and our other Thrush Green friends." What a pair of poppets they are! Won't it be lovely to see them again?'

'It will indeed,' agreed Harold, still studying his form. 'I can't make head nor tail of this bally thing. It says at the beginning "Consult your solicitor if in any doubt", and I think that's exactly what I shall do.' He folded it up and thrust it back into its envelope. 'I wonder why you always get the nice letters and I get the dreary ones,' he remarked.

But Isobel was too immersed in her letter to reply.

Later that morning, she dwelt upon the future visit of her old friends as she went about her household tasks.

Miss Dorothy Watson and Miss Agnes Fogerty had been their neighbours at Thrush Green ever since she had married Harold. Dorothy was headmistress of the junior and infant school next door, and Agnes was her loyal assistant.

In fact, it was through little Agnes Fogerty that Isobel had met Harold. She and Agnes had been at a teachers' training college many years earlier, and the two had always kept in touch. When Isobel's first husband died, she had visited Agnes and decided to look for a small house somewhere near her old friend, and in that part of the Cotswolds which she had known all her life.

The two friends, though much the same age, were poles apart in looks and temperament. Little Agnes Fogerty was only an inch or so over five feet. Her soft hair was smoothed back into a bun on the nape of her neck. Spectacles covered her kind weak eyes, and the clothes she wore were in the gentle hues of fawn and brown, as inconspicuous as her retiring nature. She had spent many years in the infants' class of Thrush Green school, and was held in great affection and respect by pupils and parents.

Isobel had always been pretty: her blue eyes sparkled, her fair hair curled, and even now in her fifties, she remained trim of figure and youthfully energetic.

In the months after the death of her first husband, her manner was subdued as she struggled to get over her loss. Agnes's quiet sympathy did a great deal to help her, and the kindness of her Thrush Green friends was an added support.

But it was Harold Shoosmith, a relative newcomer himself to Thrush Green, who proved such a staunch friend. He insisted on accompanying her on many of her house-hunting forays, knowing only too well from his own recent experiences how depressing and exhausting such undertakings can be.

Over the months the friendship grew deeper, and when Harold asked her to marry him, it was, as Isobel mischievously put it, 'the answer to all that house-hunting'; the two had settled down in Harold's house on Thrush Green, to their own delight and that of their friends.

When the two schoolteachers had decided to retire together, the Shoosmiths knew that not only would they miss them sorely but that they would have new neighbours in the school house next door. Until that time, the headteacher of the school had always lived in the school house, but now the education authority had decided to sell the property.

The new headmaster owned a house some twenty miles away, and was quite prepared to make the journey daily. He had two young children who were doing well at their present school, and his wife was happy in their house. It seemed pointless to uproot the whole family to live in a house which needed to have a great deal done to it. In any case, the thought of finding the money for Thrush Green's school house was a daunting one. He decided to let things remain as they were while he tackled his new job.

The travelling did not worry him, nor did the challenge of fresh problems at the school. But he was a little anxious about his wife's health, and hoped that the length of time he would have to spend away from her each day would not depress her.

She had been left rather frail after the birth of their second child, now aged six, and relied – rather too heavily, some of their friends thought privately – upon the cheerful willingness of her husband. She could do no wrong in his eyes, and he was blind to the fact that, like so many apparently gentle and fragile wives, she had an inner core of selfishness which relished dominating her very kind-hearted partner.

Harold and Isobel had invited them to supper soon after Alan Lester had taken up his duties at the school, and agreed that they were a 'nice couple' as they waved them goodbye. They did not see Mrs Lester again but often spoke to Alan, and liked him more and more as the weeks passed.

The school house remained empty throughout the winter, but just before Easter it was bought by a young and obviously prosperous couple called Angela and Piers Finch.

They were an exuberant pair and had great plans for enlarging the house. All through the summer they appeared at odd times in an old but dashing scarlet MG car which scandalized Thrush Green with its noise. They spent several weekends at the house, 'slumming' as they called it, while they pored over detailed plans, tidied the garden, lunched at The Two Pheasants, and visited Harold and Isobel next door.

Isobel found them exhilarating, enjoyed their chatter, and was much touched by the expensive flowers and chocolates with which they showered her.

Harold found them excessively tiring. It seemed to him that they always descended upon them just as he was settling down to read or to listen to music. He viewed their future proximity with some misgiving, especially as their plans to enlarge the modest house were being drawn up with a family in view.

But no actual building began, as it happened, and in the autumn the Finch couple arrived on the Shoosmiths' doorstep with surprising news: he had been posted overseas by his export firm at a salary which staggered Harold, and they were to fly out in a month's time to take up the appointment.

The school house at Thrush Green was on the market again.

Its fate, of course, was a constant source of speculation and surmise among the inhabitants of Thrush Green.

Mr Jones of The Two Pheasants hoped that it would be made into offices so that the staff would visit his establishment for lunch. Albert Piggott, the morose sexton of St Andrew's church on the green and one of Mr Jones's regular customers, was of the opinion that a decent, quiet couple would be best there.

'None of these 'ere yuppies, like that jazzy pair as bought it. Thrush Green don't want that sort.'

'Well, they was free with their money,' pointed out his old crony Percy Hodge, over their half pints. 'Give me three quid for a load of farm muck.'

'More fool them,' growled Albert.

Winnie Bailey, the doctor's widow who lived across the green, wondered if her nephew Richard would like to try his luck again.

'Not a hope,' he told her on the telephone. 'I'd love to live on Thrush Green, as you know, but I can't prise Fenella from London and the art gallery.'

The Reverend Charles Henstock who had the church of St Andrew's in his care, hoped that whoever took the house would support the church he knew so well, and his wife Dimity added her hope that children might live at the old school house, as it was so handy for the school next door.

And so the speculation continued, while the little house stood empty.

It was Betty Bell, the exuberant woman who kept the school clean and also charged round the Shoosmiths' house twice a week, bringing them up to date with village gossip, who came nearest to the mark.

'It'd never surprise me,' she said, unwinding the flex of the vacuum cleaner from the figure-of-eight pattern which so irked Harold, 'to hear as Mr Lester came to live next door. Real handy for the school it would be, wouldn't it?'

'He prefers to stay in his present place, I gather,' said Harold. Was it worth trying, yet again, to get Betty to wind the flex straight up and down to withstand the strain of these contortions? He decided it would be a waste of time. She liked a good tight figure-of-eight finish to her vaccuming labours, and that was that.

'It would be nice to have the Lesters next door,' conceded Isobel, 'but I should think it most unlikely. He thought about it all when he took on the post. I shouldn't think he would change his mind.'

'Ah well,' agreed Betty, crashing the vaccum cleaner against the skirting board and bending to pick up a flake or two of paint with a licked finger, 'time will tell, won't it?'

Meanwhile, news of the approaching visit of Dorothy Watson and Agnes Fogerty to their old haunts overshadowed the problematical future of the school house, which had once been the home of the two retired ladies.

Charles Henstock and his wife Dimity discussed the matter as they pottered about the lovely garden at their vicarage in the Cotswold town of Lulling, only a mile away from Thrush Green, where they had started their married life.

Dimity had shared a cottage for many years with her friend Ella Bembridge, and was still a frequent visitor. Charles Henstock had been a widower for a number of years, and lived opposite Ella and Dimity's cottage in a bleak and hideous rectory, grudgingly looked after by a formidable housekeeper.

On her marriage, Dimity had forsaken her snug quarters with Ella to share the rigours of life at Thrush Green rectory with her adored Charles; the housekeeper had returned to her native Scotland, to the relief of everyone at Thrush Green.

A year or two later, whilst Charles and Dimity were on holiday, a fire broke out at the empty rectory and it was gutted. No one mourned its loss except Charles, who had never really noticed its ugliness, its discomforts and its incongruity amongst so many lovely Thrush Green buildings.

On its site, 'arising like a phoenix from the ashes', as someone said dramatically, appeared a pleasant group of homes for old people, designed by the local architect Edward Young. He himself lived, with his wife Joan, in the most handsome house on the green, and the view of the Victorian rectory had annoyed him for years. The sight of the smoking remains after the night of the fire had given him acute satisfaction.

The Henstocks had spent several months in lodgings nearby but moved into the lovely Queen Anne vicarage at Lulling within the year. It was a great joy to Charles to find that he would still be looking after his old parishioners at Thrush Green, Lulling Woods and Nidden, as well as the more important and larger parish of Lulling in which he and Dimity now lived.

It was a morning in early May when they first heard that their old friends Dorothy and Agnes were coming back to Thrush Green for a week's visit.

The lawn was wet with a heavy dew. A pair of blackbirds ran about collecting food for their family nearby; a lark was greeting the sun with an ecstasy of song, and the great copper beech tree at the end of the garden was turning auburn with young leaves.

'They couldn't come at a lovelier time,' said Dimity. 'May is the best month in the year.'

Her husband straightened up from his weeding, a bunch of chickweed in his hand. His plump, pink face was thoughtful.

'I think I prefer April. Nearly always get Easter then. All those daffodils, and life renewed, and such a *festival of hope*, I always feel.'

Not for the first time Dimity was reminded of how closely woven into his life was her husband's religion.

'But May is *warmer*,' she pointed out, 'and the evenings are longer, and there are far more varieties of flowers to pick.'

7

'Do you think Dorothy and Agnes will go picking flowers?'

'They'll probably be visiting local gardens open to the public. I know that's the sort of thing they promised themselves when they retired to Barton-on-Sea.'

'Well, we can't compete with Hidcote or Stourhead,' commented Charles, 'but I hope they will visit Lulling Vicarage garden while they're here.'

It was Ella Bembridge, Dimity's old friend, who first mentioned the approaching visit to the Misses Lovelock. These three ancient sisters lived in a fine house in Lulling High Street, and from it they kept their sharp eyes upon the affairs of the town in which they had been born.

Ella had entered the local tea-room, known as The Fuchsia Bush, in search of a much-needed cup of coffee after carrying a heavy box of petunia plants the length of the High Street. She found the three sisters debating the merits of a fruit cake, which would last for several teatimes if the slices were cut thinly, or three scones, one apiece, slit and buttered sparingly, for that day's repast.

'I should take both,' advised Ella robustly. 'The fruit cake will last for days. Save you hunting about tomorrow.'

The sisters looked at each other. Bertha and Ada were obviously shocked by such wanton extravagance but before the protestations could flow, Violet, who was the youngest of the three and still in her seventies, nodded her approval.

'Such a good idea, Ella. Let's do that.'

She called across to one of The Fuchsia Bush's lethargic assistants who was picking little pieces of fluff from the mauve and red overall in which all the staff were arrayed, in deference to the flower named over the establishment's bow window.

The girl came across unhurriedly, looking extremely bored.

'Three scones, please,' said Violet briskly, 'with plenty of sultanas in them, and that small fruit cake. Now, how much is that?'

As she fumbled in her purse, surveyed by her two sisters, Ella broke in.

'I'm in here for coffee,' she said, heaving the petunias on to a chair. 'Come and join me.'

'We really should be getting back,' murmured Ada.

'My treat,' said Ella. 'You gave me coffee the other day, remember?'

'Well,' said Bertha graciously, 'that is most kind of you. Coffee would be very welcome, wouldn't it?'

The four settled themselves at the somewhat wobbly table and Rosa, the languid waitress, exerted herself enough to make her way into the kitchen with their order.

It was then that Ella mentioned the visit of Dorothy Watson and Agnes Fogerty.

'How nice,' said Ada. 'I know that Charles and Dimity know them well, but somehow we never came across them.'

'Not *socially*,' added Bertha.

'But of course we know them *by sight*,' said Violet.

'And heard what excellent women they were,' agreed Ada.

'Well then,' said Ella – she began to roll one of her deplorable cigarettes, but thought better of it in present company, and returned the tin containing papers and tobacco to her pocket – 'you *do* know them.'

'By *sight* and *hearsay*,' explained Bertha. 'They never came to the house.'

Ella's face must have expressed the astonishment she felt, for Violet, rather more in touch with life than her venerable sisters, spoke hastily.

'You see, the two teachers were working so much of the time.'

'But *I'm* working,' protested Ella, 'at my handiwork, of one sort and another, and you invite me to your house.'

'You are in *The Arts*,' said Bertha kindly. 'Father always encouraged artistic people. He was devoted to William Morris's principles.'

'And some of the professional people came too,' put in Bertha. 'We often had the vicar to tea, and that nice doctor whose cousin was Lord Somebody-or-other. Father was very broad-minded.'

'What about your dentist?' asked Ella, now thoroughly intrigued by these bygone niceties of social distinction.

Bertha drew herself up. 'One did not meet one's dentist *socially* in those days.'

'The very idea!' said Ada, scandalized.

'Good! Here's the coffee,' said Violet, as Rosa emerged from the kitchen. She sounded relieved.

'I think I could do with a biscuit,' said Ella, looking somewhat shaken at her friends' disclosures of times past. 'Will you join me?'

The ladies accepted with smiles and Rosa, sighing, returned to the kitchen.

'That lot in there,' she said to Nelly Piggott, who was in charge of The Fuchsia Bush kitchen, 'wants a plate of biscuits now. Fair livin' it up today them Lovelocks. I bet Miss Bembridge foots the bill.'

'It's no business of yours who foots the bill, my girl,' responded Nelly. 'It's all money in the till, and that's where your wages comes from, don't forget.'

She watched Rosa rummage in the large biscuit tin to find suitable provender for the four ladies.

'Them custard creams and bourbons are all right, and a few little wafer biscuits, but have a heart, girl, who's going to crunch gingernuts at their age?'

She whisked away the offending gingernuts, added two slender chocolate sticks, inspected the completed plate, and pushed Rosa towards the door.

'There you are! Look lively!' she exhorted.

She watched the door swing back.

'Might as well save my breath,' said Nelly, returning to the sink.

2. LOOKING AHEAD

Nelly Piggott was the wife of Albert Piggott, who was the official sexton of St Andrew's church. She had been a buxom widow when she married Albert some years earlier. If anything, she was now even more buxom, with her passion for cooking both at her place of work and in her small kitchen at their Thrush Green house.

She had little encouragement from Albert when she presented him with succulent pork pies, steak-and-kidney puddings and rich trifles, for Albert's digestive system had been ruined by the steady imbibement of alcohol over the years. Dr Lovell had forbidden a rich diet, as well as the alcohol, but Nelly was incapable of curbing her hand when it came to butter, cream and eggs in her delicious concoctions.

The kitchen at The Fuchsia Bush gave her more scope. She had started as a temporary help when Mrs Peters, the owner of the establishment, pleaded with her 'to help out for a week or two'.

So successfully had she helped that she was soon working there permanently and Mrs Peters, seeing her value, later made her a partner. It was Nelly's salary which kept the Piggotts' establishment going, for Albert worked less and less, partly through natural idleness, but also because of failing health.

Their household arrangements suited Albert perfectly. Nelly left home soon after eight and was back some time between five and six. She had her lunch at the kitchen table at The Fuchsia Bush with the rest of the staff, and Albert was left with a meal for midday. Usually he did not bother to eat the food provided, but went next door for a pint of beer, some bread and cheese with pickled eggs or onions, and a good gossip with his cronies.

On this particular May morning he found Percy Hodge already ensconced in the window seat with half a pint of bitter before him on the table. He went to join him, lowering his ancient limbs carefully.

'Ah, Perce! How's things?' he asked, when he had got his breath back.

'Rotten! I'm thinkin' of sellin' up the farm.'

'What again?'

'Two of me heifers gone lame this mornin'. The pony's kicked a gate flat, an' a fox bin and got 'alf a dozen hens in the night.'

'You don't say!'

'What's more, Willie Marchant brought me up a 'alf 'undred of forms from the Min of Ag in today's post. Don't understand one word in ten, an' that's the truth.'

Mr Jones, the landlord, put Albert's usual before him without a word. The two customers sipped noisily, and with much smacking of lips.

'You needs somethin' to cheer you up,' said Albert lugubriously. He replaced his glass carefully exactly upon the wet ring which it had made on the table. 'Take that girl of yours out,' he continued.

Percy grunted. 'Thought you didn't take to the Cooke family.'

'Nor I don't, but if you're fool enough to take up with one of 'em you may as well enjoy it,' said Albert.

Silence fell. The distant sound of children playing at the school next door could be heard above the rumble of beer barrels being rolled down into Mr Jones's cellar from a lorry outside.

'I hear as that new headmaster is thinkin' of livin' at Miss Watson's,' said Percy, changing the subject from his unsatisfactory love-life. The school house was destined to remain 'Miss Watson's' for a long time to come: at Thrush Green, as in most country places, houses are not known by the names on their gates, but by the owners who live, or once lived, in them.

'I heard as he was all set to stay in his own place,' said Albert. 'He'd have bought Miss Watson's when he took over the school, surely. I bet the price has gone up since them young flibbettigibits bought it.'

The thought appeared to give both men some satisfaction.

'Well, now his wife's bad,' said Percy, 'so I was told.'

'Is she now?' Albert became quite animated. 'What's she got? Nothing serious, I hope, with two young children to leave.'

The afflictions of other people were almost as interesting as Albert's own, but never, of course, so severe.

'I dunno,' said Percy, losing interest. He picked up the two empty glasses, wiped his mouth on his coat cuff, and made for the bar.

Albert waited hopefully for a possible refill. He was unlucky.

Percy made for the door. 'Best be gettin' back. Plenty of trouble up the farm today.'

'Sooner you sells it the better,' rejoined Albert nastily, watching his companion vanishing through the door.

When Nelly came home that evening, Albert told her about Percy's disclosure.

'Funny you should say that,' commented Nelly, busily turning liver about in a sizzling frying-pan. 'Rosa at the shop said her auntie had heard the same. Wonder if it's true?'

'No smoke without fire,' quoted Albert. He was rather proud of his erudition, and repeated the adage rather louder. Nelly took no notice.

'I could do with a rasher with that,' he said, changing his tactics.

'A rasher you won't get,' responded Nelly, 'but I'll pop an egg in for you.'

Over their meal at the kitchen table Nelly reverted again to the news they had both heard.

'You can't believe all Perce Hodge says,' said Nelly, 'but

Rosa's auntie now, she's a different kettle of fish. Strict Baptist, teetotal, and not given to tittle-tattle. I'll lay there's something in this rumour.'

'Be handy for you if they wanted a bit of charring done if his wife's poorly,' observed Albert. 'Practically next door, ain't it?'

Nelly surveyed him coldly. 'I've got more than enough down The Fuchsia Bush,' she pointed out, mopping up the liver gravy with a piece of bread, 'but there's no reason why you shouldn't take on a bit of gardening at Miss Watson's. Lord knows you've plenty of time to spare, and it might keep you out of The Two Pheasants now and again.'

She began to clear the table, bustling about the kitchen with renewed energy.

Albert sat himself morosely in the wooden arm chair, and picked up the newspaper.

'FIGHTING BREAKS OUT AGAIN' said the headline.

It seemed fair comment.

On that same evening, across the green, Ella and her friend Dimity Henstock were busy packing pots of young geraniums into a cardboard box.

'I don't care what people say,' declared Ella, through a haze of blue smoke rising from the dishevelled cigarette in the corner of her mouth, 'but I like scarlet geraniums better than any.'

'Very cheerful,' agreed Dimity.

'I've only lost two cuttings this year,' went on Ella, 'and they were some wishy-washy pink things Muriel Fuller gave me. These are much hardier. How many can you do with, Dim?'

'Twelve would be fine. Fifteen if you can spare them.'

'More than welcome. Glad to get 'em off the window-sills. We'll put the box in the porch then Charles can pick 'em up tomorrow. I've got to go to the dentist, but remind Charles where the spare key is. I still put it under the flint with the hole in it by the front step.'

'I should think all Thrush Green knows that hiding place,'

commented Dimity as they settled themselves in the sitting-room.

'Never thought of that,' said Ella. 'Not that I mind Thrush Green knowing, just the bad lots from elsewhere. Perhaps I should move it?'

'I shouldn't bother. You'd probably forget yourself.'

'True enough. By the way, I saw the Lovelock girls this morning. They get odder than ever.'

She told Dimity the tale of those who were acceptable and unacceptable at the Lovelocks' establishment in the past.

'Of course, they still live a century ago,' commented Dimity. 'All those occasional tables and whatnots, laden with silver. Who would bother with so much work these days, let alone facing the strong possibility of burglars? It has happened, after all.'

'Violet is about the only one now capable of sensible conversation,' commented Ella. 'It's my belief that Bertha and Ada are fast becoming gaga.'

Dimity looked sad. 'Charles is of the same opinion. It's Bertha's behaviour that's perturbing him. She's taken to storing some of those silver knick-knacks in her bedroom, and insisting on some of the most valuable pieces of furniture being taken up there too. The drawing-room is fast being denuded.'

'Good thing!' said Ella robustly. 'You couldn't move in there without knocking something to the ground. I should tell Charles not to worry on the Lovelocks' behalf. They've always been on the make, cadging bits and pieces from all and sundry. Come to think of it, I've not seen my Victorian sugar tongs since they came to tea in the winter. I bet they're somewhere in the Lovelocks' place.'

'If that clock's right,' said Dimity, 'it's time I went. I've promised to call at Dotty's, and there's no getting away quickly when dear old Dotty gets going.'

Dotty Harmer was an eccentric spinster who had lived alone in a cottage between Thrush Green and Lulling Woods for many years. Poor health and advancing age had made it necessary for her to have someone living with her, and she was very fortunate to have her sensible niece Connie and her husband Kit as companions.

She still insisted on tending her garden and the innumerable animals she had acquired over the years, but Connie saw to it that she was clad in warm clothing and stout shoes when she ventured forth. In the old days, Dotty had been quite content to wander about at times in her dressing-gown and slippers, much to the dismay and censure of the local inhabitants and Betty Bell in particular who did her best to keep the place in order once or twice a week.

There was a chilly wind blowing through the narrow path which led from Thrush Green, beside the Piggotts' cottage, to the open fields beyond. The sun was beginning to sink behind the trees of Lulling Woods, dark against a pale sky.

Dimity found Dotty in her kitchen, busy chopping onions with an enormous knife.

'It's good to get into the warm,' she commented, seating herself at the clear end of the kitchen table, and watching Dotty at her dangerous task. 'It's more like February than May this evening.'

'Not surprising since it's the time of the Ice Saints,' explained Dotty, ceasing her labours for a moment. 'May eleven, twelve and thirteen belong to three saints, and it is often perishing cold then. You should never shear your sheep around that time, you know.'

'I don't,' Dimity assured her.

She watched Dotty scrape the chopped onions on to a plate, and then tip them into a large saucepan which was bubbling on the stove.

'That smells delicious,' she said.

'For the hens, dear. I always add some onions at this time of year. They contain so much iron, you know, so needed at the end of the winter. Purifies the blood. My father used to eat his raw. Wonderfully refreshing, and so good for the bowels and bladder.'

Dimity reflected, not for the first time, how naturally Dotty referred to the parts of the body and their functions with no coyness. There was something appealingly eighteenth-century about her old friend, her archaic turn of phrase, her knowledge and use of herbs, and her unshaken belief that all things English were naturally best. Dotty was refreshingly free from doubts; they seemed to have come in during Victoria's reign and had become more and more potent ever since, Dimity surmised.

'Heard about Dorothy Watson's old place? Betty Bell tells me that that new man at the school may live there after all.'

'I heard something about it too.'

'Wonder why? Perhaps Dorothy and Agnes will find out when they come to stay. Have some coffee. It's dandelion – excellent stuff, I drink pints of it – but Connie and Kit still stick to Nescafé.'

'I like that too.'

'Well, I *could* make you a cup I suppose,' said Dotty. She sounded disappointed.

'No, no! Don't bother, please. I only came to give you the parish magazine and to see how you were. Are Connie and Kit out?'

'Yes. At a parish meeting. Somebody wants to buy the field at the back here. Lots of silly plans for houses. Who wants a lot of *people* living in that field? Besides, I need it for the goats.'

'Well, people do need houses, of course,' said Dimity mildly.

'And my goats need grass,' said Dotty. She began to look very obstinate, and Dimity decided that it was time to depart. If the demands of people and animals were in debate, she knew on whose side Dotty would be.

What with the approaching visit of the two retired teachers, the speculation about the headmaster Alan Lester's plans, and now this disturbing news about Bertha Lovelock's oddness, the inhabitants of Lulling and Thrush Green had plenty to engage their interests. They could be seen chatting on every corner.

The cold spell passed, and May began to show itself in all its traditional warm beauty. The lilac bushes tossed their mauve and white plumes in cottage gardens, filling the air with heady scent. Stately tulips followed the dying daffodils, their satin cups in every shade known to man.

Lulling Woods were hazy blue and fragrant with carpets of bluebells, and the last of the wood anemones and primroses starred the leaf mould. Along the road to Nidden the ancient pond teemed with tadpoles. Young birds sat bemused on the grass verges, or hopped behind their busy parents clamouring for food, all fluttering wings and gaping beaks, oblivious of the dangers around them from traffic, callous boys, or the hovering shapes of sparrow hawks which cast their sinister shadows in the May sunlight.

The cuckoo's cry, at first so welcome at the beginning of the month, now annoyed its listeners with its monotonous persistence. The rooks chattered and squabbled in the tall trees overshadowing Percy Hodge's farm, and he was already making plans for a rook shoot with a few of his cronies. Percy was partial to rook pie.

Prudent housewives were spring-cleaning and hanging out quilts and blankets to air on their clothes-lines. Those who ran to winter curtains, as well as summer ones, were folding the former and storing them away, and admiring the crisp freshness of the summer alternatives at their windows.

Paint brushes were at work, inside and out, and wallpaper patterns, bed covers, curtain materials and floor coverings were being earnestly studied in many a home. It was not surprising that amid this hopeful bustle another topic arose to engage Thrush Green's attention.

It seemed that the small communal room at the old people's homes, Rectory Cottages, would have to be enlarged. Edward Young, the architect, had had the foresight to see that this might happen, and luckily had put the room at one end of the buildings where it could be extended if need be.

There had been some doubt as to whether the old people would use this communal sitting-room to any great extent. Jane and Bill Cartwright, the wardens, had been of the opinion that the residents might well prefer to stay in their own comfortable quarters most of the time. But, as it happened, the general sitting-room was a popular feature of the complex, and it was decided to enlarge it by adding a good-sized conservatory-type of building at one end. This would give not only more room, but added light, facilities for growing plants, and a pleasant sunny spot when the Cotswold winds made it too blustery and chilly to sit outside.

The trustees had met, and had gone through the usual preliminaries of discussion, argument and anxious perusal of their finances. With everyone's consent, Edward Young had been given the task of designing the extension and he was now busy preparing plans for approval.

It was a job he relished. It was generally felt that his original plans had worked well, and that Rectory Cottages were an enormous improvement on the former rectory which had been such an eyesore on the green.

He had been given plenty of gratuitous advice by the inhabitants of Thrush Green whilst his original buildings had been in the making. For an impatient man he had been remarkably forbearing, although he grew quite heated with his brother-in-law Dr John Lovell when the latter pointed out that some outdoor steps were a hazard to old people, particularly in slippery weather. As it happened, it was poor Jane Cartwright who was the first to come a cropper, and she had been unable to attend to her duties as warden until the broken leg had mended. John Lovell, to give him his due, nobly refrained from saying: 'I told you so!'

It was quite apparent that funds would have to be raised for this new venture, and already plans were afoot for the usual Mammoth Jumble Sale, a Mammoth Summer Fête, a Mammoth Bazaar nearer Christmas and innumerable sponsored activities such as walks, swimming contests, and even an hour's silence to be kept at Thrush Green school, all in this good cause.

Ella Bembridge had been entrusted with the job of buying and making the necessary curtains and soft furnishings, and was busy co-opting various like-minded ladies to form a working party when the time came.

As the birds flew back and forth in the trees and hedgerows, building their nests and making plans for the future, so did the residents of Lulling and Thrush Green plan their own affairs, in this May world bright with hope and new life.

On the last Wednesday of the month, Isobel Shoosmith finished her domestic preparations for Dorothy's and Agnes's visit. Despite their protestations, she had persuaded the two ladies to stay at her house for a week, and the spare-room stood ready for them, complete with a vase of lilies of the valley, and a selection of reading matter on the bedside table.

She and Harold went to check the room during the

afternoon. The two friends were due at four o'clock, and Isobel still had the cucumber sandwiches to prepare.

'It all looks splendid,' said Harold heartily, surveying the twin beds, smooth and glossy in their matching bedspreads.

'I think they would enjoy Ellis Peters' latest, and Dick Francis's, wouldn't you?' asked Isobel anxiously.

'Be mad if they didn't,' Harold assured her. 'And what about a magazine or two?'

Isobel nodded agreement, tweaked a lily of the valley into place, and decided it really all looked extremely peaceful.

They made their way downstairs, and Isobel set off to the kitchen. There was a cheerful hooting from the front of the house, and there was the well-polished Metro on the drive, with hands fluttering from its windows.

'They're here! They're here!' cried Isobel, and hurried out to greet them in the greatest excitement.

3. News of Old Friends

Naturally, the arrival of the two ladies had been noticed by most of the Thrush Green residents long before the last of Isobel's cucumber sandwiches had been eaten.

The first to see the car draw up was Muriel Fuller, who lived at Rectory Cottages and immediately had taken up a strategic position on one of the seats on Thrush Green. It had an excellent view of the Shoosmiths' house, and as Muriel wore dark glasses and held a newspaper, the casual passerby would assume that she was simply enjoying the sunshine.

For most of her working life Muriel had been headteacher at the little school at Nidden, a mile or two north along the road from Thrush Green. When the school had closed, she was fortunate enough to be allotted one of the seven homes under the care of Bill and Jane Cartwright.

She had continued to give part-time teaching help with Miss Watson and Miss Fogerty, and so looked forward more keenly than most to seeing her friends again. She also intended to tell them how disappointed she was by the new headmaster's attitude: he had *not required* her part-time services, and Miss Fuller was indignant.

A close second in the race to see the visitors was Ella Bembridge. She was clipping a few early shoots from the front hedge and had forgotten about the Shoosmiths' visitors, her mind still busy on the Lovelock sisters' odd ways, as she snipped away.

Mr Jones at the public house saw them through the window of the bar, as they drew up at Harold's. Across the green Winnie Bailey, widow of Dr Donald Bailey who had attended to Thrush Green's illnesses for many years, noticed the Metro standing in Harold's drive as she washed her hands before tea. By five o'clock, eighty per cent of the local residents were happy in the knowledge that the two respected ladies had arrived safely.

But it was Ella who stumped across the green as soon as the six o'clock news had finished. Genuinely anxious to see her old friends and having no qualms about the possibility of being *de trop*, she put her head into the open front door, and gave a cheerful shout.

'Anyone home? Welcome back!'

Albert Piggott, who expected to be one of the first to see anything of note occurring at Thrush Green, was rather annoyed to miss the arrival of the retired schoolteachers. He had spent an hour or two weeding Dotty Harmer's garden and, as usual, had been held up by Dotty's scatter-brained suggestions.

'What about a bird-box in that walnut tree?' was one of her proposals. 'I'm quite sure I saw a green woodpecker there the other evening.'

As the walnut tree was about forty feet in height, and Albert suffered from vertigo, he quashed this suggestion.

'Come and see my rhubarb,' urged Dotty. 'A splendid second crop coming. Do help yourself.'

With such things had Albert been delayed, but he arrived back at the cottage a few minutes before Nelly and had exerted himself enough to put on the kettle.

'Them teachers come?' enquired Nelly, flinging a cloth over the kitchen table and whizzing plates upon it.

'Dunno. Never saw 'em. I was workin'.'

'Makes a nice change,' commented Nelly, briskly setting cutlery round the table as if she were dealing cards.

'No need to be sarky,' growled Albert. 'I was down Dotty's. Got better things to do than to poke my nose into other folks' affairs.'

This lofty attitude was greeted by a snort from his wife.

'Well, I bet you're the only person on Thrush Green who don't know if they've arrived. I saw a few curtains twitching as I come along just now.'

She set about poaching a piece of smoked haddock with her usual dexterity, and after it was consumed went to the sink to wash up, while Albert sank exhausted into his chair with the newspaper.

'I knew a woman,' said Nelly conversationally, 'who *never* washed a frying-pan after using it for fish. Couldn't face the job.' She studied her own wet frying-pan critically.

'What she do with it then?' enquired Albert, rousing himself.

'Chucked it out.'

'You'd better not start that sort of lark, my girl,' warned Albert, asserting himself as a householder.

'I might yet,' replied Nelly.

Albert returned to his paper, and Nelly to her thoughts.

She was perturbed about an incident in the shop that morning, involving Bertha Lovelock. That ancient lady had come in on her own to purchase a small currant loaf, a commodity for which The Fuchsia Bush was justly renowned.

Nelly had turned to the tray to fetch the loaf, and thought she saw, from the corner of her eye, a scone being transferred from the basket on the counter to Miss Lovelock's coat pocket.

She said nothing. She could have been mistaken, and she had no idea how many scones should have been in the basket. Some had already been sold by the assistants, and it was impossible to check. In any case, Miss Bertha Lovelock was an old customer and not to be upset.

She swathed the currant loaf in snowy tissue paper, took the money, wished the old lady a civil good morning and watched her depart. She returned to the kitchen and her pastry-making. Should she question the girls to see if such a thing had happened before? Should she tell Mrs Peters of the incident? Had there *really been* an incident?

Flouring the pastry board and wielding her rolling pin, Nelly began to grow calmer. Let the old dear have the benefit of the doubt this time. It might never happen again, and least said soonest mended. No point in alarming Mrs Peters and the girls over one scone. Nevertheless, Nelly determined to keep a sharp eye on the Lovelock sisters, and Miss Bertha in particular.

Meanwhile at the Shoosmiths, Ella Bembridge had wished the visitors goodbye, invited them to call at any time, and stumped homeward.

'Would you mind very much if we stretched our legs after our drive?' enquired Dorothy. 'That is, after we've helped you wash up these tea things.'

Isobel refused to countenance their presence in the kitchen, and gave her blessing to the proposed walk.

The two ladies naturally looked first at their old school: the playground was empty, the doors and windows shut, but all looked neat and clean, and geraniums had been planted in new window boxes.

'It looks very well cared for,' said Agnes. 'I wish we could go in. I wonder if the fish tank is still kept in my room.'

'Most probably,' said Dorothy, moving along to study the outside of the empty school house.

'I must say,' she continued, 'that it is very sad to see the state of our garden. Those roses should have been pruned, and I can't see any mower getting over the lawn if it is left much longer.'

Agnes could hardly bear to look at her old home. Here she had been so happy; here she had spent years of companionship with Dorothy, and had met so many pupils, parents and friends.

'Let's stroll along the road towards Nidden,' she suggested. 'The evening's so lovely.'

'I must say,' said Dorothy a little later, 'that the air here is better than at Barton. I know we have the *sea* now, but there is something so *pure* and *exhilarating* about the Cotswolds, and of course the trees and flowers are more abundant.'

She stopped by a magnificent elder bush, its creamy flower-heads forming a mass of luminous fragrance. Nearby, a spray of early dog roses cascaded from the hedgetop towards the roadside ditch, and buttercups brightened the grass verge.

Agnes shared her delight, and remembered countless walks with her infants class along this leafy lane. Somehow, in every season it had supplied them all with treasures. In spring, the first small violets appeared under the hedgerows, and in summer the children would return with sprays of honeysuckle or mauve pincushions of wild scabious in their hands. In the autumn, there were hazelnuts, blackberries, hips and haws and all manner of bright berries to adorn the nature table, and even in the depths of winter some treasures could be gleaned; a glossy rook's feather, a bleached snail's shell, or a sprig of frost-rimed yew or holly.

The children's joy in these discoveries was echoed by little Miss Fogerty, reflecting as it did her own childhood memories of the Cotswold village not many miles from Thrush Green.

'Good to be back,' said Dorothy.

'Good to be back,' replied Agnes.

The days passed all too quickly for the visitors. There were so many friends to see, so much news to exchange.

Winnie Bailey, Ella Bembridge, Dotty Harmer and other Thrush Green friends invited the two ladies to their homes. Charles and Dimity Henstock gave a celebratory lunch party at Lulling Vicarage, and the Shoosmiths took them out to the neighbouring villages which their visitors had known so well.

Everything went smoothly until the day before the ladies were due to return, when Agnes started a feverish cold.

'I'm sure I shall be quite well tomorrow,' she assured her anxious hostess.

'In any case, you are to stay in bed,' said Isobel, 'and if you are still groggy in the morning you are staying here until you have recovered.'

Agnes became much agitated. 'Oh, I couldn't *possibly*! There are several things we must get back to do, and I don't want to impose on you any longer, Isobel dear.'

'The longer you can stay the better I shall like it,' Isobel assured her. 'Now lie down, and try to have a nap.'

Downstairs Dorothy was reading the paper, and looked up anxiously when Isobel reappeared.

'What do you think? Should we get Dr Lovell to have a look at her?'

'Let's see how she is in the morning before we do that. Is it absolutely necessary for you to return tomorrow? We'd love to have you another day or so.'

'*Absolutely* necessary,' said Dorothy, with a return of her headmistressy manner. 'I have an old college friend coming to stay on Saturday, and must get things ready. She has been looking after her aged mother for years, and this is a rare break for her. I can't possibly put her off.'

'I can see that.'

'And then there's Teddy,' added Dorothy. 'I usually call in to see him after tea on Fridays.'

Teddy had been mentioned once or twice during the ladies' stay, but apart from the fact that he was a neighbour at Barton, Isobel knew little about him.

'Surely he would understand?' she said.

'Oh, he would *understand*,' replied Dorothy with vigour. 'There never was a more *understanding* man, but I should hate to disappoint him.'

'Well,' said Isobel briskly, 'I don't think we need to make any plans until we see how Agnes is in the morning. Would you like to come down to the greenhouse with me? I'm just going to do some watering.'

As it happened, the greenhouse was a very pleasant place to be, for although the sun still shone, as it had on most days of the ladies' visit to Thrush Green, the wind had veered to the north, and was already stripping some of the young leaves and blossom from the trees.

Agnes slept fitfully that night. Her throat was on fire, the glands behind her ears swollen, and she was feverishly hot. It was quite apparent, when morning came, that she was in no fit state to travel, even downstairs.

John Lovell called before he opened his surgery. Dorothy and Isobel awaited his verdict as they stood at the foot of the patient's bed.

The doctor was reassuring as he replaced his thermometer in its case. 'Keep her here,' he said, 'with plenty of liquids to drink. I don't think it is anything more than a heavy cold, but there's mumps about, and the wind can slice you in two this morning.'

He knew Agnes Fogerty well, and realized how physically frail she was with no spare flesh anywhere. But her spirit, of course, was indomitable, and had often kept her at school when she should have been in bed. This time, the doctor was going to see that she was properly looked after, and he was relieved that she was in the Shoosmiths' care.

'I'll pop in at the same time tomorrow,' he said, as he scribbled a prescription. 'This should take her temperature down, and the more she can sleep the better.'

He patted the invalid's bony shoulder, accompanied the two ladies downstairs, and departed across the green to his surgery.

'What is to be done?' cried Dorothy. She appeared to be extremely upset, quite unlike her usual competent self, and Isobel took charge.

'If you can get in touch with your friend and your neighbour, I suggest that you both stay on here. You are more than welcome, as I'm sure you know.'

'Dear Isobel, you are so kind,' said Dorothy, pacing the room distractedly, 'but I really must get back.'

'Then in that case,' said Isobel, 'you know we shall look after Agnes, and I will bring her back to Barton when she is fit to travel.'

'What nuisances we are!' cried Dorothy. 'I wouldn't have had this happen for the world!'

'Now stop worrying,' said Isobel. 'You drive back as arranged, and we'll enjoy Agnes's company. We can keep in touch by telephone.'

'I will go and tell Agnes about our plans,' agreed Dorothy.

'And I will obey doctor's orders,' answered Isobel, 'and go and make a jug of lemonade.'

Dorothy departed the next afternoon after an affectionate farewell to Agnes and her hosts, and many promises to keep in touch by telephone.

Luckily, Agnes made steady progress and the dreaded mumps did not appear, but John Lovell noted that the cold had left a painful cough, so forbade his patient to venture out whilst the north wind held sway.

It was during this time that Harold heard someone in the school house garden which ran alongside his own. It was almost six o'clock and he knew that the children and staff of the school should have gone long ago. Who could be trespassing?

He moved along on his side of the hedge until he came to a gap. Peering over he could see a figure, and was surprised to find that it was the headmaster, Alan Lester.

'Hello!' he called. 'Are you doing overtime?'

Alan laughed, and came to the gap.

'To tell the truth, I'm just having a recce. I'm wondering if I shall buy this place after all.'

'We'd be delighted to have you as neighbours,' said Harold. 'Are you getting fed up with the car journey every day?'

'Well, no,' said Alan. He seemed slightly embarrassed. 'That's one point, of course, but the fact is I've been offered a very good price by a friend of ours for my present house, and I'm wondering if we should be better off here.'

'Awful lot of hassle selling a place though,' observed Harold.

'That's one of the attractions with this transaction if it comes off. It could be done with the minimum of fuss and delay. Our friends are handing over to his son who has just got married, and they would be free to take over from us whenever we wanted to move.'

'Would your wife like to move here?' asked Harold, and thought he saw an expression of pain pass over Alan's face.

'I'm sure she would,' he replied.

'By the way, we have Agnes Fogerty with us at the moment. Would you like to come in and see her?'

Alan excused himself, saying that he was overdue at home, but that he hoped she would call at the school if she felt up to it.

'Actually, Betty Bell told us that she had been taken ill,' he went on. 'I do hope she will soon be better.'

'And I hope you will decide to take the school house,' replied Harold.

He returned to his own, ruminating on the rapidity with which all news circulated in Thrush Green, and with a valuable nugget of his own to share with his wife and Agnes.

As it happened, the two ladies were in Agnes's bedroom and so engrossed in conversation that Harold did not have a chance to impart his news; he returned to the sitting-room and settled down with a drink and the racing pages of the *Daily Telegraph*.

Dorothy had rung to enquire after Agnes's progress, and to give an account of her own. It was this which the patient and Isobel were discussing so earnestly. Phyllis, Dorothy's college friend, had arrived safely and Teddy was delighted to have his neighbour home again.

'Tell me,' said Isobel, 'who is this Teddy?'

Agnes turned rather pink, and plucked agitatedly at the counterpane.

'Oh, a very nice person,' she replied hastily. 'Very nice indeed.' There was a pause. 'A man,' she added.

'So I gathered,' said Isobel patiently. 'Does he live nearby?'

'Just along the road from us,' said Agnes. 'His wife died a year or so ago.'

'Has he got some help in the house?'

'Oh yes! He has to have help as he is practically blind. It's quite amazing how much he can do, but he misses his reading. That's why Dorothy goes regularly to read to him. He appreciates it so much.'

'I'm sure Dorothy enjoys it too,' said Isobel, with some cunning.

'She does indeed,' Agnes agreed enthusiastically. 'They have become great friends.'

Isobel detected a wistful note in this last comment. Could Agnes resent Dorothy's new interest? It seemed unlike her.

'I just hope,' went on Agnes, 'that Dorothy doesn't take on too much with Teddy. She used to go once a week, but lately it has been twice, and she is already on the WI committee, and helping with church affairs. She is so good-hearted,' cried her loyal friend, 'that I don't think she gets the rest she needs.'

'Hasn't Teddy got other friends to help him?'

'Yes, indeed. He has a wonderful woman who comes every morning to clear up and get his lunch, and then there is Eileen.'

'And who is Eileen?'

'A friend of his who lives across the road. She and her husband used to go on holiday regularly with Teddy and his wife. She visits Teddy quite a bit – pops in with a jam sandwich, and that sort of thing.'

'It sounds as though he gets lots of kind attention,' commented Isobel.

'Dorothy thinks he finds Eileen a little *too* attentive,' said Agnes. 'She is very effusive, talks a lot, and is always laughing. "*Guffawing*", Dorothy says. I must confess she is rather noisy. But then, Dorothy and I enjoy being quiet, just sitting with our books and knitting, and looking at nature programmes on the telly.'

'Perhaps Teddy finds her cheering,' suggested Isobel.

'Oh, I'm sure he does,' agreed Agnes earnestly, 'and she really is most generous with her time there. I think she may be lonely. She nursed her husband for months before he succumbed.'

'Succumbed?'

'To cancer, poor man. They were a devoted couple, Teddy told Dorothy. He says he has a great regard for Eileen.'

'It's good to know he has such good neighbours,' said Isobel, rising to go. 'I'm sure Dorothy will not have to do too much. It's not as though she were the only one to lend a hand.'

'No indeed,' agreed Agnes.

She sounded rather husky, and began to blow her nose energetically.

'But you see, she so *enjoys* lending a hand with Teddy,' she continued, still busy with her handkerchief. 'And, Isobel dear, I know you will understand, I can't help looking ahead and wondering if she is getting *too* fond of him. I mean, people do get married again, and he is a very attractive man, and dear Dorothy might feel . . .'

She faltered to a halt and the handkerchief went to work again.

'Now, now,' said Isobel soothingly, 'you mustn't upset yourself with needless worries. Dorothy has plenty of sense, and I'm sure she knows exactly what she is doing. Try and have a little doze.'

Agnes nodded. She looked wretched, Isobel thought. Surely these fears were groundless?

But then, she thought, as she went downstairs, love can be the very devil, and can strike one at any age. What a muddle!

Later that night in the privacy of their bedroom, she told Harold about Agnes's worries.

'It sounds to me,' said Harold, with rare male perspicacity, 'that Agnes may be a little in love with this Teddy herself.'

'Good heavens!' cried his wife, deeply shocked. 'Of course she isn't! She has the *cat*, after all!'

Harold pondered on this as he lay awaiting sleep.

Should men really have to compete with cats?

4 · BERTHA LOVELOCK CAUSES CONCERN

It was some days later that Harold remembered his news about the headmaster's interest in the school house. Agnes had returned to Barton and seemed to have recovered her composure, much to Isobel's relief. She said as much to Harold, on her return from delivering her friend.

'I think she was just a little feverish, you know,' she told Harold. 'Naturally, it upset her to think of Dorothy perhaps making a fool of herself at her age. And in any case, they have planned their retirement together, and where on earth would Agnes go if Dorothy and this Teddy-man made a match of it?'

'Don't *you* start,' begged Harold. 'Nothing will happen, you'll see. Agnes and Dorothy will be happily together for years. I can't see any man coming between them.'

He was too chivalrous to add that he thought neither lady could really inspire passion, worthy though they both were, but privately that was what he felt.

'By the way,' he said, glad to change the subject, 'I forgot to tell you that Alan Lester is considering taking on the school house.'

'Yes, I did hear that,' replied Isobel. 'Betty said something about it, and Ella seemed to think he's worried about his wife's health. Charles said he thought it might be the journey over here in the winter that was making him think again.'

Not for the first time, Harold realized that he was well behind with the local news.

'I'll never get used to the *speed* with which gossip flies around here,' he commented. 'In Africa the natives' drums were

35

reckoned pretty efficient, but Thrush Green's tongues can beat them hollow.'

Down at The Fuchsia Bush in Lulling High Street, Nelly Piggott had other things to worry about.

Bertha Lovelock had appeared less than an hour before to purchase a currant loaf. Rosa had served her.

On the counter stood a tray of rolls filled with ham and lettuce. Each was wrapped in hygienic clingfilm. Nelly herself had prepared these snacks which had become increasingly popular with drivers and delivery men in the early part of the morning. A second batch was prepared later for the local office workers and shop assistants who hurried in to fetch a quick lunch to take back to their place of work.

It so happened that Nelly pushed open the door from the kitchen at the precise moment when Bertha was surreptitiously sliding one of the shiny packets into her shopping bag. Rosa had her back to Miss Lovelock as she was dealing with the till.

Nelly's first impulse was to rush towards the old lady and demand back the goods, but prudence won. In the first place, there were several customers taking morning coffee, and she did not want a scene in public. Secondly, she wished to check with Rosa that none of the rolls had been sold: there should be ten in the tray, as she knew, having brought them through herself only ten minutes or so earlier. Thirdly, she wanted to consult Mrs Peters, the owner, about the best way of dealing with this awkward situation. Lurid headlines in the local paper would not do The Fuchsia Bush any good, and the Lovelocks were an old respected family.

As soon as Bertha had gone, Nelly counted the packets; there were nine left.

'Haven't sold any yet?' she asked the girl.

'Give us a chance,' replied Rosa grumpily. 'You only brought them through ten minutes ago.'

'Just check them,' commanded Nelly.

Rosa obeyed.

'Nine,' she said, stopped, and stared at Nelly. 'Surely, she never . . .' she began, awe-struck.

'Never you mind,' said Nelly. 'It's me and Mrs Peters' problem. You just hold your tongue.'

The girl nodded, looking shocked, and Nelly bustled back into the kitchen.

Mrs Peters was in the storeroom alone, and Nelly told her the news.

'And it's not the first time,' continued Nelly. 'That's to my knowledge, so Lord knows how long it's been going on.'

Mrs Peters sat down heavily on the step-stool. 'Gosh! What a pickle! I'm not getting the police in for this one. I think one of us had better have a word with Miss Violet. She's the only one with a ha'porth of sense.'

She looked at Nelly, who shook her head.

'Don't ask me, love. I know we're partners now, but you're better able to do it than I am. I've got the courage to face them old dears, but you'd do it more tactful, and that's the truth.'

'I don't mind doing it, if you think that's the right step.'

'Dead right. But how are you going to get Miss Violet on her own?'

'I'll ask her to call here about a private matter, and see her in the office. Meanwhile, not a word to anyone.'

'Our Rosa knows.'

'I'll deal with Rosa,' said Mrs Peters grimly. 'One squeak out of her, and she goes.'

She got up from the step-stool and patted Nelly's fat arm.

'Don't worry, Nelly. We've faced worse than this before.'

And, somewhat comforted, Nelly went back to making her gingerbread.

While his wife was coping with the affair of Bertha Lovelock, Albert was plying a broom in the churchyard.

There had been a wedding at the weekend. There had also been a high wind, which had not only played havoc with the bride's veil and the ornate coiffures of the bridesmaids, not to mention the wedding guests' hats, but had sent confetti in every direction.

Albert pottered about morosely, jabbing under shrubs, along the edges of the paths, and attempting to free the grass of its scattered finery.

It was while he was thus engaged, and counting the minutes to opening time at The Two Pheasants, that Percy Hodge appeared.

He rested his arms upon the gate top and watched the labourer.

'You busy then?'

'Whatjer think?' replied Albert, nastily. 'It's time the rector stopped all this confetti lark. Look at the mess.'

He paused and leant upon his broom.

'Ah well!' replied Percy indulgently. 'You can't blame young folks wantin' a pretty weddin'.'

'These wasn't young folks,' said Albert. 'That old fool Digby this was. Got spliced to that gel as works at Boots. A case of have to, they say.'

'Not so much of "that old fool Digby",' said Percy. 'We was at school together. Besides . . .' He halted and began to look sheepish.

'What's up?' asked Albert, coming nearer.

'Well, the fact is, I'm thinkin' of getting' married again myself.'

'You ain't!' cried Albert, dropping his broom. 'You silly juggins! What on earth do you want to clutter yourself up with a woman for?'

'There's reasons,' said Percy primly.

'Not the same as old Digby's?'

'Not the same at all, Albert. And I don't like your nasty way of thinkin'. I just want a bit of company, and the house cleaned up, and a decent dinner to come home to, same as any other man.'

'If it's that flighty Emily Cooke you've got in mind,' said Albert, bending to retrieve his broom, 'you ain't likely to get any home comforts. She's nothin' but a slattern, and got that boy Nigel as a by-blow, too. You'll be takin' on two of them. Not to mention her 'orrible old mother. You must be out of yer mind, Perce.'

The farmer's face was scarlet. 'You mind your own business! I knows what I'm doin' and when I needs your advice – which is never – I'll ask for it. That poor girl has learnt her lesson, and she'll make a good wife, you'll see. Anyway I'm fond of young Nigel.'

'More than anyone else is,' responded Albert. 'Well, they say there's no fool like an old one, and it looks as though that's right. You'll regret it, Perce. You'll regret it.'

At that moment Mr Jones opened the doors of The Two Pheasants, and Albert propped his broom against the church porch.

'Comin' over?' he queried.

'Not with you I ain't,' replied Percy coldly, and made his way towards Lulling.

Far away at Barton-on-Sea, thoughts of matrimony for the elderly were also tormenting poor little Agnes Fogerty.

She was scraping new potatoes at the sink, and wondering whether it would not be better to throw in the sponge and take to the potato peeler, so refractory were the vegetables.

Dorothy had gone to see Teddy, taking with her a cutting from the *Daily Telegraph* about pesticides which she thought might interest him.

Any excuse is better than none, thought Agnes with unusual tartness, but remained silent.

Really, she mused, as she struggled with the potatoes, there is far too much of this marrying, and giving in marriage, about. One could get on perfectly well without it, and she and Dorothy were good examples.

Nothing had been said between the two friends, but Dorothy had seemed to make a point of visiting their nearly-blind neighbour every day since she had been back. It was not only the *unsuitability* of the relationship which worried Agnes; there were also serious and practical aspects to consider.

In the first place, would Dorothy really be happy as Teddy's wife? Or anyone else's, for that matter? Dorothy was used to having her own way. She was also singularly undomesticated, able to ignore dust, spots on the carpet and windows which needed cleaning. She disliked cooking, although she was quite capable of roasting a joint and preparing a straightforward meal, but she got no pleasure from doing it. Those regular household chores such as spring-cleaning, ordering the fuel, having the chimney swept and so on, had been arranged by Agnes.

It was not that Dorothy was inefficient, Agnes told herself loyally. The household accounts, the business letters, the interminable forms for taxes, registration of this, that and the like, were all competently managed. But no doubt Teddy, or any other man, would already be coping with such things, and Dorothy's skills in this direction would not be needed. Would she find this frustrating? Would she be critical? Dorothy's patience was easily exhausted, and she would not hesitate to state her feelings. Men, so Agnes believed, very much disliked interference in their methods and habits, particularly as they grew older.

And there was an even more pressing problem for Agnes. Where could she go? There was no question of the three of them living under one roof, which meant of course she would have to find other accommodation.

Her savings were far too inadequate to contemplate buying a small house, no matter how modest. She would have to look about for a bed-sitter like the one she had had years ago at Thrush Green before she shared the school house with Dorothy. It was a bleak prospect.

Or perhaps she ought to start collecting brochures from those excellent societies who care for indigent gentlewomen. She believed that there were several connected with the church, as well as those advertising themselves as 'Homes From Homes', with photographs of stately houses with white-haired old ladies in the foreground, looking bemused in wheelchairs under an ancient cedar tree.

But even more distressing than the thought of Dorothy regretting such a step and her own financial difficulties, was the overriding misery of having to leave Dorothy and their new little home to which she was now deeply attached. She had never been so content.

How would it all end?

She gazed out of the window over the sink, the view somewhat blurred by incipient tears. The cat came and rubbed round her legs, and she bent to fondle it with a wet hand.

'Timmy, we are in a pickle! What is to become of us both?'

Would cats be allowed in these homes for gentlefolk? Come to think of it, she hadn't seen hair nor hide of an animal in those photographs. Whatever happened, Tim should stay with her.

She blew her nose, tucked the handkerchief in her apron pocket, and surveyed her handiwork. She seemed to have scraped seventeen potatoes altogether, and only six were needed.

'Well, they will just have to do for the next two days as well,' she told Tim briskly.

And putting her fears from her, she set about cleaning the sink.

The day after the unfortunate affair at The Fuchsia Bush, Miss Violet Lovelock, gloved and hatted, called next door at the shop. She was ushered in by Miss Peters, who led the way to her office at the rear of the premises.

'Do sit down,' said Mrs Peters, pushing forward the only comfortable chair in the room.

'Thank you,' said Violet sitting bolt upright, and removing her gloves.

Through the window behind the desk at which Mrs Peters was sitting, she could see the brick wall, rosy with age, which divided this garden from the Lovelocks'. At one time, a retired admiral had lived here, and this office had probably been his study, she surmised. Her father had taken a dislike to this neighbour, and threats of writs, solicitors' letters and the like had been tossed verbally across this self-same wall when she and her sisters were toddlers. It was a strange feeling to be sitting here now, awaiting Mrs Peters' pleasure.

Mrs Peters approached the matter with great tact and sympathy. She suspected that the culprit's sister, now busily folding her gloves together, had some idea of what was afoot, and in this she was right.

When at last she ceased to speak, Violet sighed heavily. 'My dear Mrs Peters, I can only apologize and hope that you will allow me to reimburse you.'

'That won't be necessary, I assure you.'

'The fact is,' said Violet, 'my sister is getting very old. Well, I suppose we all are – but dear Bertha is becoming rather eccentric with it. I suppose that one could say that this is a mild form of kleptomania, and I should tell you that she has taken to removing quite a number of objects to hoard in her bedroom. It is all most distressing, but a common symptom of senility, I believe.'

'So I have heard,' said Mrs Peters. 'The thing is, what can we do? Sooner or later, one of our customers will notice, and probably tell the police. This is why I felt it best to have a word with you.'

'You are quite right,' replied Violet. She sat very upright and dry-eyed, but Mrs Peters watched the thin hands, dappled with age-spots quivering, as she played with her gloves.

'We had absolutely no idea that this was going on,' went on the old lady. 'I mean, the scones or buns, or whatever she purloined, must have been eaten in secret. It seems such an odd thing to do. I shall have to speak to her about this at once.'

'Thank you,' said Mrs Peters, glad to see the end of this painful interview in sight. 'I wondered if you might think of consulting your doctor? He might be able to help.'

'I shall have a word with her first myself and, believe me, we shall not let her come in here again on her own.'

She rose to go, back as straight as a ramrod and hand extended in farewell, but her papery wrinkled cheeks were flushed with embarrassment.

Mrs Peters' heart was touched. What a bully one felt, but it had to be done.

'You can be quite sure that this will go no further, Miss Lovelock,' she said. 'We are all much too fond of you and your sisters to wish to see you troubled in any way.'

The old lady inclined her head graciously. 'I very much appreciate the kind way in which you have dealt with this unhappy incident,' she replied. 'I shall do my best to put things right.'

She preceded Mrs Peters through the tea-room, bowing slightly to an acquaintance in the corner. Mrs Peters opened the door for her and watched her depart next door.

The old lady mounted the three steps to the Georgian front door, steadying herself by the iron handrail. To Mrs Peters' anxious eyes, she seemed to cling rather more heavily than usual to this support, suddenly looking particularly frail.

Feeling sad, Mrs Peters returned to the office. She found that she was trembling.

'Rosa,' she called. 'Bring me a cup of coffee. Black today, please.'

Violet went straight up to her bedroom and sat down in an old sagging wicker chair by the window. Outside, in the garden which ran alongside that of The Fuchsia Bush, a blackbird piped merrily. The scent of pinks floated through the window, and some yellow Mermaid roses nodded from the wall which divided the two properties.

The scene was tranquil, but the watcher was not. Violet's heart was thumping in a most alarming manner, and she was quite unable to control the tremors which shook her frame.

The thought of confronting her sister Bertha was devastating. As the youngest of the three, Violet had always felt slightly subservient to her older sisters' demands, although recently she had come to realize that they relied upon her more and more as their own strength receded.

But this was a different matter. This was a question of being dishonoured, of inviting ridicule, of personal shame.

Violet rose from the chair, which gave out protesting squeaks, and rested her hot forehead against the cold window pane.

What should she do? How best to approach this dreadful problem? What would be Bertha's reaction? Would she deny the charge? Would she break down, and confess to even further guilty secrets?

Violet decided that it would be best to tackle Bertha after they had all had their morning coffee. She herself should be calmer by that time, and more able to face her unpleasant task.

She went downstairs to the kitchen and began to set the tray with three large cups of exquisite Limoges china and three silver teaspoons. In the Lovelock household, such plebeian objects as mugs were not used, even for morning coffee.

Going about this simple task made her feel more settled. If only they had had a brother, she thought wistfully. This was the sort of thing a man could cope with so much better.

As she waited for the kettle to boil, she toyed with Mrs Peters' suggestion that it might be a good idea to speak to Bertha's doctor, but she rejected it at once. Dr Lovell was much too young, and there might be disagreeable consequences, such as further consultations with psychiatrists and other horrors.

And then she thought of Charles Henstock, and a warm glow suffused her. Dear Charles! The complete answer! If Bertha should prove even the tiniest scrap difficult, then Violet would seek help from their old and wise friend.

The kettle boiled. Water poured on to the coffee grounds and Violet stood savouring the rich aroma, now mistress of herself.

5 . TROUBLE AT THE LOVELOCKS

July arrived, and gardeners were picking broad beans and raspberries and admiring their swelling onions. They were also, of course, spraying their roses for blackspot and mildew, and trying to cope with ground elder, couch grass, chickweed and groundsel, all of which rioted in their flower borders.

'But,' as Muriel Fuller observed to Ella Bembridge, 'there is no pleasure without pain.'

She was inclined to trot out these little sayings as though she had just thought of them, which Ella found distinctly trying.

The two ladies were meeting rather more often these days, as they were sharing the responsibility of coping with the soft furnishings for the extension to the sitting-room at Rectory Cottages.

The footings were already dug and, like all footings everywhere, looked ludicrously small, as though the room would be hard put to it to accommodate two chairs, let alone the dozen or so envisaged.

The question of curtains awaited further discussion for Edward Young, the architect, was strongly in favour of pull-down blinds being fitted to the windows inside for easy adjustment, and for an awning which could be pulled down on the outside of the glass building facing south.

The two ladies were quite content to shelve the matter of the curtains until such things as expense and necessity, should blinds be considered adequate, were settled; but they decided to go ahead with cushions and other small objects, and had prudently chosen a William Morris pattern which they were assured 'was always in stock'.

'Though that's not to say that the manufacturers may not discontinue some colour or other,' said Ella morosely to her companion. 'Still, we can't do more, and as far as I can see this pattern should tone in pretty well with most colours. The Cartwrights are having a plain hair-cord carpet, so that's a help.'

Those ignorant of the art of cushion-making might have thought that it was a simple process of stuffing soft material into an attractive bag, but Ella and Muriel were artists, and the problems were formidable. Should they be square or oblong? Should they sport a frill, or be left plain? Should they be piped, and if so, inside or out? What about silk edgings, fringes, tassels?

The discussions went on, each lady clinging tenaciously to her own ideas, but in the meantime quite a lot of local gossip was exchanged in Ella's sitting-room.

'You are lucky to be farther from the school than I am,' said Muriel. 'The noise at playtimes is quite horrendous, and I don't think the teachers are on playground duty as promptly as they were in Miss Watson's time.'

This, Ella realized, was a side-swipe at the new headmaster, whom Muriel had never forgiven for spurning her services as a part-time remedial reading teacher.

'All children get excited at playtime,' she commented diplomatically.

'But that's when accidents happen. I well remember at Nidden once . . .'

Ella let her ramble on about her old village school which was now closed, where Muriel had spent the greater part of her working life in comparative obscurity. Her attention returned, however, on hearing Muriel say that she was quite sure that Alan Lester would be coming to live in the school house.

'I doubt it,' responded Ella robustly. 'After all, he had the chance when he took over the job. Prices have gone up since then, for one thing.'

'Maybe,' said Muriel, stooping to pick up a thread from the floor, 'but Betty Bell heard it from his own lips. He was measuring the windows, and saying that he doubted if any of their existing curtains would fit.'

'That's a law of nature,' said Ella. 'Nothing ever fits the next house. That's partly why I don't contemplate moving, and I'm surprised he is.'

'They say,' went on Muriel, 'that it's because of his wife – ailing, in some way. I suppose he worries about her while he's at work.'

'Well, he'll be away at his duties in school anyway,' replied Ella, 'and if she's ailing, I should think the noise of the children would upset her even more. What's the trouble?'

'Betty Bell didn't say.' She held up an embryo cushion cover, surveying it critically. 'I wonder if a frilled ruche of toning satin ribbon would look well round the edge?'

Ella winced. 'No, it wouldn't,' she told her.

It was Harold Shoosmith who next heard more, and it was Alan Lester who enlightened him.

The children were making their way home, loitering in the dusty summer lanes, playing idly on the swings at the corner of Thrush Green, too indolent in the heat to make much noise.

Harold was clipping the privet hedge for the second time that season and thinking how remarkably unpleasant the smell of the little white conical flower-heads was, when he became conscious of the headmaster pacing at the rear of the school house.

He was accompanied by a man whom Harold felt he ought to know. Was he one of the Lulling shopkeepers? A plumber? An electrician? Someone he had met at a party?

Harold contented himself with a wave to both men and continued clipping. A pity the chap who put in this hedge had not settled for yew, thought Harold; it would only need cutting once a year. But then, he supposed, when this privet was planted it was clipped by the full-time gardener who had been kept at Quetta, as his house was once called, along with a resident cook and housemaid.

Intent on his work, he was scarcely conscious of the departure of the two men next door, until he heard a car drive away. He straightened his aching back, and saw Alan Lester emerging from the school house gate, presumably on his way to fetch his own car from the corner of the playground, where it had stood all day in the shade of an elder bush which was so rampant that it could almost be called a tree.

Seeing Harold he came over to speak to him. Harold lowered his shears with relief.

'That's a job that's waiting for me at home,' he observed to Harold. 'I keep putting it off. I'm not all that fond of privet, it grows too fast.'

'My view entirely,' agreed Harold. 'Here, come in and have a drink before you go home. I'm stopping for a bit anyway.'

'Thank you,' said Alan, following his host to the open front door. 'It's hellishly hot today. The children have been drooping all over the place, and I don't blame them.'

Isobel was out, so the two men sat alone in the cool sitting-room. They both settled for Isobel's homemade lemonade, and the ice chinked comfortingly in the misted glasses.

'That was a friend of mine who was with me,' announced Alan. 'He's a local builder, Johnson by name. I came across him at Rotary, and he's having a look to see if we can enlarge one of the rooms without too much hassle and expense.'

So that's why I felt I knew him, Harold thought.

'So you really are going ahead – with buying the place next door?'

'Definitely. I should like to have everything signed and sealed before next term. I had great hopes of getting things done during the summer holidays, but I can see that's out of the question.'

'It's no good getting impatient in these affairs,' agreed Harold. 'Simply asking for a heart attack. I've yet to meet anyone who has got into his house at the date first given.'

They sipped their cool drinks in companionable silence. Outside, a blackbird scolded furiously. A child called to another. Someone was mowing a lawn across the green, and the curtains stirred in the light summer breeze.

'It's a very good place to live,' said Harold, at last. 'I'm sure you won't regret the move. The natives are friendly – I know from experience!'

'I've discovered that myself.'

'Will your wife mind uprooting herself? I always think the women have to do so much more in adapting to a different house.'

'I think a change is just what she needs at the moment. She's not been too well, and I shall be able to keep an eye on her more easily.'

'Nothing serious, I hope?'

'No, no. Nothing like that. But both children are at school all day, and I'm away from soon after eight until getting on for six some days. She gets rather lonely, I feel, and she's never been one to make a lot of friends.'

His voice trailed away. He turned his empty glass round and round, his eyes upon it. He looked very tired.

'Let me get you another,' said Harold rising.

Alan Lester came to with a start. 'No, many thanks. I must get back to my own privet hedge. I've held you up long enough.' He put his glass on the tray. 'And thank you again for that life-saver.'

Harold went to the gate with him. The scent from the lime trees filled the warm air. The statue of Nathaniel Patten hard by was throwing a sharp shadow across the grass. Some sparrows were busy in a dust bath at the edge of the road.

'Well, I'm sure you will find Thrush Green very welcoming,' he assured the headmaster. 'And it will be good to see the school house occupied again. We all miss Dorothy and Agnes. You and your wife should be very happy here.'

'I sincerely hope so,' replied Alan.

He was smiling as he said this, but Harold had the feeling that, despite the brave words and the bright smile, some small doubt was lingering.

What was it, Harold wondered, picking up his shears, that was worrying the poor chap?

At the Lovelocks' house, Violet had made little headway with her problem. She had expected either fierce denials and a frightening display of temper from her sister Bertha, or a complete collapse and confession accompanied by a storm of tears.

Either would be quite dreadful, but had to be faced, and she had confronted the culprit when Ada was safely out of the way. It was a shock to find that Bertha neither denied nor confessed. Instead, she gazed at Violet with a look of utter stupefaction on her face.

'What on earth are you trying to tell me, Violet?' she said coldly. 'You seem very distressed about something.'

Violet explained all over again, only to be met with shrugs and shakes of the head.

'I don't think you are quite yourself,' said Bertha. 'I refuse to listen to any more of these silly remarks. You are giving me a headache. I shall take two aspirins and lie down, and I advise you to do the same.'

Thus dismissed, Violet was thrown into even greater confusion. Should she tell Ada? She doubted if she would get any further help from that source. Ada had always hated trouble, and would probably be as scathing as Bertha in dealing with the problem.

She went to the telephone and rang the Henstocks' number.

'Come whenever you like,' said Charles's reassuring voice. 'I shall be here all day, and shall look forward to seeing you.'

At half past two, Violet emerged from the front door of her home and made her way up the High Street towards the vicarage. The lime trees cast pools of welcome shade on the hot pavements. Bees murmured among the lime-flowers, and Violet thought how much pleasanter it would be sitting in a deck-chair in the garden at home than embarking on this worrying project. She had left her two sisters dozing there, as she crept away, feeling like a conspirator.

She crossed the large green at the southern end of Lulling; the great parish church of St John's dominated the scene, its benevolent presence comforting the distraught woman.

She found Charles in the vicarage garden, his hands full of groundsel, his shirt sleeves rolled up. He waved her towards a rustic seat beneath the cedar tree, and sat on another opposite her.

'We shall be quite undisturbed here,' he told her. 'Dimity has gone shopping with Ella. Something to do with cushions. Lots of talk about *ruching* and *piping* on the telephone. It had rather a Highland Games' flavour, I thought.'

He beamed at her, his spectacles glinting in the sunlight. He put the bunch of weeded groundsel on the ground, dusted his hands, and put them on his plump knees.

'Now, what's the trouble?' he enquired.

His voice was so kind and gentle that Violet was afraid she might weep, but Lovelocks did not show emotion under pressure, and she forced herself to remain calm.

'It's about Bertha,' she began, and told him the whole sad tale.

He listened without interruption, noting Violet's fluttering hands, and her voice husky with emotion. Certainly this old friend of his had suffered much, and needed all the help he hoped that he might be able to give her.

'And I still don't know if I should have consulted John Lovell first, but really, Charles, he might have felt that she should be sent to some mental specialist, or one of those clinics dealing with kleptomaniacs. I know so little about these things, but I do know that Bertha would absolutely refuse to have medical advice in this case.'

She paused for a moment, her eyes downcast, and her fingers plucking at the silk of her skirt.

'So I came to you,' she added.

Charles leant across and put his pink (and rather dirty from the groundsel) hand upon her own agitated ones. It was like holding a bird, he thought; there was the same fragility, the panic, the brittle feel of small bones.

'My dear,' he said, 'you should not have to suffer like this. I'm glad you came to me first. We may have to consult Lovell at some time, but not yet.'

'But what can we do?' cried Violet. 'I mean, we simply can't watch her behaving like this! It's not only a case of "what-will-the-neighbours-say?" It is *fundamentally dishonest*, and I can't let Mrs Peters and heaven knows how many other tradesmen be at the mercy of Bertha.'

'It is that which is the main problem,' agreed Charles.

Violet went on to tell him of Bertha's strange ways of moving objects of value from all over the house into her own bedroom.

'She's always been excessively possessive,' Violet told him. 'She would never lend Ada or me any of her things, not even a belt or a pair of gloves for some particular occasion.'

'And did she borrow yours?'

'Oh, frequently! We rather treated it as a joke when we were girls. "Go and look in Bertha's room", we used to say to each other, if we missed a brooch or some other trifle.'

Charles nodded. 'It sounds as though it has simply grown more obsessive as the years have passed,' he said. 'Do you think she has any inkling of what she is doing?'

'I can't say. Somehow I think she *does* know that she is at fault, but she is so clever at evading the issue that I simply can't tell. It is as if she shuts her mind to the consequences of her actions. And I'm quite sure this isn't just forgetfulness, as it would be in dear Ada's case. Bertha is a much more ruthless person, I'm afraid, as I know to my own cost after all these years.'

They sat in silence for a time. Bumblebees tumbled about in the border nearby. A thrush stood, still and statuesque, at the edge of the lawn, before running purposefully to a spot which he jabbed energetically with his beak. There was a distant cackle of laughter from the almshouses nearby, where two ancient neighbours, it seemed, were sharing a joke.

Charles sighed. 'Leave this to me, Violet. You have done all you can, and I can only suggest that you make sure that Bertha is accompanied wherever she goes, so that nothing is taken. Mrs Peters, I imagine, will see that nothing is said?'

'Mrs Peters is the soul of loyalty and discretion,' replied Violet. 'I trust her absolutely. If others have been robbed I only hope they will tell *me*, and not the police.'

'If you have heard nothing, then I should assume that nothing has happened.'

'But will you speak to her, Charles, or just wait to see if this is her only slip?'

Charles looked thoughtful. 'I rather think I shall have a word with her. It will follow up your own efforts, and also make her realize that her actions are being noted.'

'She'll certainly take more notice of you than she does of me,' said Violet, getting up from the seat.

They began to walk towards the gate. Violet stopped suddenly and faced the clergyman.

'Charles, I can't begin to thank you. You are a tower of strength, and I feel so very much better for talking to you.'

'I've done very little,' said Charles. 'You have done most of the work. Mine lies ahead.'

He watched her as she retraced her steps across the green. She looked old and frail, but the Lovelock back was as straight as ever, Charles noted with admiration.

It grew hotter and more humid as the month of July went on. The grass at Thrush Green became brittle and brown, and the gardens of the houses around it needed watering every evening. Hoses, sprinklers and watering cans went into action as soon as the sun began to sink behind Lulling Woods, but all house-holders awaited the grim warning from the council banning the use of the life-saving liquid for the crops and flowers.

'It's the same every year,' grumbled Percy Hodge to Albert in The Two Pheasants. 'We gets fair flooded out in February and March – water butts overflowin', puddles up to your hocks, gumboots on day in and day out – and then comes three weeks dry, and we're told we've got a drought!'

'Gets in your chest, too,' said Albert, fingering an empty glass.

'What! The drought?'

'That's right. The dust like. Brings on me cough.' He essayed a short spell of somewhat unconvincing hacking.

'You best have another 'alf,' said Percy, not moving. His own glass was half full.

Seeing that there was no possibility of being treated to his drink, Albert shuffled to the bar to get a refill.

'Got two weddin's this Saturday,' he said on his return. 'What with the dust, and them old lime trees shedding their muck, not to mention rice and confetti, I'll be at it all Saturday evenin' clearin' up for Sunday.'

'Well, it's your job, ain't it? What you gets paid for? Weddin's is to be expected.'

'And when's yours to be expected?' asked Albert sharply. 'You havin' it here? White, and all that? I'll look forward to seein' you all dolled up in a mornin' suit and topper.'

Percy looked at him coldly. 'Ah! Very funny, Albert Piggott! I hope I knows how to behave at the right time.'

He pushed aside his glass and made for the door, slamming it behind him.

'You shouldn't have said that,' said Mr Jones, mopping down the counter. 'It's his own business, after all.'

Albert looked faintly embarrassed. 'Well, we all knows he's makin' a fool of himself if he takes up with that Cooke girl. Don't do any harm to twit him now and again.'

'There's such a thing as playing with fire,' the landlord told him, wringing out his cloth. 'How would you feel if some chap made nasty remarks about your Nelly?'

Albert stared stolidly at him across his empty glass. 'I'd join him,' he said.

6. CHARLES HENSTOCK DOES HIS BEST

Percy Hodge's courtship had been common gossip, in a somewhat desultory way, to all Thrush Green and Lulling. The death of his first wife some years earlier, followed by the departure of his second and their subsequent divorce, had left Percy lonely and on the lookout for a new wife.

At one time he had paid unwelcome attention to Winnie Bailey's companion, Jenny. He had been repulsed, and Jenny was one of those most relieved to hear that Percy's hopes of matrimony might come to fruition in the near future.

She and Mrs Bailey were discussing the matter as they washed up the breakfast things together, for Jenny lived in, in a comfortable flat upstairs in Dr Bailey's old home. It was a happy arrangement. Winnie had found, to her shame, that she was nervous alone at night after her husband's death, despite the many friends around her. When Jenny's parents went into a retirement home, she was offered her present quarters, and the two women had settled together with the utmost satisfaction.

'I must say,' said Jenny, rinsing cups under the hot tap, 'that it'll be a relief to see Perce settled.'

'Nothing like the relief I felt when you turned him down,' replied Winnie. 'What should I have done without you?'

'There was never any chance of me taking on that fellow,' said Jenny briskly, 'and Emily Cooke's a fool if she does.'

'Well, she does have her little boy to consider,' replied Winnie tolerantly. 'I suppose she feels it is best for Nigel to have a father – or stepfather, I should say.'

'It won't be Nigel she'll be thinking about if she takes on

57

Percy,' said Jenny. 'It's her own comforts that'll be on her mind.'

'Percy is certainly what my husband's people used to call "a warm man", with that big house and quite a bit of land.'

'It'd take more than that to persuade most women to saddle themselves with Percy Hodge,' said Jenny.

At that moment they heard a thud in the hall, and Winnie went to collect the post from the door-mat. Willie Marchant, the postman, was making his way back to the bicycle which was propped up by the gate.

Winnie took the letters back to the kitchen, and sat at the table.

'Two for you, Jenny, and one enormous packet for me. What can it be?'

It turned out to be a book, most carefully swathed in tissue paper and then stiff brown paper, with a label addressed in what Winnie suddenly realized was Agnes Fogerty's clear print.

There was a letter enclosed which Winnie read attentively.

'It's a book I lent Miss Fogerty when she was laid up at the Shoosmiths. I wish she hadn't bothered to return it. The postage is so expensive, and they are bound to be coming up again.'

'How are they?' enquired Jenny, propping her two postcards on the dresser.

'They sound busy, and seem to have made quite a few friends. Dorothy is doing good works, including reading to a blind man called Teddy.'

'Poor chap!' said Jenny. 'I reckon being blind is the worst of the lot. My old people were both stone deaf towards the end, and that was bad enough.'

'Losing any of your five senses is dreadful,' agreed Winnie, stuffing Agnes's letter back into its envelope.

'Have you ever thought,' commented Jenny, busily swabbing the draining board, 'that if you can't see you're called *blind*, and if you can't hear you're called *deaf*, but if you can't smell anything, like Bill Cartwright, there's no word for it?'

'Oh, but there is,' Winnie informed her. 'My old uncle always said he was *snoof*!'

A little later that morning, Winnie was pegging out some washing when she was hailed by her neighbour Phyllida Hurst who lived next door. Winnie approached the useful gap in their common hedge, where one of the hawthorn bushes had expired and never been adequately replaced.

'I've promised to do the flowers for the church this week,' said the younger woman, 'and I wondered if you could spare some of your copper beech twigs.'

'Of course, Phil. Come round whenever you like. Is there anything else of use here?'

'Can I come and see? All I appear to have here are dwarf begonias and nasturtiums. Not quite the stuff for church decorations really.'

She squeezed through the gap, and the two women paced round the garden, assessing Winnie's floral produce.

It was perfectly true, Winnie thought, that the next door garden never did as well as her own. Something to do with the soil, no doubt, but also the several years of complete neglect before the Hursts had taken it over.

The former occupants of Tullivers had been an elderly couple, Admiral Josiah Trigg and his sister, Lucy. To be sure, Josiah had tended his flower border assiduously, and a jobbing gardener had cut the grass and hedges in his time, but when the admiral had died Lucy had done nothing to the garden.

Hedges became spinneys, lawns became meadows, and the seeds of thistle, dandelion, and willow herb floated into neighbouring gardens. Brambles and nettles invaded the place, and the inhabitants of Thrush Green grieved over Tullivers' sad condition.

Nothing had been done to the house either for that matter, Winnie remembered. She had been perturbed by the condition of her neighbour's house; the grimy windows, paths and steps, and the utter neglect of all that was inside.

It was not as if Lucy Trigg were senile, far from it. Winnie knew her as a formidable bridge player and solver of crossword puzzles, and she had trenchant views on current events. But her surroundings meant nothing to her, and her meals were as erratic as dear old Dotty Harmer's at Lulling Woods: an apple crunched as she read the newspaper, or a doorstep of brown bread spread with honey, as she filled in the crossword, sufficed Lucy.

It had been a relief to everyone when a young woman, then Phyllida Prior, had taken over the house and set about tidying up, with the help of her little boy and a succession of local amateur part-time gardeners. It was Harold Shoosmith who had really done most of the reclamation in the early days, and although the garden was much improved, it was not until Phil married again, an older man called Frank Hurst, that the place became trim, although it was never as fruitful as some of the other much-loved gardens at Thrush Green.

Winnie and Phil collected an armful of beech sprays, some roses, lupins and Canterbury bells.

'It seems a motley lot,' observed Winnie, surveying their harvest. 'I suppose you really want some trailing stuff for the pedestals. You can quite see why the Victorians liked smilax to drape everywhere.'

'This is splendid,' Phil assured her. 'I'm only in charge of the humbler efforts at the foot of the lectern and the font. The real high-fliers like Muriel Fuller are the only people let loose on things like pedestals.'

'That reminds me,' said Winnie, sitting on the garden seat and patting the space beside her. 'I heard from Dorothy and Agnes today. They do seem to have settled very happily at Barton.'

'They'd make friends wherever they went,' replied Phil. 'You get good training at Thrush Green in the art of sociability.'

'I think you are right. I only hope that Alan Lester's wife will think so too. As the headmaster's wife, she'll be scrutinized pretty thoroughly, I'm afraid. It's not easy, you know, living on top of the job like that.'

'Agnes and Dorothy managed it,' said Phil.

'Agnes and Dorothy,' responded Winnie, 'were two remarkable women, whose lives were outstandingly exemplary and virtually an open book.'

'Well, let's hope the Lesters will prove the same,' said Phil, rising to return next door.

'Let's hope so indeed,' echoed Winnie.

While the two ladies were conversing in the garden at Thrush Green, the subjects of their discussion were studying a Trust House Hotels' brochure with much interest. It had been Dorothy's idea that another short break would do them both good.

'After all, Agnes,' she said, 'you had to spend quite some time in bed when we were at Thrush Green. The visit really didn't do you the *benefit* it should have done. What about somewhere further north?'

'Scotland, do you mean?'

'No, no, no! There's no need to go somewhere as extreme as that, all mist and murk.' She turned the pages briskly.

'I'm really quite content to stay here,' ventured Agnes.

'I'm sure you are,' said Dorothy, 'but the fact remains that in this humid weather Barton seems as hot and sticky as most places. I should like somewhere more wooded, and with a few nice hills.'

'What about Wales? Are there any Welsh hotels in that brochure?'

'Quite a few.' She browsed in silence for a time. 'What I like about these Trust House places is that they have a kettle in the bedroom.'

Agnes looked bewildered.

'For tea, dear, or coffee,' explained Dorothy in the tone she used to address somewhat dim-witted children in her teaching days. 'It does mean that one can have a cuppa in the privacy of one's room rather than having to be civil to strangers in the lounge.'

It was quite clear to Agnes that they would certainly be setting off for another few days' holiday within the next few weeks, and she adapted herself to the idea, though with some remaining misgivings.

'What about your meetings? And Teddy?' she added.

'We can pick a time when we haven't any commitments; and I have no doubt that Eileen would be only too pleased to read to Teddy.'

She sounded a little waspish, Agnes thought. She disliked Eileen's noisy ways as much as Dorothy did, but recognized the fact that Eileen was a lonely woman, and also extremely kind-hearted. In fact, Agnes remembered, with a wave of gratitude, she had offered to look after dear Timmy if they were away.

'There's Timmy—' she began.

'Well, we know all about Tim,' said Dorothy, shaking out the brochure impatiently to find the map. 'We faced the problem of Tim when we took him on. No doubt one of the neighbours will feed him.'

'I was just going to say so,' said Agnes. 'Eileen mentioned it only the other day. Anytime, she said, she would look after him, and I'm sure she meant it.'

'I'm sure she did,' agreed Dorothy, spreading the map on the table. 'There's nothing Eileen likes more than seeing inside other people's houses.'

Agnes fell silent. It was the only thing to do when Dorothy was in this mood.

'There seem to be some nice hotels in the Derbyshire area,' said Dorothy.

'Isn't that rather a long way to drive? Isn't Birmingham in the way?'

'Well, Birmingham doesn't stretch *right the way across*! We could drive to the left or right of it, if you see what I mean.'

Agnes joined her friend and studied the map too.

'There are certainly some lovely old houses to see,' she

agreed. 'Kedleston Hall and Hardwick, and lots of others. And, of course, we should get the hills, shouldn't we?'

At that moment the telephone rang, and Dorothy hastened into the hall to answer it. She was smiling when she returned.

'It was that nice Terry Burns,' she told Agnes, naming one of the churchwardens. 'He's bringing round some gardening books at about six. I wonder if we've any sherry? He likes it dry, I seem to remember.'

'There's some of the Tio Pepe left that Isobel gave us,' Agnes reminded her, relieved to see how much happier Dorothy seemed now that Eileen was forgotten.

'Perfect,' replied Dorothy, folding up the map. 'What should we do without our friends?'

A few days after Violet's visit to the vicarage, Charles Henstock made his way down the High Street to call upon the Misses Lovelock, and Bertha in particular. His heart was heavy. This was one of those duties which had to be undertaken, but it filled him with foreboding. However, he had promised Violet that he would have a word with her sister, and so it must be done.

Violet opened the door to him; her expression of joy and relief as she greeted him was more than compensation for the good rector's endeavours.

'Ada is shopping,' said Violet, 'and Bertha is in bed, not too well. I will lead the way.'

Charles followed Violet's bony legs upstairs and along a dark landing to a bedroom overlooking Lulling High Street.

'I've brought you a visitor, Bertha,' said Violet.

'Well, what a nice surprise,' replied Bertha, removing a pair of steel-rimmed spectacles. 'How kind of you to call, Charles.'

She extended a fragile hand. It felt almost like a bird's claw as Charles held it in his own plump one.

'Would you like coffee?' enquired Violet.

'Not for me,' said Bertha.

'Not for me, many thanks,' smiled Charles.

He was aware of Violet's agitation by the unusual flush

which now suffused her face and neck, but he could not help admiring the aplomb with which she was carrying out her duties as hostess.

'Then I shall leave you to talk,' she said. 'If you will excuse me, I will go back to my kitchen affairs.'

She closed the door, and Charles had a chance to look about the room as Bertha busily folded up the newspaper she had been perusing. It certainly was uncomfortably crowded, and Charles recognized one or two pieces of furniture which had once had their place in the drawing-room downstairs.

A glass-fronted china cabinet was squashed between the dressing-table and wardrobe. It appeared to be crammed with exquisite porcelain, and on top stood a heavy silver rose-bowl which Charles knew had once been presented to the sisters' father.

More silver pieces were lodged on top of the mahogany wardrobe: Charles could see mugs, salvers, wine coasters, jugs and at least three silver teapots. A little Sheraton sofa table, another exile from the drawing-room, stood by Bertha's bed, and this too carried a host of miniature silverware. Charles recognized a dolls' tea-set, a miniature coach-and-four, and a windmill.

There was certainly something very odd happening in this house, and Charles felt a shiver of apprehension. Here, he knew, was madness – madness of a mild kind, no doubt, but something strange, sad and ominous.

'And how is dear Dimity?' enquired Bertha.

'Very well, thank you, and sends her love.'

Bertha inclined her head graciously. She seemed to be completely in charge of herself, but Charles noticed that the bony hands which smoothed her bed-covers were quivering.

He decided to broach his painful duty. 'I see you have had some things transferred from downstairs.'

'I like to have pretty things around me.'

'But don't your sisters miss them?'

Bertha looked at him sharply. 'They are not their property. And in any case, they can see them when they come up here.'

Charles decided on another approach. 'But don't you find they get in the way? It must be quite difficult to move around with so much in here.'

'I can manage,' she snapped.

Silence fell. A car hooted in the street below, a baby wailed, and a dog barked. The life of Lulling continued as usual outside in the fresh air, and Charles became aware of the stuffiness of this cluttered bedroom.

'I *want* the things here,' said Bertha at last. 'Ada and Violet don't appreciate them, and never have. I've taken them into my care, and I intend to see Justin Venables about changing my will.'

'Changing your will?' echoed Charles, much bewildered.

'Everything in this room is to go to St John's church in gratitude for Anthony Bull's ministrations.'

Charles was stunned. He felt as if he had been struck with a hard and heavy object, and was conscious of his head throbbing and his heart behaving in a most unusual fashion.

'Would you mind if I opened the window a little, Bertha?' he asked.

'Please do. Violet is inclined to keep the windows closed.'

Charles struggled from his chair, and heaved at the large sash window furthest from Bertha's bed. It was a relief to see the normality of Lulling outside, and the cool air revived him. He took several deep breaths and returned to his chair.

'My dear Bertha,' he began, 'it is a most generous gesture of yours, but before you do anything about the will, please consult your sisters and tell them what is in your mind.'

'I shall do nothing of the sort,' Bertha rapped out. She looked at him suspiciously. 'You are on their side! They've put you up to this!'

'I'm on nobody's side,' protested poor Charles, 'and no one has "put me up", as you say, to anything.'

'I shall tell Justin to call here,' replied Bertha. She was now very flushed and breathless. Charles knew that it was useless to try to reason with her. He had failed in his mission, and it was time to depart. It was obviously going to be impossible to go into the matter of taking things from The Fuchsia Bush at this stage.

He got up from the chair and approached the bed. He took Bertha's hand and patted it.

'I am sorry to have upset you, Bertha, and I'm going to leave you to rest now. But please think about my suggestion. I hope you will decide to talk to Ada and Violet.'

'I told you – I shall certainly *not* consult them.'

Charles released the hand. 'Then I beg of you,' he said earnestly, 'to consult your conscience instead.'

And with that he left.

Violet was fluttering about in the hall as he descended the stairs.

'Come into the drawing-room,' she whispered.

They sat down facing each other.

'Well?' queried Violet.

'Not well at all, I fear,' said Charles. 'I haven't really helped much.'

He told her, as gently as he could, about her sister's plan to alter her will, virtually laying claim to all that was in her bedroom. However, he purposely did not tell Violet about Bertha's idea of leaving all the treasures to St John's church. There was no point in burdening her with this extra problem, and he disliked the idea of this crazy plan of Bertha's being discussed in the parish.

'And she intends to see Justin?' gasped Violet. 'What shall we do?'

'I should do nothing while she is safely in bed,' replied Charles. 'I gather that the only telephone is in the hall down here, and any letters will pass through your hands. If she does propose getting in touch with him, then I think you must speak to him first and explain matters. If need be, I will have a word with him whenever you give me permission.'

'Charles! I hope it won't come to that.'

'So do I. In any case, I am sure that Justin will know exactly what to do in this sort of situation. I seem to recall something at the beginning of a will to the effect that: "I, being of sound body and mind etc." and I'm sure it is now sadly plain that Bertha is *not* of sound mind at the moment.'

'I fear not,' agreed Violet, much agitated.

'I must go,' said Charles. 'I'll come again in a day or two to see how things are going. Get in touch at once if you are worried, but I'm sure we can only wait and hope that she will realize how foolish she is being.'

'Thank you, Charles, for everything. I shall take your advice.'

As Charles returned to the vicarage he felt a great sense of failure. He also turned over in his mind Bertha's strange intention to leave everything to the church. The fact that the gift was to be a tribute to his predecessor Anthony Bull, who now had a parish in London, did not perturb or surprise him. Anthony was an old friend, and Charles was the first to recognize and appreciate his dynamic qualities.

Anthony Bull's outstanding good looks, his charm of manner, and his almost theatrical delivery of his sermons, had won the hearts of all who met him. It was not surprising that Bertha Lovelock had felt such burning affection for him. She was only one of many in his congregation to whom he had brought colour and comfort.

It was also quite logical that she should wish to repay the inspiration he had given her, and to do it through the church she had always attended rather than as a direct bequest to the man himself, showed a certain delicacy of feeling, and a sense of propriety quite consistent with the attitude of the Lovelocks.

But Charles hoped sincerely that nothing would come of Bertha's alarming plans. Rumours of her incipient kleptomania were already rife in Lulling, and Dimity knew that he had made today's errand in the hope of being able to help. He would have to tell her that he had failed in his mission, but that he hoped to try again.

The business of the will, he decided, should remain secret.

7. PREPARING TO MOVE

It came as no surprise to anyone to find that the school house at Thrush Green had little to show in the way of additions when the school holidays began. To be sure, there was an area at the back of the house which had been marked out with pegs, and one morning in early August a lorry had backed in and deposited a load of sand.

Betty Bell remarked on it when she was at the Shoosmiths one morning, giving them what she termed 'a good turn out'.

'I'll bet my bottom dollar them poor Lesters won't be in that place before next Christmas. I thought the old people's place was taking its time; but this lot haven't even got started.'

'Well, I believe the Lesters are on holiday for a week or so,' said Isobel. 'I expect they'll chivvy things up when they return.'

'Gone to the seaside, have they?' asked Betty, turning a dining-room chair upside down and tackling the legs with a generous dab of polish.

'No. The Peak District, I think. They're touring, and Mr Lester hoped to go to the opera at Buxton.'

Betty's ministrations were arrested. 'I went to the opera once,' she said. The tone was of one recollecting a nasty session at the dentist's.

'Didn't you enjoy it, Betty?'

'No, I didn't! The *noise*! What with all that screeching, and the band on top of that, I had a splitting headache. I really prefer the telly – you can switch it off.'

She resumed her polishing with renewed vigour.

'So when's he hoping to move in?' she enquired somewhat breathlessly.

'I believe he hoped to move in during August,' said Harold, who was looking out of the window to the house next door.

'He'll be lucky,' commented Betty.

And Harold was inclined to agree.

But a week later, Alan Lester's car drew up outside the property and out tumbled two little girls followed, more decorously, by their parents.

Interested inhabitants of Thrush Green watched the schoolmaster unlock the front door to allow his family some folding-chairs, several large baskets and assorted packages into the empty house.

'That looks more hopeful,' commented Harold to Isobel. He watched Alan Lester return to the car to retrieve an unwieldy bundle of brooms, a bucket and a vacuum-cleaner.

'Don't be such a busybody,' said Isobel. 'You are as bad as the Lovelocks, peeking behind curtains.'

Harold laughed, and went into his study to write some letters. They could hear the children playing next door, exploring the playground and peering in the hedge for abandoned nests.

When it became time for mid-morning coffee, Isobel suggested that Harold might call next door to invite them over. The Lesters seemed delighted to down tools, and the four of them joined the Shoosmiths in the garden.

'I must say,' said Harold, 'that we didn't dare hope to see you quite so soon. You really have bought it, then?'

'It was a case of moving quickly,' said Alan. 'The fellow who bought my house had the ready money and was anxious to move in quickly as his wife is expecting their first baby shortly. It suited us, too.'

'It's good news for us,' Isobel said. 'We've hated seeing the place standing empty. Is there much to do?'

'Basically, no. The extension will simply have to be done while we are in residence, but in some ways that will be a good thing. We can keep an eye on affairs.'

'What we *would* like,' said Alan's wife, 'is somebody to give the place a good scrub out. Can you suggest anyone?'

'Domestic help is pretty thin on the ground at Thrush Green,' replied Isobel. She told her about Betty Bell, but Margaret Lester was adamant that she would not employ someone who was already heavily engaged.

'It's the quickest way to make enemies,' she said smiling, 'but perhaps she might know of someone? We want to move in in about ten days' time, and it would only be this one occasion. I don't think I shall need regular help.'

Isobel promised to make enquiries, and the conversation turned to such matters as milk deliveries, reliable grocers and butchers, the rarity of jobbing gardeners and the everlasting boon of The Two Pheasants.

The two men, followed by the little girls, then went on a tour of the Shoosmiths' garden, while Isobel and Margaret sat talking.

'I do so hope it will all work out,' said the latter. 'It's all been done in such a hurry, but Alan was worried about me, I know.'

'Do you have health problems?'

Margaret sighed. 'I've really not been quite as fit since Kate was born. There's nothing that the doctors can do, so they say, but I get the most appalling headaches, and they leave me terribly low and depressed.'

Isobel made sympathetic noises. Privately, she wondered if Margaret Lester was something of a hypochondriac; she seemed almost pleased to be discussing her symptoms.

'In that case,' said Isobel, 'I'm sure Alan is doing the right thing by moving here where you can be together so much more. And you will find Thrush Green people are very friendly. As for the air here, it's absolutely a tonic in itself. I'm sure you will all feel the benefit.'

'Well, I certainly hope so,' said Margaret wanly. 'I really can't face feeling like this for the rest of my life!'

'You won't have to,' replied Isobel sturdily. 'Come round here if you need anything while you are working next door; the telephone is here, and a couch if you feel like a rest.'

'You are so kind. We are having lunch at The Two Pheasants and Mr Jones has said exactly the same. I think we are going to settle in nicely.'

'I'm sure of it,' said Isobel, and watched the woman making her way towards the family, and then next door to resume her labours.

Later that day, Isobel voiced her fears about Margaret Lester's possible hypochondria, but Harold was dismissive of such conjectures.

'I thought she was a very nice little woman. And after all, they are obviously having quite a lot of worry at the moment, with all the upheaval of moving, and getting the little girls used to the idea of going to the same school as their father. It's not surprising that she seems a little low at the moment.'

Isobel said no more, but reserved her judgement.

True to her word, Isobel spoke to Betty Bell about the cleaning of the school house.

'Well, now,' said Betty, 'I'd dearly like to take it on myself, but I've got my old auntie coming for a bit, and I shall be tied up with her.'

'Don't worry, Betty. Mrs Lester didn't really expect you to do it, just to suggest someone, if possible.'

Betty Bell ruminated, picking automatically at what appeared to be congealed marmalade on the edge of the kitchen table.

'Tell you what,' she said at last, 'have a word with Nelly Piggott. She might do it, and if not she'd know of someone, I don't doubt.'

That evening Nelly Piggott was busy frying what she termed 'a nice bit of rump' when Isobel called to make her request.

'Come in, come in,' cried Nelly, shifting the sizzling pan to one side of the stove, but Isobel made her request from the doorstep, not wishing to disturb Nelly's labours.

'I'd do it myself if I'd the time,' Nelly told her. 'Nothing I like more than a bit of steady scrubbing, but we're a bit short-handed at the shop, what with holidays and that. I'll have a word with a friend of mine, Mrs Lilly. I know she might be glad to earn something.'

This was good news, and Isobel explained that Nelly's friend should get in touch with the Lesters, if she were interested, and gave Nelly their telephone number. She returned home feeling that she had done her duty.

The evening was hot and humid. Tiny black thunder-flies were everywhere, speckling the white paint and crawling over bare skin in the most irritating manner.

Isobel sank thankfully into a chair and brushed her tickly arms. 'Heavens, I'm tired!'

'What have you been up to?' queried Harold.

Isobel told him.

'Now for pity's sake, don't go rushing about on the Lesters' behalf,' he said crossly. 'They are quite capable of coping with their own affairs, and there's no need to wear yourself out.'

'I haven't done much,' protested Isobel. 'Only tried to find someone to clean the house for them before they move in.'

'Well, don't let them impose on you,' said Harold, who could not bear to see Isobel worried in any way.

'You sound like my mother,' laughed Isobel, 'who used to say: "Start as you mean to go on!"'

'And quite right too,' agreed Harold. 'Now stay there, and I'll get you a drink.'

Meanwhile, replete with rump steak, fried potatoes, onions and baked beans, Nelly took herself down the hill to the road where Gladys Lilly lived.

It was one of the smaller, older terraced houses in the street, a 'two-up-two-down' cottage where Gladys had lived alone since the death of her husband.

A year or so earlier, in the last few months of Miss Watson and Miss Fogerty's reign at Thrush Green school, a daughter Doreen had kept her mother company. The girl had a young son, and had worked for a time at the Lovelocks, leaving the child with his grandmother. It was not a happy arrangement. Doreen had hated her job, and to give the girl her due it was hardly surprising, for the Lovelocks' house was large, over-furnished and difficult to keep clean. The three sisters were demanding and paid a poor wage. Gladys got used to listening to a string of complaints about life in Lulling when Doreen came home from work each day.

But it was a considerable shock to Gladys when the girl sneaked away with the child one day, leaving no message and no address. It was soon apparent that she had run away with the young man who was her little boy's father. Apart from a sparsely-worded postcard, on which the postmark was so blurred that it was indecipherable, Gladys had heard no more, and had resumed her solitary existence with both resentment and relief.

She was delighted now to see Nelly, and the kettle was put on at once for a cup of coffee. While it boiled, Nelly broached the purpose of her visit, and handed over the slip of paper bearing the Lesters' telephone number.

'What are they like?' asked Gladys.

'To tell the truth, I've never clapped eyes on *her*,' replied Nelly, 'but *he's* a nice enough chap. Good with the kids. I haven't heard anyone criticizing him yet, and that's saying something after all those years Miss Watson and Miss Fogerty were there.'

Gladys nodded ruminatively. 'Well, I'm game,' she said at last. 'I keep the chapel clean these days, but I don't do much else. The money would come in handy, too. I'll give them a ring later on.'

The two ladies then turned their attention to other matters.

'What's all this I hear about the Lovelocks pinching things?' enquired Gladys.

Nelly, for all her love of a good gossip, had no intention of discussing this matter which so intimately concerned The Fuchsia Bush.

'Don't know much about that,' she asserted, 'but is there any news of Doreen?'

Thus diverted, Gladys imparted exciting news. Doreen, it seemed, had rung the next door neighbour and left a message.

'And what was it?' asked Nelly, equally agog.

'Just to say she was all right. Might be coming down sometime.'

'But where is she? And who with? And is the little boy all right? Is she still with that fellow of hers?'

Gladys responded to this spate of questions, with a sad shaking of the head.

'She never said no more. Makes me wish I'd got the telephone myself. I could have found out more. The money run out evidently, and she just rang off.'

'Well, that was bad luck,' said Nelly, with genuine sympathy.

'Still, you do know she's all right. Be nice to see her again, won't it?'

'A mixed blessing, I expect,' replied Gladys. 'She's not turned out as I'd have hoped, brought up chapel too, and kept respectable. Makes you think, don't it?'

The ladies sighed in unison.

'Must be off,' said Nelly, getting up.

'I'll come as far as the phone box with you,' said Gladys, picking up the slip of paper.

'Can't you ring from next door?'

'I *could*,' replied Gladys, 'but I don't want everyone knowing my business.'

Nelly nodded her approval, and the two friends walked to the foot of the hill to Thrush Green and parted there by the telephone box.

'Well,' murmured Nelly, as she puffed homeward, 'I suppose I've done my good deed for the day. And now for the washing-up.'

It so happened that Charles Henstock saw the two women in the distance as he returned from a stroll by the River Pleshey. It was one of his favourite walks, and one which he always found himself undertaking when particularly perplexed in mind.

There was something about running water which healed the spirit as surely as sleep did. For Charles Henstock, the company of the river was indeed: 'Balm of hurt minds, great nature's second course,' and he usually returned from it calmed and comforted.

He sat by its side on a grassy bank, watching the secret life of the water creatures: a dragonfly alternately darted and hovered above the surface; while a water vole emerged from a hole on the opposite bank, fearless of the still figure so close, and paddled across, its hairy muzzle and bright eyes just clear of the water, leaving a wake behind it as neat as an arrow.

Flies studded the glistening mud at the edge of the bank, and a trio of butterflies played among a patch of nettles. An ancient willow tree stretched a gnarled arm over the water, and a flycatcher sat, still and erect in between its rapid darts, to secure an unwary insect.

Purple loosestrife and wild mint stirred in the light breeze, setting free the river smell, 'unforgettable, unforgotten' which brought back to the watcher on the bank a hundred memories of other loved rivers. Charles sat there for almost half an hour, letting the magic work its spell, and then he rose to return home.

The sun was beginning to sink behind Lulling Woods, and midges hovered in gauzy clouds over the river. In an hour or so the owls would be out, and the bats and moths, all busy above the glimmering water in their search for food. The river creatures of day and night might be different, thought Charles, setting off for home, but the river was unchanged in its steady progress eastward and the music of its voice.

Charles strode along the footpath until it emerged into the most westerly road of Lulling within a mile or two of the vicarage. He was calmer and more refreshed than when he had set out, but his mind was not entirely at ease.

It was the plight of Violet Lovelock which worried him. He had kept his word and returned to see Bertha again, hoping that she might have faced the fact that she had been at fault, and determined to overcome her weakness.

But his visit had been in vain, as he suspected it would be. Bertha was as evasive as ever, admitted nothing, was even more autocratic than was usual, and now that she was up and about appeared to be determined to go out as soon as possible.

Violet had been unable to get Charles alone on that occasion, but cast him appealing looks which rent poor Charles's kind heart. Later, he had spoken to her on the telephone, urging her to call at the vicarage whenever she felt the need. She had sounded resigned and exhausted, which Charles found even harder to bear than her earlier agitation, but there seemed little more that he could do.

As he walked up the High Street of Lulling in the failing light, he came to the Lovelocks' house and paused. There were lights in the drawing-room. They were not very bright lights, to be sure, probably just one or two table lamps containing low-watt bulbs, just enough to give adequate light to the sisters' knitting or crossword puzzle.

On impulse, Charles mounted the steps and knocked. Footsteps approached, and there was a rattle as the chain on the door was removed. Bolts were shot back, the door opened, and Violet stood silhouetted against the dim light of the hall.

'Oh Charles!' she cried. 'How lovely to see you. Do come in.'

Her two sisters fluttered to their feet as Charles came into the drawing-room, expressing delight and offering sherry or coffee.

Charles declined and apologized for disturbing them.

'The fact is,' he explained, 'I simply saw your lights on and couldn't resist calling to see you.'

'How very kind,' said Ada.

'Very kind,' echoed Bertha.

The room seemed stuffy and chilly at the same time, but Charles told himself that it was probably his own walk in the fresh air that made this present situation so enervating in contrast.

The usual polite enquiries were exchanged about health, gardens and the like, until Bertha announced with some pride: 'Tomorrow I am taking Ada and Violet to lunch at The Fuchsia Bush.'

There was a gasp from Violet, and a puzzled look from Ada; it was quite apparent that this was the first they had heard of it.

'Are you sure, dear?' enquired Ada.

'I had prepared a little chicken in a casserole,' said Violet.

'No, no!' said Bertha, with some vehemence. 'I *particularly* want to go next door tomorrow.'

There was a pause.

'Very well,' said Violet at last. 'I'm sure we should all enjoy it.'

'I must be off,' said Charles. 'Dimity will wonder where I am. So good to see you looking so well.'

Violet accompanied him to the front door. 'One moment,' she whispered. 'I will walk part of the way with you.'

She returned to the drawing-room briefly, and then joined Charles. He was surprised to see that she did not put on a hat or gloves, as was her wont, but simply drew on a jacket which was hanging in the hall. Charles helped to arrange it round her skinny shoulders, and they descended the steps into the deserted street.

'I felt I must have a word with you,' began Violet, as they set off towards the vicarage. 'You have been *such* a support through this awful time, and I just wanted you to know that I am feeling so much better about the whole affair.'

'Is she over it? Faced things? Or has John Lovell seen her?'

'No, no, nothing like that. She still refuses to admit anything, but I have made up my mind that we can only do so much and no more. It's I who have faced things, Charles.'

She slowed to a stop. It was now almost dark. Moths fluttered around one of the street lamps which were beginning to come into light along the High Street. A black-and-white cat trotted purposefully under the shadow of the shop fronts, intent on its nightly business. In a nearby front garden, the night-scented stocks sent out a heady perfume.

'I shall keep a sharp eye on Bertha, and accompany her whenever she goes out. Luckily, I don't think she is able to slip away unnoticed. And if she transfers any more things to her bedroom, I shall simply ignore it.'

'Has she said any more about the will?'

'Not a thing. But I am quite prepared to have a private word with Justin if she broaches the subject again.'

'I don't think you can do more at this stage,' agreed Charles, 'and I must say I am so relieved to hear that you feel that you can cope with her.'

'What else can we do? She is my sister, and I am devoted to her, infuriating though she is at the moment. I know I can ask you for help, and if need be I can speak to Justin and John Lovell. Meanwhile, I live in hope that she will come to her senses.'

She gave a sudden shiver.

'You are getting cold,' said Charles anxiously. 'The wind is quite chilly. I think you should go back, and I will come with you to the door.'

'No, no, indeed! It is only a few steps, and I shall hurry back. But I wanted to tell you how things are. No better really for Bertha, but much more settled for me.'

'Call on me if ever you are worried,' replied Charles, and watched her scurry back to her home.

Later that evening he told Dimity about his visit to the Lovelocks' establishment.

'You are not still worrying about Bertha's little weakness?' said his wife. 'It is general knowledge, you know, and most people are very understanding about it.'

'I hadn't quite realized,' replied Charles, somewhat taken aback, 'that the Lovelocks' affairs were generally known.'

'Good heavens, Charles,' cried Dimity, 'you've lived in Lulling long enough to know how news gets about! All that I bother about is seeing you so worried. I suppose poor Violet has been unburdening herself to you!'

'I'm truly sorry I've been a worry to you,' said Charles. 'I should have realized that you are ever-watchful. But I really think that things will be easier now in that unhappy household.'

He told her a little of Violet's attitude, and of her reaction to Bertha's strange ways.

'It certainly sounds more hopeful,' said Dimity, folding up her sewing in preparation for bed time. 'Now I shall get a hot drink. You look tired and cold, as well you might with the Lovelocks' burdens upon you.'

She kissed the top of his shiny bald head as she passed his chair on the way to the vicarage kitchen, and wondered if his parishioners really knew how completely he lived for them.

8. TERM BEGINS

Gladys Lilly had performed her cleaning task at the school house with exceptional zeal and speed, and Thrush Green was pleased to see a large removal van draw up at the Lesters' gate one morning.

'They've got a lovely sofa,' Jenny told Winnie Bailey as they made the beds together. She was standing at the window, plumping up a pillow as she gazed across the green. 'Like my old folks had, only their springs had gone. And I wonder what's in them crates?'

'Jenny, do come on! I've left the gammon boiling, and it will be all over the stove.'

Jenny wrenched her attention from the Lesters' affairs, and returned to the bed-making reluctantly.

'I wonder what they'll find missing at the end of the day,' she remarked, as she tucked in sheets in an efficient hospital corners' way. 'It's usually something small like the tea strainer, or the washing-up brush.'

'Bound to be something vital,' agreed Winnie.

Of course, the rest of Thrush Green was equally enthralled by the Lesters' arrival. Joan Young and her husband Edward reminded each other of the upheaval they had experienced when settling Joan's parents into their new abode.

Muriel Fuller, sorting out material with Ella Bembridge, told her of the horrors she had endured when it came to packing up her old school's property, and her own personal belongings as well.

'It's not so much what you want to *keep*,' she said, 'as what you simply *have* to throw away. I nearly had a nervous breakdown. Dr Lovell was so understanding. He said I'd been living with my nerves for years.'

'You wouldn't be much use without them,' said Ella bluntly, and Muriel withdrew into affronted silence.

Isobel Shoosmith, the soul of hospitality, would have liked to ask the Lesters for morning coffee, but in view of Harold's earlier remarks about doing too much for their new neighbours decided to leave any invitations until later in the day. It was possible, she thought, that Harold himself might make overtures over the hedge.

But the most concentrated attention came from Albert Piggott who had taken up a strategic position in the churchyard. Ostensibly, he was weeding round the edges of the plot, and had a bucket beside him in which he occasionally deposited a handful of grass, chickweed or groundsel. The more virulent intruders such as young brambles, stinging nettles and the like, Albert ignored. Young Cooke could get on with those – what was he paid for?

Albert noted a nice plain green carpet going in, followed by a set of book cases and two upholstered arm chairs. Getting the sitting-room done first, thought Albert with approval. They'd need a good rest this evening. A number of tea chests were carried in next; they clanked rather noisily, and Albert surmised that they held kitchen equipment.

He moved round inside the churchyard wall to get a better view, just in time to see a single divan bed being hoisted from the pantechnicon. Now would that be for one of the children or for the master or his wife? Albert watched closely from behind a tombstone erected to 'Ezekiel West 1798–1860, Beloved By All' (an assertion which Albert had always considered unduly optimistic) and watched as one more single divan followed the first.

Albert hoped these would be for the parents. He and Nelly

had separate beds, in fact, they had separate rooms, and Albert appreciated it. Nelly snored, although she hotly denied it.

Having satisfied himself about the sleeping arrangements, Albert left Ezekiel West's resting place, and shifted to 'Patience Wellworth, Devoted Wife and Mother' whose dates of birth and death were obscured by some tendrils of ivy which Albert had no intention of removing. Resting his arms on the top of Patience's granite cross, he observed with pleasure that the landlord of The Two Pheasants was opening his doors.

At the same moment, he became conscious of a large object being manhandled through the school house's front door, to the accompaniment of warning shouts. It was a large double bed, and Albert's hopes were thrown to the wind.

He put down his half-empty bucket and sought solace in the pub.

Betty Bell, returning from her labours at the Shoosmiths that morning, called to see Dotty Harmer on her way home. As well as her regular visits to that house, Betty often 'popped in', as she said, to keep an eye on the old lady, although this was not so vital now that Kit and Connie were there to look after their eccentric relation.

Dotty was busy trying to rake dead leaves from the surface of her little pond. She was not being very successful, and the half-dozen displaced ducks were squatting moodily nearby, occasionally giving a protesting quack.

She abandoned her task and motioned Betty to the garden seat, taking her place beside her. Betty was not surprised to see that Dotty's shoes and stockings were soaking wet, and that she had a streak of mud on one cheek.

'I'd let Mr Kit do that job,' said Betty. 'It's too much for you. And you ought to get your shoes off. Catch your death, you will.'

'Don't fuss, Betty,' responded Dotty. 'You're as bad as Connie. A little dampness never hurt anyone. After all, we are three parts water I believe, and originally evolved from water creatures.'

'Some time ago,' Betty pointed out reasonably. 'You on your own?'

'Kit and Connie are getting back for lunch,' said Dotty. 'Which reminds me, I'm supposed to turn on the oven.'

'Well, let's go and see to it,' said Betty, used to Dotty's vague ways, 'and I'm going to see you take off them wet shoes, and give you a cup of coffee. I don't suppose you've had any?'

'Well, no,' admitted Dotty, 'I've been rather busy.'

Betty shepherded the old lady into the kitchen, peered into the oven, turned it on, and then filled the kettle. Within ten minutes, Dotty's stockings and shoes were removed and replaced with dry ones, and the coffee was made.

'Is this the milk?' queried Betty, sniffing at a small jug. 'Smells a bit off to me.'

'Oh, that will do, dear. I really don't mind it slightly cheesy.

After all, the Tibetans always use rancid milk in their tea – and *yak's* milk at that.'

'I think I'll have mine black,' said Betty, and the two settled happily at the kitchen table for ten minutes' gossip about the newcomers to Thrush Green.

It so happened that Isobel saw nothing of her neighbours for several days as she and Harold had an unexpected invitation to have a few days with friends in Wales. On their return, Isobel rang the Lesters to enquire how things were going. Alan answered the telephone.

'We're settling in nicely,' he said cheerfully. 'We shall be pretty straight indoors before term starts next week.'

'That's good,' replied Isobel, 'and how's the building getting on?'

'Far too slowly, but I'm not sorry really as poor Margaret is under the weather again.'

'Oh dear! Can we help?'

'No, no, it's just this wretched migraine. She gets an attack now and again, and bed's the only place until it passes.'

'I expect she's been doing too much,' said Isobel. 'Let us know if there's anything we can do.'

'You are kind. She'll soon be over it, I'm sure. We're quite geared to this sort of thing.'

'I wonder,' said Isobel to Harold some time later, 'if they've decided to move here because of these migraine attacks?'

'Maybe,' said Harold engrossed in the crossword. 'Have you ever heard of "Taxonomy"?'

'Never.'

'Nor me. These crossword setters must be born in the knife-drawer, as my mother used to say. Far too sharp for me.'

Term began at Thrush Green school and Alison and Kate Lester were enrolled as new pupils, along with half a dozen new five-year-olds who were escorted to the classroom which had once been the domain of little Miss Fogerty.

On the same day, far away at Barton-on-Sea, Agnes was watching a little knot of children making their way to school. She was moved to see the small ones, obviously new entrants, clutching their pristine school bags and wearing school blazers which were rather too large, 'to allow for growth'.

'Do you ever wish you were back at Thrush Green, Dorothy?' she asked.

Dorothy was poring over a form which had just come in the post. 'Well, of course I do,' she replied. 'But not at the school.'

She had heard children's voices, and knew from neighbours that this was the first day of term. She also knew, from her long association with Agnes, exactly what was going on in that kind lady's heart.

'Not at the school?' echoed Agnes, somewhat surprised.

Dorothy put down the form. 'Pure gobbledegook this is! Why these so-called communications can't be expressed in plain English I cannot understand.' She surveyed Agnes with sympathy. 'No, I can assure you, I would not want to return to teaching. I did over forty years, as you did too, and I am very happy to have retired.'

'Yes, of course,' agreed Agnes. 'It's just that seeing the new babies going along just now, so trusting and *clean*, you know, it brought it all back.'

'It should also bring back the memories of tears and tantrums and puddles on the floor, which marked the first morning of term,' said Dorothy briskly. 'And do you remember that terrible boy who bolted home? We caught him half a mile up the Nidden road. Wretched child!'

'He was a Cooke,' said Agnes.

'That,' replied Dorothy, 'does not surprise me. Now, about this form. I think you have to sign it, too, but I'll slip along to Teddy later on and read it to him. He's bound to know what it means.'

She was as good as her word, and in her absence Agnes busied herself in the garden. The dahlias were making a fine show of scarlet and gold, and the roses still showed a few late blooms, but there were signs of autumn already. The new pyracantha, pushing its way valiantly up the wall by the porch, was a mass of berries just beginning to turn orange. The birds would be grateful, thought Agnes, watching some blue-tits squabbling over the peanut-holder nearby.

She sat down on the seat to enjoy the sunshine, and hoped that Dorothy would not be too long with Teddy. It was so difficult to time the potatoes exactly when she went out in the morning. She ruminated again about Dorothy's attitude to this new friend. He certainly seemed to take up a great deal of her time, but she remembered Isobel's sensible words. Dorothy was a wise person, and would not be likely to do anything rash. It would be quite dreadful if she let her kind heart rule her head though, and succumbed to Teddy's pleas to marry him.

At this alarming thought Agnes pulled herself together. Now, who on earth had said anything about Teddy proposing marriage? Or about Dorothy accepting him? It really was unfair to either of them to think this way. Teddy, after all, was a good, decent, well-educated man, with beautiful manners and a voice not unlike dear Anthony Bull's of Lulling. Perhaps, thought Agnes, with a return of the flutters, that was what made him all the more dangerous! Anthony Bull had often been called a charmer; was Teddy equally irresistible?

What rubbish! Agnes rose from the seat and set about deadheading pansies with unusual violence. And one really must trust Dorothy's judgement in this situation. She was simply being kind to an afflicted neighbour. The fact that he was *male* was beside the point. *Any* neighbour, Eileen say, who had been blind, would have been treated by Dorothy with the same selfless kindness which was one of her great qualities.

But Eileen? The ubiquitous, noisy, laughing Eileen, who also called so frequently upon Teddy? *Would* Dorothy do as much for Eileen?

Agnes dismissed the doubt from her mind and deadheaded an innocent yellow pansy with such violence that the whole plant came up in her hand. She decided it was high time to put on the potatoes.

At Lulling that same morning, Ella Bembridge and her old friend Dimity Henstock were enjoying coffee together at The Fuchsia Bush.

'And how goes the new extension at Rectory Cottages?' asked Dimity. 'I keep meaning to come up and have a look, but Charles keeps me informed about its progress.'

'It's taking shape well,' responded Ella. 'It didn't take the men long to erect the glass part, and it will be marvellous for the old folk when it's done. I've just been to see about the curtains.'

'So it is to be curtains after all?'

'Yes. Muriel and I had a word about it with the committee. It would have been rather bleak, we thought, just with those blinds Edward wanted. Sometimes I find Edward's ideas a trifle *Scandinavian*.'

'Scandinavian, Ella? Well, what's wrong with that?'

'Cheerless,' asserted Ella, helping herself to a piece of Nelly Piggott's gingerbread. 'Angular, cold – not right for us anyway.'

'What did Edward say?'

'Nothing. We told him that old people living in the chilly Cotswolds would want something cosier than just glass all round them in the winter.'

'I expect he wanted the blinds because he was thinking of the heat in the summer,' said Dimity, feeling rather sorry for Edward Young who had obviously met his match in Ella and Muriel.

'More fool him,' pronounced Ella rather indistinctly through the gingerbread. 'We have far more cold days than hot ones. Anyway, top and bottom of it is that Muriel and I are coping with the small curtains at the side, and the main ones, which are enormous, are being made by Prouts. I've just been over there to check the headings and fixtures.'

She went on to such technical matters as pulleys and

pinch-pleating which meant nothing to Dimity, but she was brought back to earth by hearing Ella say that Muriel had called on the headmaster's wife.

'She was looking very poorly,' Ella said. 'Red-eyed and rather snuffly. Probably getting a cold, Muriel didn't stay long in case she caught it.'

She dived into her handbag, producing several keys, a man's handkerchief of red-and-white spotted cotton, and a large sheaf of booklets which she deposited on the table.

'Raffle books,' she announced.

'What for?' enquired Dimity, feeling for her purse and about to do a vicar's wife's familiar duty.

'The extension, of course. The money's coming in quite well, but the autumn is going to be a mad whirl of whist drives, concerts, jumble sales and the usual things. How many can you manage, Dim?'

'Ten, I think,' said Dimity. 'I'm still coping with RSPB, Save The Whales, RSPCA and Blue Cross raffle books.'

'But they are all *animals*,' protested Ella.

'I prefer them,' replied Dimity simply.

When Dimity returned home that morning she found Charles searching for a box of tissues.

'I think I have a cold hanging about,' he said. 'I'll go and gargle. Such a nuisance so near to Sunday.'

Dimity remembered Ella's remarks about Mrs Lester's cold, and became extra solicitous.

At eight o'clock that evening Charles confessed that his head ached, and he thought that he should go to bed. He slept in fits and starts, and Dimity heard him tossing and turning in the other bed, occasionally mumbling incoherently.

At first light he awoke to find Dimity standing beside him, thermometer in hand.

'It's John Lovell for you,' she said firmly on reading the result.

'But I have to take a funeral,' protested Charles.

'It will be your own,' Dimity told him, 'if you don't do as you are told.'

Charles knowing when he was beaten, put his aching head back on the pillow.

Within three hours, of course, it was known that the rector was seriously ill, with complaints ranging from a heart attack, a fall downstairs, appendicitis and pneumonia to tonsilitis and influenza.

John Lovell's diagnosis was a combination of the two latter afflictions, but knowing how easily Charles contracted severe and painful chest troubles, he pumped a good measure of anti-biotics into his victim, left a list of medicaments with Dimity, and strict instructions to see that his patient remained in bed.

'And as for that funeral he is fretting about, it will have to wait,' said the doctor, his mind naturally full of his duties towards the living rather than the dead.

Dimity, secretly shocked, said that she had already been in touch with the clergyman at the neighbouring town, who had kindly offered to stand in.

She closed the front door behind John, and made her way into the kitchen before going upstairs to assure her husband that everything was arranged, and that he could now relax and concentrate on his own affairs for a change.

But John Lovell's single-minded attitude still troubled her. Fancy saying that the funeral could wait! What about the relatives' unhappiness, and such practical matters as the cater-ing for all those people who might have come from a distance? And think of all the flowers being made into beautiful sheaves and wreaths, and all the cards and letters? Really, men were so thoughtless, so inconsiderate!

Putting off a funeral, indeed!

Full of righteous wrath, Dimity set about making a jug of lemon barley water for the invalid. Thank goodness Charles was such an exceptional person, so unlike the usual run of men.

Thus dwelling on her good fortune, Dimity's rage gradually

simmered down, and she was able to bear aloft the soothing drink in her usual gentle frame of mind.

Harold Shoosmith was one of Charles's first visitors.

'Well, I must say you look pretty comfortable up here,' he remarked, looking down at the sunny garden and his old friend propped up on the plump pillows enjoying the view. 'Far better than the first time I visited you as an invalid, when you were in the clutches of that ghastly housekeeper at Thrush Green rectory.'

'Oh, really,' protested Charles, 'poor Mrs Butler did her best.'

'Well, it wasn't good enough,' maintained Harold. 'I remember her martyred expression as she puffed into your bedroom with a couple of water biscuits and a wizened apple for your lunch. I wonder you didn't succumb with malnutrition as well as bronchitis.'

'I must say Dimity is a first-class nurse, and I'm being thoroughly spoilt.'

'Now, what can I do? Any errands to run? Messages to deliver? Parish magazines to take round? Just say.'

'I think Dimity has most things in hand, but I am supposed to be introducing things at Joan and Edward's coffee morning later this week. It's for the old people's extension. Could you do that?'

'Of course.'

'Otherwise I'm just having to put things aside until I'm out and about again. It's the visiting which worries me. I have met Alan Lester, of course, but when I called to see his wife she was upstairs with a severe headache.'

'That's often the way,' Harold told him. 'I feel very sorry for Alan.'

'Indeed, yes,' said Charles, his face puckered with concern. 'It must be dreadful to have an invalid wife.'

'I'm not sure myself,' said Harold slowly, 'that she is an invalid in the sense you mean.'

Charles looked mystified. 'Not an invalid? But if she is so often prostrate upstairs what else can it be?'

But at that moment, Dimity came in with a tea tray, and Harold was spared the necessity of answering.

9. FAMILY AFFAIRS

Charles Henstock was confined to his bed for over a week. Both Dimity and John Lovell saw to that, despite protests from their patient who kept remembering parish duties of the most urgent nature which, so he maintained, could only be undertaken by himself.

His pleas fell on deaf ears.

'Do you want me to send you to hospital?' threatened the doctor.

'Do think of yourself for a change,' pleaded Dimity.

In the end it was simpler to give way, and the good rector had to admit to himself that it was really pleasant, apart from some aches, to loll back among the pillows and look forward to appetizing meals being brought at regular intervals and, even better, the visits of old friends.

Among them, to Charles's delight, was his predecessor Anthony Bull, who blew into the bedroom like a breath of sea air, and laughed to see Charles's astonishment.

'I'm on my way to Bath for a conference,' he explained, after enquiries about the patient's progress, 'and I couldn't pass so near without calling. Dimity has kept me in touch. Tell me the news.'

Charles rattled away, and was sorely tempted to tell him about Bertha Lovelock's alarming intentions concerning her will. But one of his favourite precepts was: 'Least said, soonest mended', and with that in mind he simply gave a brief account of Bertha's growing eccentricity and poor Violet's worries.

'And I've news for you,' said Anthony. 'Gladys Lilly's

daughter Doreen turned up the other day, and I very much hope that she will decide to come back to Lulling.'

'What has been happening to her? And why didn't she go back to her employers? Didn't they live near you?'

'Indeed they did – and still do. But I don't think she had the pluck to go back after deserting them. She seems to have left the so-called husband, but she looked pretty pathetic, so did the child. I did my best to persuade her to go back to her mother, but all she would promise was to get in touch by telephone.'

'I believe Dimity heard that she had,' said Charles.

'At the moment she says she is staying "with friends". I only hope they are female,' commented Anthony. 'I have promised to give her her fare home, and she says she will be in touch. We fitted her out with some clothes from the church box, and the boy too, but she wouldn't give us the "friends'" address. Do you know if her mother is on the telephone?'

'I can find out, but I doubt it. Maybe a neighbour is.'

Anthony looked at his watch, then rose and went to the window to survey the garden which had once been his.

Charles looked at his handsome back in its well-tailored dark suit. His silver hair was as abundant as ever, his bearing youthful and his face unlined. How soon, Charles wondered hopefully, would he be made a bishop? Somehow it seemed inevitable, and how well Anthony's elegant legs would look in gaiters!

'The garden looks better than ever,' said Anthony. 'Do you know, I think we were happier here in Lulling than in any other living. We loved everybody here.'

'It was reciprocated,' Charles assured him, as they made their farewells.

Harold Shoosmith carried out his duties at the coffee morning with the general approval of Thrush Green.

'Well, if it couldn't be the rector,' one of the inmates of Rectory Cottages was heard to remark to her neighbour, 'then you couldn't do better than Mr Shoosmith.'

And this, Harold reckoned when told the tale, was high praise indeed.

Although the morning was overcast, and the Youngs' garden was already showing signs of autumn, it stayed dry and pleas-

antly warm. Butterflies rested on the Michaelmas daisies, opening and shutting their dappled wings. A pair of collared doves strutted about among the visitors, alert to any crumb which might fall.

Mrs Curdle's old gipsy caravan, which now had a permanent resting place in the Youngs' small orchard, was being used as a bring-and-buy shop that morning. Ben, Mrs Curdle's grandson, and his wife Molly were in charge, and pots of jam and marmalade, lavender bags, handkerchiefs, homemade fudge and all the other familiar bring-and-buy objects were changing hands at a brisk pace, while the small drawer, where old Mrs Curdle had kept her takings for so many years, was in use again and chinked steadily with a stream of coins.

Winnie Bailey had suggested to Margaret Lester that they should go together since it would be a good opportunity for the headmaster's wife to meet people. She was then going to Winnie's for lunch.

Certainly the newcomer seemed to be enjoying herself, and talked animatedly to those she met. She was quite pretty, Winnie decided, when she forgot her troubles and joined in the general activities. It was important, Winnie felt, that Alan's wife should be seen to be pleasant and approachable, for a man in his position would be very much in the public eye, and his family under scrutiny. As the widow of the local doctor, Winnie knew that the wife of a leading resident played a part as vital as the man himself.

It was a relief to her to see the pleasure with which her friends greeted Margaret. She had been so much of a recluse since moving in, suffering from those mysterious headaches, that very few people had met her. Now everyone was anxious to welcome her to the small world of Thrush Green.

Muriel Fuller seemed particularly effusive in her greetings, and went to some length to say that she had called at the school house on several occasions and had been perturbed to hear of Mrs Lester's indisposition.

Winnie, seeing that the two were getting on so well, excused herself and went across to Ella and Dimity.

'And what news of Charles?'

'Getting on steadily, and dying to get out and about again.'

'Sure sign that he's on the mend,' commented Winnie.

'And far more difficult to control,' added his wife, 'than when he was really too groggy to go far. With luck, he should be back on light duties next week.'

They had both met Margaret Lester, and agreed that it was splendid to see that she was fit again.

At that moment, Winnie noticed that a car had stopped outside her gate, and a man was walking to her front door. Even at that distance, Winnie could see that it was her nephew Richard who had the disconcerting habit of turning up without warning.

'Oh dear,' cried Winnie, 'I'd better go across and see what's going on. I'll just let Margaret know where I'm going.'

She spoke to the headmaster's wife, and then hurried across

the grass. Trust Richard to arrive when there was only one trout apiece for lunch! Why couldn't it have been steak and kidney, or something equally *stretchable*, a casserole perhaps?

Richard was in the kitchen with Jenny sipping coffee, and he greeted his aunt affectionately.

'I'm on my way to pick up Fenella and the children. They've been staying with an old cousin of hers. I must say, I'll be glad to have them back. The place has been like a morgue without them.'

Winnie thought this sounded most satisfactory. Richard's marriage had had its ups and downs, and sometimes Winnie had wondered if Fenella might leave him. She was a strong-minded young woman who ran a picture gallery in London where the family lived. Sometimes Winnie suspected that it was the main reason for keeping the family together, and wished that Richard would provide the home as most husbands did. Fenella definitely called the tune, but Winnie was the first to admit that Richard was a difficult fellow to live with, and perhaps it was as well that Fenella could hold her own.

When the school house had been on the market, Richard had made an attempt to buy it, but Fenella had refused point-blank to leave London and her livelihood.

'Do stay for lunch,' said Winnie.

'No, I'm due at the cousin's at twelve-thirty,' replied Richard. Immediately Winnie ceased trying to think of how to stretch the three trout so it would not have looked too contrived, and relaxed at once.

'Call in on your way back if you can.'

'We'll have to stop for tea with the old lady,' said Richard. 'Fenella says she's very proud of a fatless sponge she makes, and we are in duty bound to sample it and congratulate her. Damn dry it is, too,' he added.

'It's all right if it's eaten the same day,' Jenny said stoutly, defending a fellow cook.

'Old Cora must make hers a week before,' said Richard.

'I must go back to Margaret,' said Winnie, kissing her nephew. 'Nice to have had a glimpse of you.'

He had gone when the two ladies returned from the Youngs' garden shortly before lunch.

'Sherry?' asked Winnie, in the sitting-room before lunch.

'Do you happen to have some gin?' asked Margaret. 'I find I can take a little gin,' she explained, 'without getting an attack of migraine. Sherry seems to bring it on.'

Winnie poured her a generous tot, and they sat back to enjoy their drinks. Winnie was a little surprised to see her visitor's glass empty so quickly – and even more so when her offer of 'the other half' was accepted.

Quite soon, Jenny appeared to tell them that lunch was ready, and the three sat down together.

Normally, Winnie and Jenny were content with a glass of water apiece with their meal, but today they had provided a bottle of white wine in honour of their guest. It was empty by the end of the meal.

Jenny brought them coffee in the sitting-room, but would not join them.

Margaret, now rather flushed, rattled away about her new kitchen cupboards, and the pleasure she was getting from her new oven. It was two-thirty by the time she rose to go. She seemed unsteady on her feet, and Winnie said that she would walk across the green with her.

People were clearing up in the Youngs' garden; Winnie could see Ben and Edward carrying trestle-table tops to the shelter of the garden shed, and Molly Curdle and Joan Young seemed to be stacking crockery on trays. They waved to them as they passed.

Winnie left Margaret at the gate of the school house. Children were playing in the playground, and Winnie thought, with a pang, how often she had seen Dorothy and Agnes among their charges. She missed them sorely.

The sun had come through and as she made her way back,

Winnie sat down on one of the seats on the green. She felt very tired. The lunch had gone well, and it had been good to see Richard, but there was no doubt that entertaining, even with Jenny's incomparable efficiency, was getting increasingly burdensome. It was old age, she supposed, looking across at Rectory Cottages where even more aged friends lived.

Her thoughts turned to the new one she had just accompanied home on the other side of the green. There was definitely something wrong there. Winnie, as a doctor's wife for many years, was quite accustomed to seeing patients who were over-fond of alcohol, and knew the misery that it could bring to a family.

She roused herself from the bench and returned home. Jenny was on her knees putting away the best china, and looked up from the low cupboard with a welcoming smile.

'Nice party,' she said. 'But my word, she can put it away, can't she?'

It would not be long, Winnie realized, before a great many people would be of Jenny's opinion, and what might that augur for the happiness of the Lester family?

The former occupants of the school house were in the throes of packing for a few days away in Wales. It was Dorothy who took longer over this chore than Agnes. Possibly it was because Agnes owned far fewer clothes, and was not distracted by having to make a choice between six or eight different cardigans, say, or four or five frocks suitable to wear in the evening.

Dorothy too was more clothes-conscious altogether and, as a headmistress, had always made sure that she looked well turned out. Agnes, much less perturbed by her appearance, aimed to be neat, clean and unobtrusive. So when it came to packing, she was at a distinct advantage.

'Now, if I take my black,' Dorothy said, 'it means putting in my black patent shoes which are most uncomfortable and will take up far too much room.'

'I shouldn't take the black,' advised Agnes. 'I think the green, and that pretty new fawn dress should be ample for evenings. Then your brown shoes would look right with both.'

Dorothy looked undecided. 'It means wearing each one twice,' she said.

'I don't suppose anyone will have the vapours if you do,' retorted Agnes with unusual tartness. 'I'm only taking one skirt for evening with two dressy blouses, and people will have to put up with it.'

Dorothy nodded abstractedly.

'In any case,' continued Agnes, 'they will be worrying about their own appearance, not ours.'

'I'm sure you are right,' responded Dorothy, putting the black dress back in the cupboard.

'I'll just go down and check Timmy's provisions,' said Agnes. 'It's so good of Eileen to take him on. He's becoming quite devoted to her.'

When Dorothy appeared downstairs, case in hand, she found that Agnes was about to fill a flask with coffee for their picnic lunch.

'I'm popping along to say goodbye to Teddy,' she announced.

'But I thought Eileen was going in this morning,' replied Agnes, jug poised.

'She is,' agreed Dorothy, 'but I thought it would look more friendly to say we were just off, and leave our telephone number with him.'

'But I left it with Eileen!' protested Agnes.

'No harm in letting them both know where we are,' said Dorothy. 'I shall only be a minute.'

She vanished, to leave Agnes sitting on the kitchen chair watching Tim cleaning his handsome whiskers.

'Teddy this, and Teddy that,' sighed Agnes. 'Where will it all end?'

The coffee morning brought in almost three hundred pounds, a record sum at Thrush Green for such an event. Much cheered, the inhabitants braced themselves for further efforts during autumn, and watched the progress of the new extension with renewed proprietorial interest.

The topic was discussed by Nelly Piggott and her friend Mrs Jenner as they made their way down the hill to Lulling one evening, bound for an evening's diversion at Bingo. Nelly thoroughly enjoyed her regular outings, not only for the possible thrill of winning some money, but also for the more practical pleasure in sitting down after a day on her feet at The Fuchsia Bush.

Mrs Jenner was one of the oldest residents of Thrush Green, and sister to Percy Hodge the farmer. She lived a short distance along the road to Nidden, had once been a nurse, and was mother to Jane Cartwright, one of the wardens at Rectory Cottages. In any emergency it was ten chances to one that Mrs Jenner was called first, before the doctor or the vet, or the police or the fire brigade. She was indeed, as the rector often said: 'A very present help in trouble.'

Both Charles and Dimity knew this from first-hand, for when the rectory had gone up in a blaze that fateful night, it was Mrs Jenner who had offered them a home for several months and given them comfort as well as shelter after their shock.

She and Nelly had met at Bingo, and struck up a friendship. Mrs Jenner appreciated Nelly's good sense, her industry and cheerful disposition. She felt some pity, too, for her role as Albert Piggott's wife. She had known Albert since their school days, and knew also that he was incapable of changing his curmudgeonly ways.

The evening was fine, the two ladies agreed, but there was a definite nip in the air. At the bottom of the hill they saw Gladys Lilly hurrying towards them. Occasionally she joined the Bingo-players, but as a devout chapel-goer she sometimes had qualms about games of chance which her old father had roundly condemned as 'the devil's work'. Tonight, it seemed, she was about to put aside her doubts and was going to enjoy an evening out.

'Such news!' she gasped, as she approached the two friends. 'My Doreen's back!'

Nelly and Mrs Jenner said how pleased they were and they expressed their gratification as the three made their way up Lulling High Street together.

'She just turned up at midday. Some fellow she'd met, a window-cleaner in London, was off to see his mother in Cirencester, and he gave her a lift.'

'Is she staying long?'

'That I couldn't say.'

'And the little boy?'

'Into everything. Had my dripping bowl over before he'd been in the house five minutes. I'm going to have my hands full, I can see.' By now they had reached the hall where more people were going in. Gladys Lilly lowered her voice. 'There's one snag about all this. Glad though I am to see the girl, she's expecting again, and I've no doubt she'll reckon to stay with me till it arrives.'

Mrs Jenner had gone ahead and was talking to a friend.

'Oh lor!' said Nelly. 'The same fellow, is it?'

'Who's to tell?' replied Gladys despairingly. 'She won't, that's for sure. And to think I brought her up strict chapel.'

The chilly spell of weather which had been blamed for Charles Henstock's illness and a host of other people's ailments, now changed to warm sunshine.

Harold Shoosmith, who was at the end of his garden survey-ing the view across to Lulling Woods, wondered if anything could beat a sunny, dewy early September morning.

The harvest was now in, and most of the fields sloping away to the Pleshey valley had already been ploughed or drilled, ready for planting. The one immediately adjoining Harold's was still bristling with stubble, and Harold was pleased about that. For one thing, at night it had a strange luminosity which had a beauty of its own. More practically, it provided food for a covey of six partridges which sometimes wandered through the hedge and delighted Harold and Isobel as they sat at breakfast.

This morning they were not to be seen, but Harold became conscious of noises coming from next door in the school house garden. The children were in school and Thrush Green lay peacefully in the morning sunlight; gradually, Harold became aware that Margaret Lester was pottering about at the end of her garden, just as he was.

'Hello!' he called. 'Lovely morning.'

'Oh, you made me jump,' gasped Margaret. She came towards the hedge, and Harold approached her.

'Enjoying the sunshine?'

'It is rather nice,' she said vaguely. 'I've really been too busy to notice.'

There was a sound which Harold surmised was a hiccup.

At that moment, Isobel appeared to say that he was wanted on the telephone. She waved to Margaret, and the Shoosmiths excused themselves to hurry indoors.

'Margaret Lester doesn't look well,' commented Isobel as they traversed the garden.

'Margaret Lester,' said her husband shortly, 'is drunk.'

10. CRISIS FOR VIOLET LOVELOCK

On that same bright September morning, Violet Lovelock was busy in the garden, too. Girded in a hessian apron and wearing leather gardening gloves, she was cutting a few late roses for the drawing-room's silver trumpet-shaped vases, and deadheading the dead ones at the same time.

Violet liked gardening, unlike Ada whose arthritis hindered her from stooping. She limited her gardening activities to watering geraniums in pots at waist level, while her younger sister bent and stretched, trundled the wheelbarrow, and enjoyed comparative agility.

Among the roses, Violet thought about Bertha; so far, nothing untoward had happened. John Lovell had had to be called when Bertha had developed pains in the chest after the ubiquitous cold germ had done its worst in Lulling, and Violet, finding herself alone with him downstairs, had told him, somewhat guardedly, about Bertha's eccentricities.

John Lovell, who had heard the rumours anyway, was reassuring, simply saying that it would be best to accompany Bertha everywhere in her present state, and that if her symptoms gave cause for anxiety she was to get in touch at once.

On these carefully ambiguous phrases they had parted company, and since then Violet had been comforted by the thought that both Charles and John would now be at hand for support if needed. Meanwhile, it seemed that Bertha, who had soon recovered, was behaving in a normal manner although her bedroom still remained crammed with articles from all over the house, and every now and again some fresh piece of china or silver was added surreptitiously to the collection upstairs.

After Violet's gardening session, the three sisters partook of their usual sparse lunch, took a rest, and spent the remainder of the day in various domestic pursuits. The roses were much admired in the drawing-room that evening as Violet did the crossword, with equal help and hindrance from her sisters, and Ada and Bertha knitted.

At ten o'clock, as the grandfather clock in the hall was striking, the three ladies retired to bed.

Violet remained wakeful. A large moth, pattering against the window pane, obliged her to get out of bed and rescue it. No sooner had she settled again, when she found that the moon, as large and round as could be, was sending brilliant beams across her pillow. She stirred herself again to adjust a curtain, and returned to bed.

This time it seemed she was about to find rest, and was in that pleasant state of drifting between conscious thought and the dreams awaiting her when she was startled to hear loud cries emerging from Bertha's room across the landing.

She struggled once more from her bed, envisaging a dozen emergencies from a severe stroke to a bat which had lost its way during its night-time pursuits, and hurriedly put on her dressing-gown. She heard Ada's door bang along the passage and her voice raised. Within half a minute, the three sisters had met in Bertha's room.

Bertha herself was sitting bolt upright in bed, and a very alarming sight she posed for her two agitated sisters. She was wearing what was known to her as 'my boudoir cap', a confection of pink net decorated with a rosette over each ear, and fastened with pink ribbons under her wrinkled chin. Under the pink net were a dozen or so bumps denoting hair-rollers.

But it was not the boudoir cap which so alarmed Ada and Violet, for they were quite accustomed to Bertha's night-time appearance. What made this particular night's costume remarkable was the cascade of necklaces around their sister's neck.

Gold chains, ropes of pearls, and an Edwardian opal pendant which had been one of their mother's favourites jangled, together with strands of glass beads of every colour, two amber necklaces and one of jet.

Pinned to Bertha's pink bed jacket were over a dozen brooches ranging from regimental marcasite-and-silver badges to gold horseshoe tie pins with seed pearls for nail-heads. Gold jostled silver, agate vied with lapis lazuli, and an outsize Italian cameo brooch dwarfed the diamond cluster and the solitary ruby beneath it.

Bertha's bony fingers were ablaze with rings, and there was even a man's signet ring adorning one thumb. Overturned jewel boxes of every shape and size lay on the bedspread, and she was busy scrabbling in another which seemed to hold earings.

'What's the matter, Bertha dear?' enquired Ada, intent on

ignoring her sister's bizarre appearance, and rather hoping that what she saw before her was a mirage.

Violet, strengthened with the indignation of one snatched from sleep all too often, was more positive in her approach. 'What on earth are you doing with all the jewellery? It ought to be in the bank anyway.'

'Rubbish!' retorted Bertha. 'It's far better off here where it belongs, and I can keep my eye on it.'

'It is simply inviting a burglar,' pronounced Violet, 'and in any case, why were you shouting for us in the middle of the night?'

'I simply wanted to find out where the watches and bracelets are,' said Bertha, with a dignity which did not match her bedizened appearance. 'Have you girls moved them from the bottom of the wardrobe drawer?'

'Indeed no,' quavered Ada, now beginning to sound tearful. She had always been the timid one.

'I had no idea all this stuff was here,' responded Violet with spirit, 'and the best thing would be to put it all back.'

She advanced upon the bed, but Bertha began a shrill screaming which made the two sisters recoil. At the same time she began to tug at the ribbon which secured the boudoir cap, her scrawny neck twisting this way and that in her struggles. The multi-jewelled collection of necklaces tinkled and jangled, sending out gleams from gold and flashes of fire from precious stones, and all the time the high-pitched screams continued.

When at last she had flung the cap to the floor, she tore out the plastic rollers which it had concealed, hurling them one by one after the cap. Her hair stood out from her scalp in wild spikes, her breathing came in noisy gasps and her eyes rolled in an alarming way.

With considerable courage, Violet strode towards her and slapped one withered cheek smartly. The screaming stopped and Bertha fell back upon her pillows.

For a moment there was a dreadful silence in the room, then

Ada began to cry, the pathetic frightened snivellings of a scared child.

'Go back to bed,' said Violet to her sister. 'I can cope now.'

She kept her gaze upon Bertha, but was conscious of Ada's retreat and the sound of her bedroom door closing.

Violet could hear her heart drumming in the most alarming way, and longed to be able to telephone for help, to get John Lovell with his panoply of remedies, injections, pills, inhalants, and the overall comfort of his authority.

She was afraid of madness. She was afraid of violence. She was mortally afraid of doing something, in her terror, which would seriously damage her sister. But something had to be done to restore some sort of order, and at least the appalling screaming had ceased.

'Sit up,' she commanded. 'We're going to put all this stuff back.'

Bertha struggled from her pillows. She was trembling and looked shocked.

'You *struck* me, Violet,' she whispered. 'How dare you *strike* me?'

'I shall do it again,' Violet said stoutly, 'if you don't help me to take off all this jewellery.'

With shaking fingers, she began to unravel the tangle of necklaces, undoing clasps, hooks and complicated fastenings. Bertha slowly began to slide off the rings, fumbling with various ring-boxes on the counterpane, and watching vaguely as one or two of the trinkets rolled to the floor.

'I thought all this was in the bank,' fumed Violet. 'You know we agreed that you would send it there years ago.'

'I changed my mind,' said Bertha. 'And you are pulling my hair.'

Violet scooped a handful of released necklaces into one of the largest jewel boxes. It was a faded green leather one which had come from Siena on their mother's return from her honeymoon. What would that sweet gentle soul think if she could see her daughters now? Violet pushed this thought away, and concentrated on disentangling a fine silver chain.

'What possessed you to try and keep all this?' demanded Violet, freeing the last of the necklaces. 'It's asking for trouble. Heaven knows what this lot is worth now. It hasn't been valued for years.'

'I want it here,' replied Bertha, with a return of her dominating manner. 'Everything in this room is mine. Possession is nine-tenths of the law.'

'Rubbish,' said Violet, bundling the boxes into a drawer. 'You know quite well that everything in the house, *including* everything in this room, is divided equally between the three of us. Justin has Father's will, and it is perfectly plain.'

She stooped to pick up two rings from the carpet, and realized how dizzy she was with exhaustion. It had been a long day.

'I shall get Justin to change it,' said Bertha, with some spirit.

'You will do no such thing,' responded Violet. 'Tomorrow I shall get John Lovell to call to see you.'

'I shan't see him.'

'We'll see about that in the morning. Meanwhile, lie down and sleep. Even if you don't want to, at least let Ada and me have a few hours rest.'

She tucked in the bedclothes, found a stray brooch which she recognized as one of her own, and left her sister in comparative peace.

Ada's door opened a crack as Violet returned to her bed. 'Is she all right?'

'As right as she'll ever be,' responded Violet despairingly. 'We'll talk in the morning.'

And that won't be long in coming thought poor Violet, climbing once again into her crumpled bed.

The news of Doreen Lilly's return and, of course, her interesting condition, was soon spread about Lulling and Thrush

Green. Speculation upon the possible paternity of the expected child also gave considerable pleasure to the gossips.

Charles Henstock rang his friend Anthony Bull to let him know the whereabouts of the girl he had befriended. Anthony had heard nothing since his earlier encounter, but was glad to hear that she had returned to her mother.

'What are her plans, do you know?' he enquired.

Charles admitted that he had no idea, but intended to call at the Lilly household, and would keep him informed of any developments.

They rang off after suitable messages to their families, and Charles decided to put aside his weekly sermon-in-the-making, and call on Doreen and her mother that afternoon.

Already the lime trees in Lulling High Street were dropping a few crumpled leaves. There was an autumn freshness in the air, and the sky was of that pellucid blue particular to early autumn. Great cumulus clouds towered in the north, lit brilliantly by the sunshine. It was a day when cares were cast aside and the world of nature offered refreshment of spirit.

Charles was admitted by Mrs Lilly who told him that Doreen had gone shopping, taking the little boy with her.

'I've called because I let my friend Anthony Bull know that she was here. As you know, she turned to him when she was worried in London. He has been anxious.'

Mrs Lilly expressed surprise. 'I thought she'd written to him,' she told Charles. 'She said she was going to. He was very good to her.'

Charles brushed aside her apologies with a smile. 'The thing is, what is she going to do now?' asked the rector.

'She'll stay here for a bit,' said Mrs Lilly. 'Maybe you know she's expecting again?'

'I had heard so.'

'She'll have to get a little job – part-time, say, to bring in a bit. The boy can go two mornings a week to play-school down the road. I found that out yesterday.'

'An excellent idea.'

'Doreen was with the Lovelock ladies before, but I don't think she'd fancy going back.'

Charles's private opinion was that the Lovelock ladies would certainly not have her back. She had previously left them in the lurch, and it was generally thought that she had helped the burglar who had broken into that house some time before, Doreen Lilly would certainly not be welcome there.

'Well, we'll keep in touch,' said Charles rising, 'and if I hear of any work which might suit Doreen I will send a message. I'm sure Mr Bull would be very glad to have a letter from her.'

'I'll see she sends one,' promised Gladys, opening the door. 'And it's very nice of you to call.'

She did not actually say the words, 'as you are church and I'm chapel', but Charles felt that they hovered somewhere in the air as he made his farewells.

Harold Shoosmith's blunt assessment of Margaret Lester's condition had shocked his wife. Isobel had not said a great deal about it, but naturally it was very much in her mind. Did the two little girls have any inkling? What misery it must be for her husband! Was that, she wondered, why the family had moved, so that Alan could keep a closer eye on Margaret?

At breakfast the next morning Isobel said to Harold, 'Surely Margaret couldn't be drunk so early in the morning? I can't believe it, you know.'

'Habitual drinkers,' replied Harold, reaching for the marmalade, 'are pretty well sozzled all the time. We had a fair number in Africa. Not a lot you can do for them.'

'But we must do something,' protested Isobel. 'Can't we help?'

'We can help her best by keeping quiet about it, and being at hand if Alan and the children want some first-hand support,' said Harold.

At that moment, Willie Marchant arrived with the letters, and Harold and Isobel examined their post.

'A lovely card from Agnes and Dorothy,' said Isobel. 'What a stupendous Welsh waterfall!'

'Where is it?' asked Harold.

Isobel studied the card more closely. 'It's a place with a long name, which has no vowels in it, beginning with two Ls,' she said.

'You surprise me,' said Harold.

On the morning after the Lovelocks' disturbed night, Violet rang the surgery to ask if Dr Lovell would call to see her sister.

'Dr Lovell,' said the new young receptionist, 'is out on an emergency case.'

'When will he be back?'

'In emergency cases,' said the voice with hauteur, 'we have no way of assessing the time needed.'

'Naturally,' replied Violet, with equal frigidity.

'Dr Lovell's assistant *could* call, of course.' She made it sound as if, despite innumerable difficulties, such as physical paralysis, overwhelming commitments to urgent cases and extreme exhaustion, the new doctor might possibly martyr himself to the extent of struggling into his car to drive half a mile to see the patient.

Violet, holding the receiver, knew that it would be hard enough to persuade Bertha to see John Lovell – the new doctor would not have a chance of being admitted.

'Don't bother him,' said Violet, 'I will ring another time.'

'That would be best,' conceded the receptionist graciously, and rang off.

Bertha, the cause of Violet and Ada's exhaustion, was in considerably better shape than her sisters. She received her breakfast tray happily, commented on the sunshine with pleasure, and seemed oblivious to the night's mayhem.

Violet was not amused, and was determined to get at least some of her problems solved.

'John Lovell is engaged at the moment,' she told Bertha, 'but I intend to consult him.'

'A lot of fuss about nothing,' commented Bertha.

'And I am getting in touch with Jenkins to revalue the jewellery. Then it is going to the safe-deposit at the bank.'

'Jenkins died last Easter,' said Bertha.

'Jenkins' son is running the shop,' responded Violet quickly, 'and very competently too.'

'I can't see why you make such a to-do about the stuff,' said Bertha.

'It's too valuable to have lying about. Those gold chains alone are worth a great deal of money, and there are several diamond and sapphire rings.'

'But we may want to wear some of it,' cried Bertha, dropping a piece of toast, butter-side down, on the top sheet.

'We can keep back a few favourite things,' replied Violet, 'but the rest goes to the bank.'

'I think you are being *quite* unreasonable,' stated Bertha, attending to the buttery patch with an even more buttery knife.

Violet, who had suffered much, was stung into action.

'*You* are the unreasonable one, and well you know it! Any more of these tantrums and Dr Lovell will be obliged to refer you to a *mental specialist*, and you know where he might well send you!'

At this, Bertha really did look a little shaken. She pushed aside her tray, and was temporarily deprived of speech. She suddenly looked very old and very frail, and for a brief moment Violet felt compunction.

But this weakness did not last long. Picking up the tray she made her way to the bedroom door. 'The best thing you can do, Bertha, is to lie there, think things over, and decide to mend your ways.'

And with this patting shot she made for the stairs.

The fact that Doreen Lilly was back in Lulling soon reached the ears of Violet and her sisters. As Charles surmised, they were determined never to let her into their house again.

It was at the next Bingo session that Doreen's future employment was settled, and that was through the practical good sense of Mrs Jenner.

Nelly Piggott, Gladys Lilly and Mrs Jenner were enjoying a cup of coffee and bourbon biscuits during the interval in the Bingo hall, discussing Doreen's plight.

'At least,' said Gladys, 'she's got the child enrolled at the play-school: Tuesdays and Thursdays from nine-thirty to twelve, so at least I'll have a few hours to myself.'

'If we had a vacancy at The Fuchsia Bush,' said Nelly, 'I'd give her some work there and could keep an eye on her for you, but the fact is we're fully staffed just now.'

'Would you like me to have a word with Jane?' enquired Mrs Jenner, putting down her cup. 'She sometimes likes some extra help with the old people. It might not be much, general cleaning probably, but it wouldn't be far for her to go, and she would be earning something.'

'That would be ideal,' said Gladys warmly, 'and she could pick up Bobby on the way home.'

'Well, I can't promise, of course,' said Mrs Jenner, 'but I'll speak to Jane, and she'll get in touch with Doreen, one way or the other, and your girl can decide if she likes the idea.'

'She'd better,' said Doreen's mother grimly, stacking the cups and saucers in readiness for the next half of the Bingo session.

11. WHERE IS EMILY COOKE?

It was Mrs Jenner's intention the next morning to go to visit her daughter Jane at Rectory Cottages, as soon as she had finished her breakfast. She always rose early, a legacy from her nursing days, and knew that she would find Jane, who had also trained as a nurse, well on the way with her morning duties among her elderly charges.

Mrs Jenner was putting away the last of the breakfast washing-up when there was a thumping noise at the back door. On opening it, she was not unduly surprised to find Mrs Cooke who lived some quarter of a mile away on the road to Nidden.

Mrs Cooke was a byword in Thrush Green and Lulling. Her large family was known to most of the residents, the rector, the probation officers and the local police force. Very few months passed without a mention of one or another of the Cooke family in the local paper, usually concerning a hearing at the Lulling Magistrates' Court.

Mrs Jenner, as midwife, had attended several of Mrs Cooke's lying-ins, and later had been called into the house for various crises such as a broken arm, beads stuffed into infant Cookes' ears and noses, sudden rashes on Cooke chests, or lacerations on rather grubby Cooke feet.

She let in her agitated visitor and offered her the kitchen chair. What did she want now, wondered Mrs Jenner? Medical advice? Help with an official form? Money 'for the meter'? A cupful of sugar?

All these things and many more had been asked for over the

years, but today her visitor produced a crumpled piece of paper, and thrust it towards her.

She read:

'Gone of for a bit back by Satday
Nigel's
shoos need mending
    Emily.'

'Oh dear!' said Mrs Jenner.

'Oh lor!' howled Mrs Cooke, throwing her apron up over her face and head, like someone at a wake in an Irish film. She began to sway back and forth emitting harsh cries of grief.

Mrs Jenner put on the kettle.

After a minute it began to hum comfortingly, and Mrs Cooke replaced her apron. The yells changed to sobs and hiccups, and Mrs Jenner reached for the recently emptied teapot.

'What she want to go and do this for?' sniffed the bereaved mother. 'Leaving me with all yesterday's washing up. *And Nigel.*'

'What's happened to Nigel?' asked Mrs Jenner, making the tea. 'Is he alone at your house?'

She knew from experience that any young Cooke left alone in a house could create havoc, and Nigel was no exception.

'I pushed him off to school,' said Mrs Cooke, 'afore I come up here.'

She accepted the cup of tea and spooned in three teaspoonfuls of sugar.

'Well, have you any idea why she's gone?'

'I blame St Giles for this,' said Mrs Cooke, stirring her tea morosely.

'What's he got to do with it?'

'Who?'

'St Giles.'

'St Giles' *Fair*, up Oxford. She *would* go. Took young Nigel too, and they never got back till past midnight. That's where she met this chap. He's at Oxford.'

'You mean he's one of the college boys?'

'No, no! He *works*! Up Cowley, I think.' She sipped noisily at her tea cup, the hiccups subsiding.

Mrs Jenner studied the note again. 'I don't think there is much to worry about,' she told her visitor. 'She says she'll be back on Saturday. If she doesn't turn up then, you could tell the police.'

'*Tell the police?*' echoed Mrs Cooke indignantly. 'I don't want that lot scratting around! We're respectable folk.'

Mrs Jenner, with remarkable self-control, refrained from comment.

'I come up here really,' went on Mrs Cooke, 'to see if you'd heard anythin' about my girl. I knows your brother Perce takes an interest in her.'

Mrs Jenner realized with some shock that she had completely failed to link Emily with Percy. He had made so many attempts, over the past months, to find a companion that she had dismissed the rumours out of hand. In truth, she had little in common with her brother, and the two rarely met, although their gardens adjoined.

A terrible thought struck her: if Percy ever married Emily Cooke (heaven forbid), she would be related by marriage to this dreadful old woman before her.

'I know nothing of that,' she said as calmly as she could. 'If I were you I should leave things alone. Emily's old enough to know what she's doing, and ten chances to one she'll be back on Saturday as she says.'

Mrs Cooke gulped down the last of her tea, and stood up.

'Well that's that. Maybe you're right. Best wait and see.'

Mrs Jenner opened the back door for her.

'Oh, by the way,' said Mrs Cooke on the doorstep, 'you couldn't give me a lend of half a loaf? I was that upset about Emily I forgot the baker.'

Mrs Jenner returned to the kitchen, cut a loaf in half, put the bread into a paper bag and handed it, without a word, to the waiting woman.

'Ta ever so,' said Mrs Cooke, walking briskly to the gate.

Somewhat later than she had intended, Mrs Jenner arrived at Rectory Cottages. As she had expected, Jane was there sorting out a first aid kit which was an important part of her warden's equipment.

'You remember Doreen Lilly,' began Mrs Jenner.

'I should hope so. She was in my Brownie pack years ago. What's happened? I thought she'd left home.'

'She's back,' said her mother, and proceeded to tell her about Doreen, her present condition, the problem of Bobby, and the concern of Gladys Lilly.

'If she's not too proud to do a bit of cleaning, windows, hoovering, that sort of thing, I'd find her a job here for two mornings a week. She could give a hand with the vegetables too. One or two of the old dears are poorly, and I get them a midday meal while they're under the weather.'

'Then shall I tell her to call?'

'Yes do, Mum. It won't be permanent, but it should help her out.'

That matter settled, Mrs Jenner told Jane about Emily Cooke and her mother's visit.

Jane looked unusually perturbed. 'It'll upset Uncle Percy, won't it?'

'Oh, there's nothing in that,' replied her mother dismissively. 'You know what a silly old thing he is.'

'But I think he's quite serious about this one,' said Jane, rolling up a loose bandage and securing it neatly with a safety pin. 'He ought to be married, you know.'

Mrs Jenner got to her feet. She found all this very unsettling. Perhaps she should have kept a closer eye on Percy's philanderings.

'I can't see any woman with a ha'porth of sense taking on your Uncle Percy,' she said flatly. She kissed her daughter's cheek. 'Thank you for helping out with Doreen, I'll tell her to get in touch. Now, I must get back. I've a nice little chicken to put in the oven, and dear knows when that'll get dished up, with all this to-ing and fro-ing.'

She waved cheerfully to several of the residents who were watching her departure, and made her way briskly along the road to Nidden. To passersby, she appeared her normal self – calm and capable. But Mrs Jenner's emotions were in turmoil. Surely Percy, stupid though he was, and always had been, could not seriously be thinking of making an alliance with a *Cooke*?

Tongues wagged, of course. They began to wag even more busily when Saturday was over and the girl had not returned. Mrs Jenner kept her worries to herself, and even felt a slight gleam of hope. Did this mean that Percy was out of the running altogether?

Percy, on the other hand, seemed to want to tell all and sundry about his blighted hopes. Albert Piggott, who had managed to evade him, was finally button-holed on Monday morning when he was defenceless in the churchyard, sweeping up the shower of autumn leaves which rustled round and round the church paths and porch.

'You heard about my Emily?' queried Percy lugubriously.

'Yes,' said Albert, flicking his broom along the edge of a flowerbed with unwonted energy.

'It's a terrible thing,' sighed the rejected lover. 'She could be anywhere.'

'That's right,' agreed Albert.

'With anyone.'

'Right. She could.' He negotiated a tricky corner by one of the drains with a twist of the broom.

'Could be abroad even.'

'Probably is,' said Albert.

'Not that I think she is,' said Percy. 'Len Matthews said he saw her in Oxford.'

'Well then,' said Albert, activity arrested at this mention of an old acquaintance, 'what you fussin' about?'

He looked searchingly at his companion. He did look pretty

rough, come to think of it. Even Albert's flinty heart was moved.

'Here, come and sit in the porch out of this pesky wind. Jones hasn't opened yet. We'll go over when he does.'

They sat together on one of the stone benches which lined the venerable porch. It was a chilly seat on a misty October morning, and Albert hoped that Percy's confidences would not take long, as gloomy thoughts of piles and other unpleasant afflictions went through his head.

'So what did Len say?' he urged, hoping to hurry along the proceedings.

Percy gave a gusty sigh. 'Not much. Just said he saw her in Cornmarket with this young chap. Laughin', she was.'

'Not one of them young chaps at college? She don't want to get mixed up with them. There's Deans and Masters and that, they gets proper shirty with any of their blokes as gets girls into trouble. Send 'em somewhere, they do, or sack 'em, or somethin'.'

'It wasn't one of that lot,' said Percy, dismissing all university men in one sentence. 'I heard it's some fellow up Morris's.'

'Oh well,' replied Albert, 'he ought to know better, workin' up Morris's.'

The conversation lapsed. Only the rustle of the leaves around their feet broke the silence. Albert began to find the cold more than he could bear. He rose from his chilly seat and surveyed his sorrowful companion.

'If you wants my opinion, Perce—' he began.

'I don't,' said the sufferer.

'Well, you're goin' to get it,' replied Albert with spirit. 'You wants to snap out of this 'ere mood you've got yourself in. No girl's worth it, and that Emily Cooke—'

He broke off as Percy leapt to his feet, red in the face with rage. 'You shut up about my Emily!' he shouted. 'Ain't I got enough to bear without you bein' insultin'?'

Albert picked up his broom defensively. 'All right, all right! Keep your hair on! No fool like an old one, they say, and that's true enough!'

He skipped dexterously out of the porch, and began to sweep again at a safe distance.

Muttering under his breath, Percy shuffled through the leaves to the church gate. At that moment, the welcome sound of the doors of The Two Pheasants being flung open could be heard. Without altering his pace, Percy made for the inn. Albert, judging discretion to be the better part of valour, decided to wait until a glass of beer had quenched Percy's ardour.

But it was really very annoying.

Autumn seemed to arrive particularly early that year. Albert Piggott was not alone in cursing the volume of dead leaves which created a major problem for all gardeners, as well as the Lulling Council leaf-sweeping vehicles that plied up and down Lulling High Street, doing their best to cope with the prodigal vegetation from the lime trees.

Against the golden stone of the Cotswold buildings, pyracantha berries glowed, and the palmate leaves of Virginia creeper clad many a house with vivid colour ranging from wine to cream. Variegated ivies and winter jasmine, as well as dying clematis and wisteria clothed the walls, and in the country hedges wild bryony threaded its necklaces of bright beads.

There were elderberries, late blackberries and sloes in plenty that year, and families were busy collecting this natural harvest. In Lulling Woods the bracken was turning crisp and auburn, providing shelter and bedding for the small animals which were already thinking of hibernation.

It was the season when redoubled activity in fund-raising reared its head, and Ella was just utilizing some of the remnants left over from the soft furnishings of Rectory Cottages' extension when her door bell rang.

Winnie Bailey stood on the step, a basket of apples at her feet. 'Are these coals to Newcastle, Ella?' she enquired.

'Far from it. Come in,' replied Ella, lifting the basket, and leading the way to the kitchen. 'I'll make some apple jelly. It always goes like hot cakes at produce stalls, and I'm getting stuff ready for the Mammoth Harvest Bazaar.'

'I wonder why everything is "Mammoth" in Thrush Green?' mused Winnie.

'Just a local habit,' said Ella. 'Coffee?'

Coffee being declined, the two ladies went into the sitting-room, and Ella picked up her smouldering cigarette and gave a grateful puff at it. The air was blue and acrid with the smoke, and Winnie hoped that her eyes would not water too noticeably.

As if reading her thoughts, Ella stubbed out the remains of the cigarette. 'Sorry about this filthy habit. I keep meaning to give it up. Tell myself about cancer of the lungs, and other people's revulsion, and how much I should save if I packed it in.'

'So you have tried?'

'Lord, yes! Time and time again. I can get through twenty-four hours, and then I crack.'

'It could be worse, I suppose.'

'How come? Drink, do you mean?'

Winnie was silent. Margaret Lester had come suddenly into her mind. She picked up some of the remnants of chintz which littered the sofa. 'And what are you going to make with these?' she asked.

'Well, I'm keeping some to make oven gloves, and Muriel is dead keen to make egg cosies and those rather sissy clothes' hangers. Does anyone *want* egg cosies anyway? My boiled egg doesn't have time to get cold, I can tell you, and all my coat hangers are those nice functional wire ones the cleaners give you free.'

'As a matter of fact,' said Winnie, 'I like a few padded hangers for special silk blouses and other delicate things. I'm sure Muriel's efforts will be snapped up.'

She was just congratulating herself on evading the dangerous topic of alcoholism when Ella spoke again.

'We thought it might be an idea to ask Margaret Lester to make things for the bazaar. I hear she's a good needle-woman. Tapestry rugs and all that. Besides, Muriel says she thinks she needs company. Gets depressed evidently.'

Winnie wondered how much Ella knew. Not much escaped those shrewd eyes behind their usual veil of cigarette smoke.

'It's a kind thought,' said Winnie. 'She doesn't seem to have made many friends, but of course it's early days. I know the Youngs have invited them to play cards once or twice.'

'And I bet those useful migraine attacks have cropped up,' commented Ella. 'Tell me, Winnie, what's your opinion?'

'Well, I hardly know—' began Winnie, feeling cornered.

'I do,' said Ella. 'She's on the bottle, and most people in Thrush Green know it.'

At Barton-on-Sea, Agnes and Dorothy were busy clearing the garden ready for winter and going through all the decision-making which gardeners face at this time of the year.

'Shall we try and keep some of these geraniums?' asked Agnes. 'They could stand in the porch.'

'No room. Better put them on the compost heap.'

'But Dorothy, they cost a great deal of money.'

'And they'll cost us a great deal of inconvenience stuck in the porch all through the winter.'

Agnes, brought up much more thriftily than her friend, put the dying geraniums into the wheelbarrow with some reluctance.

'We'll split these penstemon,' said Dorothy, struggling with a small hand fork. 'They make a good show, and we could do with some more in the front garden.'

She heaved at the plant, becoming red in the face with effort.

'Please, Dorothy,' begged Agnes, 'please leave it for Peter to do.'

They were fortunate in having the help of a young man now and again who 'obliged' when he needed extra money.

'It's certainly tough!' puffed Dorothy, straightening up.

'You have to have two large forks back to back, and sort of *ease* them apart,' explained Agnes. 'It's really a man's job.'

'Well, Peter's welcome to this one. Now what about a new shrub to climb up by the shed? Now's the time, I believe, to plant one.'

'Certainly that clematis has been most unsatisfactory,' agreed Agnes. 'What shall we have instead?'

'I'll ask Teddy,' replied Dorothy, and Agnes's heart sank. Why must Teddy – charming fellow though he was – be brought into everything? Even a little autumn clearing up seemed to need his assistance.

'I promised some of our pink Michaelmas daisies to the flower ladies for Harvest Festival,' continued Dorothy, unaware of Agnes's feelings. 'Miss Jones asked particularly, and I said we could spare some.'

Agnes, pulling up handfuls of chickweed, did not reply.

'I really think they make too much of Harvest Festival here,' went on Dorothy. 'Apparently they are having an *anthem*. Something about the corn.'

'I hope it's "The valleys stand so thick with corn that they laugh and sing",' said Agnes.

'I believe it is. Rather far-fetched, I think. Have you ever seen a *valley* laughing and singing?'

'Poetic licence,' said Agnes.

'And Eileen is singing a solo.'

'Oh good! She has such a lovely voice.'

'I find it rather shrill,' replied Dorothy. 'And I'm not sure she is quite true on her top notes. I think she needs some of her solos transposing to a lower key. But then she wouldn't be able to boast about her high Cs.'

'Oh come, Dorothy! She doesn't *boast*!'

'She does to Teddy,' answered Dorothy.

Agnes threw a handful of chickweed into the wheelbarrow.

'Let's go indoors for a cup of coffee,' she said, with unusual firmness. 'I've had enough of this.'

And enough of Teddy too, was her private comment, as she went back into the house.

At Rectory Cottages, Doreen Lilly was proving surprisingly useful. Whether it was the fact that she was working for her former Brownies' leader and felt obliged to do her utmost to please Brown Owl, nobody could say, but she seemed to enjoy spending two mornings a week with Jane Cartwright, while young Bobby was at play-school, and the old people liked her.

Jane, who had really only given Doreen some work out of the kindness of her heart, was pleasantly surprised at the girl's competence. She had always thought that Mrs Lilly's brisk efficiency had meant that her daughter did little in the house and, like so many daughters of bustling mothers, was content to drift about keeping out of the whirlwind's way.

Evidently, when allowed to, Doreen could tackle a household chore as well as her mother, and Jane found her invaluable. She cleaned brass, copper and silver, she scoured baths and washbasins, polished and dusted, and even coped with such recalcitrant objects as faulty cisterns and clogged-up drains. She was in the early months of her pregnancy and Jane, knowing much about such things from her nursing experience, watched her carefully and made sure that she did not overdo things.

She told her own mother how pleased she was with Doreen's work one morning.

'Well,' said Mrs Jenner, 'don't sound so surprised. Gladys Lilly's renowned for hard work, and Doreen's dad worked at the baker's all his life. He used to go along there at four-thirty every morning. Could set your clock by him, people said. Doreen may have been a silly girl over that young man of hers, but she comes of good stock. Does she ever talk of Bobby's father?'

'Never a word, and I don't question her. But it's going to be hard for her when the baby arrives. There's mighty little room in her mother's house, and neither of them want to live together anyway.'

'They'll have to sort out that problem when the time comes,' said Mrs Jenner.

12. An Accident in Lulling

The whereabouts of Emily Cooke, which was still the subject of much conjecture, was settled by the arrival of a letter to the girl's mother. Miss Watson and Miss Fogerty would have been appalled at the grammar, spelling and general grubbiness of their former pupil's literary effort had they been in a position to see it, but Mrs Cooke seemed surprisingly thrilled.

'She's bin and got married!' she shouted to Mrs Jenner, who was tidying her front garden.

Mrs Jenner went to the gate. A less diplomatic woman might have commented: 'And about time too!', but Mrs Jenner was more circumspect. 'You must be relieved,' she said kindly. As I am too, she thought, remembering the narrow escape she and Percy had had from an alliance with this deplorable family.

'Oh, I'm over the moon!' cried Mrs Cooke, beaming broadly. 'Just think of it! Our Emily married at last! I never thought to see her with a wedding ring.'

'Where is she now?' enquired Mrs Jenner.

'Up Oxford. Headington way, she says, and I'm to go over next Sunday to tea.'

'And what about Nigel? Will he be going to Oxford to live?'

'I expect so. Emily don't say anything much about that in her letter, but I'll take him with me on Sunday.'

Mrs Jenner wondered if Emily would want to be reunited with her young son; she had left him without a qualm. Would Mrs Cooke be left 'holding the baby' yet again? It would not be the first time she had been the unwilling minder of her grandchildren.

'Well, I'm sure it will all work out for the best,' she said. 'You must excuse me. I've left some washing out, and it looks like rain.'

She made her escape from Mrs Cooke, and went round the house into the back garden where a line of washing billowed in the autumn wind.

She was struggling with the sheets when she was hailed from the hedge which divided her property from her brother Percy's. With some vexation, she deposited her bundle on the garden seat, and went to their common boundary. Percy's face, pink and lugubrious, loomed above the clipped hawthorn hedge.

'Saw you with Mrs Cooke. She tell you about my Emily?'

'Percy, she's not "your Emily". Why do you make such a fool of yourself? Yes, she did tell me. Something you probably know already. Emily's married and living in Oxford.'

'No need to be snappy,' responded Percy. 'A bit of sympathy wouldn't come amiss at a time like this.'

'Well, you won't get it from me, Perce. All Lulling's laughing at you. Keep your grizzling to yourself, and stop feeling sorry for yourself too. A day's work is the best medicine.'

'You always was a hard 'un,' moaned Percy. 'Don't my broken heart mean nothin' to you?'

'Nothing at all,' said she briskly. 'And I reckon you've had a lucky escape. Don't get caught again now, Percy. Pull yourself together. What about a few days' steady gardening? Your thistle seeds have been blowing over here for weeks now.'

She bustled back to her washing line before Percy could think of a retort.

Later that morning, Percy told his sad story to Albert Piggott as they sat in The Two Pheasants. Albert's reaction was much the same as Percy's sister's, and it soon became apparent that sympathy was not going to be offered.

'Best thing that could've happened,' maintained Albert. 'She was always a bit of no good. That Oxford chap don't know what he's taken on. You forget her, Perce.'

Even Mr Jones, the soul of propriety, added his contribution.

'Albert's right, you know. You put her out of your mind, Percy. Plenty of good fish in the sea.'

'But they don't seem to swim my way,' said the disconsolate suitor, with a sigh.

'Here, have another half on me,' said Albert, with unwonted generosity. 'Nothin' like a drop of beer to put new heart in a man.'

'That's right,' agreed Mr Jones.

One bright October morning, soon after the news of Emily's wedding had rustled round Thrush Green, Winnie Bailey saw Margaret Lester emerge from her gate and set off towards Lulling. She carried a shopping bag, and Winnie guessed correctly that she would come back on the bus that left Lulling High Street at eleven-thirty with the shopping bag full.

She herself, and most of the Thrush Green shoppers, were grateful for that particular bus. It was a pleasure to trot down the hill with an empty bag in the cool of the morning, when one was fresh; it was quite another thing to struggle uphill from Lulling with a bag heavy with potatoes, celery, carrots and groceries an hour or so later.

Margaret had told her one day that Alan did not like her driving alone. He was afraid that she might be overcome by a sudden migraine attack, she said. Knowing a little more now, Winnie guessed that Alan dreaded a mishap when Margaret was at the wheel, and a breathalyser being produced. Poor fellow, thought Winnie, he must live under the most appalling strain.

Other eyes had also noted Margaret passing.

Replenishing the stocks, thought Ella Bembridge.

Wonder what she's off to buy? thought Albert Piggott, unlocking the church door.

She's looking better this morning, thought Jane Cartwright. But all three had bottles in mind.

Nelly Piggott, putting a basket of croissants in the window of The Fuchsia Bush, watched her neighbour going purposefully into one of Lulling's three supermarkets. The thought of bottles crossed her mind too, but the appearance of Bertha Lovelock, with Violet in close attendance, put all conjecture about Margaret Lester from her mind.

She opened the door for the two ladies, and noted with approval that Violet steered her sister to a table farthest from the display of cakes, scones and other delightfully tempting titbits on the counter.

'Now what can I get you?' she asked. 'Coffee as usual, I suppose? And I'm just bringing through some Eccles cakes. Would you like to try 'em?'

Violet agreed to all these suggestions, and Nelly hurried away.

She and Mrs Peters had been relieved to see the Lovelocks again. They had wondered if the unfortunate affair of Bertha's pilfering would mean the end of their visits, but Violet had been as good as her word, and Bertha was now never seen unaccompanied on their shopping expeditions.

The Fuchsia Bush was exceptionally busy that morning. A number of people who intended to catch the popular eleven-thirty bus which made its way north, passing through Thrush Green as it went, had called in for refreshment, their heavy bags and baskets littering the floor.

As the time grew near, half a dozen or so paid their bills and departed to join the little knot of waiting travellers at the bus stop immediately outside the tea-room.

Nelly Piggott, replenishing the basket of croissants in the window, saw the bus pull up, and the queue mounting the step.

At that moment she saw Margaret Lester, with a laden bag in each hand, hastening awkwardly across the road. The bus began to pull away when she was halfway across Lulling High Street, but it stopped abruptly as presumably someone had pointed out Margaret's plight to the conductor.

Obviously quite breathless and flustered, she hurried forward – and tripped over the kerb, her bags flying forward on to the pavement.

The conductor leapt down to the sprawled figure, two passersby set about rescuing the shopping, and Nelly Piggott hurried out to help.

'I'm all right,' gasped Margaret. 'Quite all right.'

But it was immediately apparent that she was not. Blood was beginning to ooze from a badly grazed knee, and her hands were covered in dirt.

'You come into the shop,' said Nelly, taking command. 'You can't get on the bus like that. You come and rest for a bit.'

'You going to be all right?' asked the conductor solicitously. A row of concerned faces in the bus window watched anxiously.

'I'll see to her,' said Nelly, collecting the bags. 'You get on. You've got your bus to look after.'

'I'm a bit late now,' confessed the conductor. 'Righto, missus. Hope you'll soon be all right.'

One of the bags seemed to be intact, but it was plain that the other had a broken bottle in it, as a trickle of liquid was running freely across the pavement. Nelly investigated, and found one bottle of gin with its neck shattered. Ruthlessly she poured the remaining liquid into the gutter, tested what appeared to be a second bottle in the bag, and found that intact.

Margaret was leaning against the bus stop post, shaking visibly and near to tears. A little knot of spectators were offering sympathy and advice, but all, Nelly noticed, were quite aware of the broken bottle and its contents. The smell of spirit alone was enough to give it away.

One of the men carried the bags into The Fuchsia Bush, and Nelly supported Margaret through the tea-room and into a chair in the privacy of the office. Rosa was dispatched for a bowl of warm water and the first aid kit, and Nelly set to work on her patient.

Margaret was in a state of great agitation. 'I must get in touch with Alan,' she cried. 'I must ring him. He'll be so worried if I'm not home.'

'As soon as I've done this,' said Nelly, 'I'll ring him, and tell him to fetch you home in the car.'

But at that moment Mrs Peters appeared, offered sympathy, and said she would do the telephoning.

Meanwhile, Rosa and Gloria had gone through the shopping bags. One held a few groceries, some toiletries from Boots, and one bottle of gin wrapped in a carrier bag from one of the supermarkets. Nothing appeared to be damaged.

The second bag held the remains of the broken gin bottle, which had been wrapped in another carrier bag from a second supermarket. The third bottle, luckily undamaged, was wrapped in a bag from yet another of Lulling's supermarkets.

The girls said little, but exchanged meaningful glances as they settled the undamaged bottle in the grocery bag. The dripping carrier with its shattered glass was put into the café's dustbin.

'Well, if that's sorted out,' said Mrs Peters, bustling in and out, 'for pity's sake get back to the tables. I can see to things here.'

Alan Lester had sounded remarkably agitated on the telephone, she thought. She had done her best to minimize his wife's injuries, but he sounded quite distracted.

'I'll be down immediately,' he told her. 'I wouldn't have had this happen for the world.'

He had the car outside within ten minutes and Margaret, now calmer, and sporting a neat bandage on her knee, was helped into it by Nelly.

Alan was full of gratitude towards the two good Samaritans when he went back to the tea-room for the bag of shopping. Rosa handed it over, obviously full of excitement at this unexpected fillip to the day.

'One bottle was broke,' she said brightly, 'but me and Gloria put the good one in with the other.'

Alan Lester looked startled, but simply thanked her before making his way to the car.

Mrs Peters surveyed her assistant coldly. 'There was no need to say anything about the breakages,' she pointed out. 'Mrs Lester is quite capable of explaining things to her husband, even if she has got a cut knee.'

'Well, I just thought he ought to know,' replied Rosa sulkily.

'It's not your place to tell him,' said Mrs Peters. And in any case, she thought to herself, no doubt the poor fellow knows well enough, without anyone telling him.

The news of the accident was soon the subject of local interest. The fact that it had occurred in Lulling High Street, amidst so many spectators, meant that there were varied accounts of the incident, and plenty of confirmation about the contents of the publicly shattered gin bottle.

To be fair to the inhabitants of Thrush Green and Lulling, it was concern for Margaret and her family rather than censure which was paramount. There was widespread sympathy for the headmaster in his domestic difficulties, and there was great care in keeping the matter as quiet as possible.

Even Betty Bell, who had summed up the situation early on, checked her ebullient tongue, although Dotty Harmer was less restrained when they met.

'I hear that Mrs Lester is a drunkard,' she remarked brightly to Betty one morning. 'Fell down in the High Street, they tell me.'

'She tripped,' began Betty.

'Such a nuisance when drink gets the better of anyone,' continued Dotty. 'The best thing is to have a drink constantly at hand.'

'But that's just what—' protested Betty, but was cut short again.

'An *innocuous* one, of course. A really strong herb tea, cold preferably. I used to make up a bottle for our old cook when I was a girl; she couldn't resist the cooking sherry, I remember. We soon weaned her on to my nettle beer, and later to a light apple juice.'

'I expect Mr Lester knows how to deal with things,' said Betty.

'I wonder if he does. I might get Connie to run me up there with a bottle or two of my own medicinal brew, and explain how to use it. He must be a very worried man.'

Betty privately thought he would be far more worried if Dotty appeared, jangling bottles and advising on the methods of tackling alcoholism. At any time Dotty was alarming; in the rôle of witch doctor she would frighten the life out of anyone.

And yet, thought Betty, one could not help admiring the direct and outspoken way that Dotty encountered trouble. It was a change from the muted remarks being passed around when the Lesters were mentioned. Here was Dotty, talking frankly of drunkenness, and offering practical help with honest sympathy.

'We had quite a bit of drink trouble in our family,' she went on with the utmost cheerfulness. 'One of my uncles was so bad when in his cups – violent and most abusive – that he couldn't keep a job. In the end, my grandfather was obliged to ship him to Australia.'

'But would anyone want him there?' asked Betty, feeling that it was hardly fair to the Australians to have to put up with such a reprobate.

'Oh, he went out to a *job* there,' said Dotty airily. 'Rounding up sheep, I think. Or kangaroos perhaps.'

'And how did he get on?'

'I've no idea. When one went to Australia in those days, one hardly ever came back.'

'My cousin,' said Betty, trying to guide the conversation away from alcohol, 'had a holiday there last year. He took a month off. Said it was lovely, when he got back. His photos took us all evening to get through.'

'That's what I mean,' said Dotty. 'In my uncle's time, when people were sent off to Australia you could be quite sure that you wouldn't see them again. Now it seems they hop up and down over the Equator like so many yo-yos. Very disconcerting.'

'Well, isn't that a good thing?' asked Betty.

'My grandfather wouldn't have thought so,' said Dotty firmly.

The new extension to Rectory Cottages was officially opened one wet and windy day at the end of October.

The local member of Parliament had been invited to declare it open, but at the last minute was unable to come as he had been obliged to attend to government business overseas.

Charles Henstock feared that yet again he would have to deputize for a guest of honour at short notice. It was Dimity who suggested that he should ring Anthony Bull to see if he could come.

'When? Wednesday? Fine, I should thoroughly enjoy a trip to see you all,' said Anthony.

He promised to arrive in time for lunch, and everyone, particularly the rector, looked forward to seeing him again.

As many friends as possible had been crammed into the premises. As well as the new room, all the residents had thrown open their own accommodation, and there was a general air of festivity. Flowers were everywhere, windows shone, furniture gleamed and on the table in the forefront of the extension stood a magnificent iced cake, and some bottles of champagne.

The only disappointment was the fact that Prouts had failed to deliver the large curtains in time. Agitated messages had been sent throughout the week prior to the party, and Prouts had surpassed themselves with excuses ranging from shortage of staff to a change in the dye of the lining material.

Ella and Muriel were in rare unity over the affair. Their own smaller side curtains hung proudly in place, and their strictures on the firm of Prout were severe.

Edward Young who, as architect, was among those present, would have liked to have said how much more satisfactory it would have been if his suggestion of *blinds* at the windows had been adopted. However he was magnanimous enough, and mellowed by the champagne, to keep these thoughts to himself.

Anthony Bull, of course, was welcomed rapturously, and seemed genuinely delighted to be among some of his former parishioners.

Through the windows overlooking the green, the bonfire could be seen awaiting November the fifth. It was a noble pile already, and everyone knew that the schoolchildren would be hard at work making the guy that would rest on the top.

Anthony looked at it with pleasure. 'And does Percy Hodge still supply potatoes to bake in the ashes?' he asked Jane Cartwright.

'Indeed he does! My Uncle Percy gets as much fun out of Guy Fawkes' night as the children do.'

'Delicious cake,' mumbled Anthony, through a mouthful. He spotted Doreen Lilly across the room. She had been invited to lend a hand, not only with preparing for the party, but to help with the waiting.

'I must go and speak to Doreen,' he said, wiping his fingers on a snow-white handkerchief. 'Does she work here regularly?'

Jane explained the position, and added how well she had fitted in. 'And she's so good with the old people,' she added.

'She certainly looks a lot happier than when I saw her last,' commented Anthony.

'It's good for her to be back in Thrush Green,' said Jane. 'She's a country girl at heart, and I hope she decides to stay here.'

'She couldn't do better,' agreed Anthony.

It was dark when the party ended. The wind was almost at gale force, and as Anthony Bull and his friend Charles drove through Lulling to the vicarage, the rain lashed across the windscreen, giving the wipers a hard task to keep pace with it.

Leaves from the lime trees whipped across the High Street. Lights from The Fuchsia Bush gleamed across the dark wet pavements, and the street lamps were reflected in murky puddles which were ruffled by the wind.

'You're going to have a rough ride back to town, I'm afraid,' said Charles. 'Are you sure you won't change your mind, and stay the night?'

'I wish I could, but I've two meetings tomorrow morning, Don't worry, Charles. I've been much refreshed by my visit. It's so good to see old friends.'

He went on to comment on the improvement he had seen in Doreen Lilly.

'She certainly seems to have found her feet,' agreed Charles. 'Who knows? She may marry again. I think that is what her mother would like above all things.'

'Maybe,' agreed Anthony, turning into the vicarage drive, but he sounded doubtful. 'She may not relish matrimony after all that has happened to her,' he went on.

'Well, we must live in hope,' said the rector, trying to open the door against the howling gale. 'One thing, she looks remarkably bonny. Let's hope fortune continues to smile upon her.'

13. PERCY HODGE'S BUSY DAY

For the past several years Percy Hodge, now middle-aged, had lived alone, but he did not enjoy his solitary state. Now that Emily Cooke had finally deserted him for another, his loneliness was even more acute.

He woke, on this particular November morning, to the usual sad contemplation of his single life. It was still dark, for the luminous bedside clock showed ten to six, and the bedroom was chilly.

'Been a frost, I don't doubt,' said Percy aloud, swinging his legs out of bed. He made his way across the landing to the bathroom to perform his brief ablutions. Ten minutes later he went downstairs to the kitchen which was warm and welcoming. The Aga stove made this the most comfortable room in the house, and Percy spent most of his time there.

His dog Gyp leapt from his basket near the stove to greet his master. It was this animal that had collided with Dorothy Watson's car some time ago, causing that lady considerable anguish. Luckily, the dog's injuries had been slight and he bore no scars.

Percy had kept a dog, and sometimes two or three, throughout his life. Normally they had slept in one of the barns or outhouses on the farm, but Gyp had been more privileged since Percy allowed him to sleep indoors. The truth was that Percy enjoyed his company since the death of Gertie, his first wife, and then the disappearance of his second, whom he had later divorced. He chatted to Gyp as he would have done to a human companion and the dog, a particularly affectionate animal, responded in the most satisfactory manner.

This morning he gambolled about his master's legs as the Aga was filled with a scuttle of solid fuel, and only desisted when Percy put down a dish full of dog biscuit and meat scraps.

Percy set about getting his own breakfast: he lifted down a large, heavy frying-pan from a hook on the wall, and placed it on the hob. He put in four large rashers and two sausages, for Percy believed in a substantial meal at the beginning of the day. He cut two thick slices of bread ready to put in when the bacon and sausages were done, and set the basket of eggs handy for the last addition to his meal.

Meanwhile, the kettle had been moved to the hottest part of the stove and was singing cheerfully. The large enamel teapot, which he and Gertie had bought in the early days of their happy marriage, was warming nearby.

Percy did not bother with such niceties as a tablecloth, but set out his knife and fork on the bare wooden table, and stood the milk bottle nearby. By now the bacon was sizzling, and Gyp had finished his breakfast, clattering the dish about the floor as he licked the last crumbs.

'Now out you go, old man,' said Percy fondly, opening the back door into the yard, and the dog ran out.

Percy adjusted the old wooden calendar which stood on the mantelpiece above the appetizing smells wreathing from the stove. As he turned the small knob showing the date, November the fourth, he remembered that the scoutmaster had promised to pick up the sack of potatoes ready for the morrow's celebration of Guy Fawkes' night. Percy had already sorted out some large beauties, and they awaited collection in the back scullery.

He was just shifting the rashers in the frying pan when Gyp's furious barking disturbed him. Dropping the fork, he hurried to the back door. It was beginning to get light and, with a countryman's eye, he automatically noticed the heavy frost on the nearby cabbages and the ice on a shallow puddle.

Gyp was growling and sniffing at the crack of the door of Percy's shed which stood close to the back door. Here were kept such useful things as the paraffin can, garden tools, a hand mower, two bins of chicken food and a pile of useful sacks.

On opening the door and bidding Gyp to 'Sit!', it was on this pile that Percy discovered a startled man. He was fully dressed, if dressed you could call it, in a long dirty overcoat tied at the waist with binder twine, with a tattered scarf round his neck, and a pair of broken boots inadequately covering bare feet. Blue rheumy eyes gazed at Percy from a stubble-decorated face.

'What you doin' here?' growled Percy. He was not unduly alarmed, or even surprised at this encounter. Over the years he must have come across a dozen or more travellers who had used his buildings for a free night's accommodation. He had been lucky, he knew, that not one of them had done damage, though he suspected that a few turnips and stored apples and carrots had been carried away in the usual capacious pockets. Some of his farmer friends had suffered arson at the hands of these gentlemen of the road, and Percy was thankful it had never happened to him.

Gyp kept up a menacing growl as the two men surveyed each other.

'I never done no 'arm,' pleaded the tramp, rising to his feet. 'Just 'ad a kip overnight.'

He sniffed noisily, and wiped his rheumy eyes with dirty knuckles. It was a child's gesture which Percy found strangely moving. He moved aside to let the tramp out.

From the kitchen, the neglected rashers and sausages sent out delicious smells.

'Cor!' said the tramp. 'I'm that 'ungry I could h'eat a h'ox.'

Percy looked at him. He was a most unsavoury fellow to have at the breakfast table, but there was no reason why he should not have some victuals in the shed.

'I could set the dog on you,' Percy told him sternly. 'You bin trespassing! For all I know you've filled your pockets with my stuff.'

'Ain't got no pockets,' protested the tramp, pulling some filthy rags from the side of the dilapidated overcoat. 'See 'ere, mister.'

Gyp growled afresh, longing to rush at the interloper. A distinct smell of burning now began to waft towards the group, and Percy started towards the house.

'You can wait at the door,' he told his visitor. 'I'll give you a bite, and then you're on your way.'

He hurried in and was just in time to rescue the rashers and turn the sausages. He scooped them to one side, and put in the bread.

Gyp remained in the scullery facing his foe at the back door, but ready to hurry to his master's side if needed. He welcomed this diversion at the beginning of the day, and the unusual smells emanating from their visitor were most exciting, almost fox-like.

Percy made the tea, looked out an enamel plate and mug which had been used for just such emergencies before, and set out some of his own breakfast portion for the tramp. Plate in one hand and steaming mug in the other, he pushed past Gyp and handed them to the waiting figure.

'Cor! Mister!' cried the man.

'Eat it in the shed,' ordered Percy, 'and don't forget to bring the plate back. And the mug.'

He shut the door sharply and returned to his own food. Gyp sighed contentedly, and stretched himself in front of the stove.

It was very quiet in the kitchen. Only the ticking of the great wall clock and the humming of the kettle broke the silence as Percy mopped his plate with a piece of bread. It was at times like this that sadness pervaded him. Breakfast time with Gertie had been a busy occasion when they discussed the day's plans and then washed up together, for Percy had always been more domesticated than most farmers, and his sister, Mrs Jenner, had made sure that he did his fair share of the chores when they were young together in this very same kitchen.

He thought about the fellow outside. Had he ever had a home, he wondered? A poor life for a man, everlasting roaming the country. Worse than his own. At least he had a roof over his head, a fire and victuals in plenty. It was just company that he missed.

He was about to take his plate to the sink when he heard the knocking at the back door, and found the tramp proffering the empty plate and mug.

'Thanks, mate. That went down good,' he said.

Percy put the plate and mug on the battered scullery table, and surveyed his visitor. He was certainly a sorry sight. It was the pink flesh showing through the gaping boots that struck Percy as the most pathetic part of the general air of destitution.

'You goin' far?' he asked.

'Makin' to Banbury way. Got a mate there. Do a bit of beatin' for the toffs' shoots.'

'You won't get far in those boots,' commented Percy, eyeing

a pair of his old gardening boots standing hardby. They looked, though Percy would not have known it, very like the famous lace-up pair belonging to Gertrude Jekyll, well-worn but serviceable.

'Take them,' he said, 'and chuck those wrecks in the dustbin.'

He left the man on the floor coping with his new acquisitions, and went back to the kitchen. An ancient pullover, knitted years before by his sister, lay on one of the chairs awaiting washing. Well, it would save him doing that chore, thought Percy, taking it to the scullery.

The man was busy lacing up one boot. Percy suddenly remembered Gertie on just such an occasion, asking one long-past traveller anxiously what size he took. He had teased her when the man had gone. Didn't she know he could stuff newspaper round the gaps, or cut a slit if they pinched?

But Gertie, child of a Lulling shopkeeper, had not had much first-hand knowledge of tramps and her ignorance had amused Percy enormously.

The sudden remembrance softened Percy now. He handed him the pullover. 'Keep out the cold,' he said gruffly. 'Want a hunk of bread to take with you?'

The man stood up, stamping in his new boots.

'They're great, mate, and you're a real gent.'

'Well, don't tell your friends,' warned Percy. 'I ain't usually so generous.'

He went back to the kitchen. He had no intention of inviting the man farther into his domain for he would be as verminous, he had no doubt, as a stray dog.

He rolled up the end of the loaf in a page from the *Radio Times*, adding a lump of cheese from the nearby cheese-dish on the dresser.

His visitor stood, still admiring his boots.

'Right! There you are, and now be off with you,' said Percy, opening the back door.

'God bless you, guv,' said the tramp fervently, and Percy

watched him striding away, in his old boots, into the frosty morning.

'Sometimes,' remarked Percy to Gyp, as he poured another cup of tea, 'I reckon I'm too soft.'

An hour later the scoutmaster called for the sack of potatoes, and Percy helped him load it into the boot of his car. He was on his way to work at the bank in Lulling High Street, and Percy thought how nice it must be to have a job which started halfway through the morning, as it seemed to him.

He himself had already seen to the cattle, mended a fence, rung the corn chandler, prepared a mash for the chickens, filled in a form for some ministry or other which meant nothing to him, looked out another pair of boots, demoted now from everyday to gardening, and left his dishes and the tramp's in the sink to soak.

Just before ten he decided to take the shabby Land Rover down to Lulling to get the tyres looked at, praying that he need not go to the expense of a new one on the off-side which was definitely suspect. Then he would seek refreshment and a little company at The Two Pheasants. Tuesday today, he thought, as he trundled down the hill; might be a lardy cake at The Fuchsia Bush, and that was just the thing on a frosty day.

He trod on the accelerator. You never knew – that Lulling lot might have cleared out all the lardy cakes if he didn't look lively.

At Rectory Cottages Doreen Lilly was busy at work. She had left Bobby safely corralled in the nursery school with a pair of blunt-nosed scissors and some coloured paper.

Today she had been asked by Jane to tidy the store cupboard and clean the shelves. It was a pleasantly straightforward job, stacking packets and tins in a small room with deep shelves on three sides, which was lit by a large window at the end.

All went well until Doreen noticed how dirty the hopper of the window had become. It was a small slanting pane, always ajar to air the place, and was liable to catch any dust and debris which the main part of the window missed.

She went to fetch the short pair of steps, which only stood hip-high and had a useful padded top which could be used as a stool. Doreen was fond of these steps: Jane had warned her about too much stretching at the present stage of her pregnancy, and they were a great help to her.

She opened them now and made her way up them, a damp cloth in her hand. The shelf was wide, and stacked with innumerable tins. Doreen found it difficult to reach across them to her target.

'Drat it all,' she muttered, and stepped on to the padded top to give her better access to the window.

It was at this point that the steps skidded away. They fell with a hideous clatter, and Doreen ended up lying awkwardly across them still clutching the cloth in her hand. Half a dozen tins, dislodged in the upset, dropped painfully upon her, and she cried out.

Jane came running, took in the situation at a glance, and soon had the girl sitting in the kitchen. She had the sense not to scold her. It was apparent from the girl's ashen face that she was upset enough already. She was bent double, and holding her stomach.

'Got an awful griping,' she gasped, and Jane's heart sank.

'You'd better come and lie down,' she said, helping the girl to her feet.

As soon as she had the girl flat on the bed she rang the surgery to explain the situation. John Lovell answered the telephone himself and, having faith in Jane Cartwright's nursing knowledge, said he would be over immediately.

'I've just finished surgery,' he said. 'In fact I was on my way to the car. I'll be with you in a couple of minutes.'

By the time the doctor arrived, Doreen was tearful and in great pain. John Lovell gave a brief examination, and straightened up.

'I want her in hospital,' he said quietly to Jane. 'May I use your telephone?'

Some ten minutes later the inhabitants of Thrush Green were greatly intrigued to see an ambulance drawing up outside Rectory Cottages, and a stretcher being carried in.

One of the poor old dears, thought Ella, surveying the scene from her landing window.

'Someone's been took ill,' Jenny told Winnie Bailey, as they made the bed together.

'I hope that's not poor Muriel Fuller,' said Isobel to Harold, catching sight of the ambulance as she put out the milk bottles. 'She was very shaky in church last week.'

Not one of the interested viewers guessed that the youngest person in the place was the victim.

Albert Piggott and Percy Hodge had just emerged from The Two Pheasants, Albert to continue his desultory tidying-up, and Percy to drive the Land Rover back to the farm.

'Wonder who that is?' said Percy, watching the laden stretcher being returned to the ambulance, accompanied by his niece Jane Cartwright and Dr Lovell.

'One of them old 'uns, no doubt,' responded Albert. 'You has to expect it at their age.'

His tone was dismissive, and he was already turning away towards the church. But Percy, whose sight was clearer than his companion's, still watched attentively.

'That's the Lilly girl!' he exclaimed. 'Doreen, or somethin'.'

The ambulance doors clanged shut. Dr Lovell raised his hand to Jane as he departed, and she, to Percy's surprise, came hurrying towards him.

'Uncle Percy, do me a favour.' She seemed unusually agitated.

'What's that?'

'Young Doreen Lilly's had a fall. She might have a miscarriage. What's worrying her is that her little boy's at playschool and she usually fetches him at twelve. Could you take a message to her mother? She'll be able to collect him, I'm sure. Do you know the house?'

'Lord, yes! Where the baker lived. I'll drive down now.'

'Thanks very much. I dare not leave my old folk. And tell her to ring the hospital direct. Visiting hours are six to seven-thirty. The hospital will tell her if the girl's up to seeing her.'

Percy clambered back into the Land Rover, and turned to drive down the hill. He was somewhat perturbed at the delicate task before him, and sorry for the young woman whom he had always considered unusually pretty. Percy, particularly now that he was alone, was susceptible to female attractions.

He found Gladys Lilly busy with a mound of ironing; there was a pleasant scent of clean linen, and a clothes' horse bearing innumerable small garments, presumably belonging to her grandson.

'Oh my!' cried Gladys, on hearing the news. 'What a thing to happen! It was all going so well too. What a blessing it was that your Jane was there to look after her.'

Percy added the message about telephoning the hospital and the visiting hours.

'I'll pop in next door and ring from there as soon as I've fetched Bobby,' promised Gladys. 'If you'll excuse me a moment, I'll go and get a coat.'

Percy was left alone in the kitchen. It was warm and tidy. A pile of newly-ironed pillow cases and sheets stood nearby, and something delicious sizzled in the oven. On the hob stood a freshly cooked rice pudding, with a nice brown crinkled top smelling of cinnamon. It reminded Percy sharply of the dinners his mother had cooked for them years ago, in that same kitchen along the Nidden road where his breakfast dishes still awaited attention in a scummy sink. It was a good thing, he thought, that his mother could not see it now.

Mrs Lilly, somewhat calmer, reappeared, and Percy offered to give her a lift to the school, but she refused.

'It's no distance, thanks all the same. You've done enough, Mr Hodge.'

Percy was touched by the rather formal address.

'Well, let me take you up to the hospital this evenin',' he said. 'It's a good step, and they've promised us rain after dark. Shall I pop down, say at half past six, and see how things are?'

'That's uncommon kind of you,' said Gladys. 'I'd really be glad of a lift.'

They left the house together, Gladys hurrying along to the school, and Percy making his way back to his midday bread and cheese. That rice pudding, he thought wistfully, would have gone down a treat.

At half past six he reappeared at Gladys Lilly's door. He had exchanged his working jacket for a somewhat cleaner one, wore a tie and had brushed his hair.

Mrs Lilly, who was already in her outdoor coat, climbed into the Land Rover. She looked tearful, and Percy was at a loss to know what to say.

'All right to visit then?' he said at last.

'Yes. Hospital folk said it was OK. Sad though. She's lost it.'

'Lost what?'

'The baby. Didn't you know? She was having her second.'

Percy did know now that he came to think of it, but his apparent ignorance was easier in the circumstances.

'Is she all right?'

'Will be, they say, but she's got to stay in a day or two.'

'She's a nice lookin' girl,' ventured Percy, driving circumspectly up Lulling High Street.

'Takes after her dad,' said Gladys. 'I was never no beauty.'

She sounded quite matter-of-fact, and was certainly not angling for compliments, which Percy approved.

'Yes, he was a handsome chap,' he agreed. 'You must miss him.'

'Thirty-three years we was married, and him in the same job up at Carters in Grain Street all that time. He was a baker, you know.'

'I did know,' said Percy, turning into the hospital gates. 'Used to make first-class lardy cakes. I had one from The Fuchsia Bush today, but it's not a patch on Carters!'

He stopped the Land Rover, and watched his passenger clamber down.

'You coming in? There's a kiosk where they sell coffee and tea.'

'No. I'll wait here for you. Don't hurry yourself,' replied Percy.

He had parked at the side of the hospital, and sat looking at the row of lighted windows before him. The glass was frosted, and he could only discern human shapes passing to and fro about their business.

A little nocturnal animal scrabbled under the laurel bushes in front of him, and somewhere a child was wailing inconsolably, probably missing his mother and the warm security of his own bed.

Poor little devil, thought Percy. He knew how he felt, lost and alone, and away from all the comforts of home. It was getting unpleasantly cold with the engine turned off, and Percy decided to take a brisk walk around the car park.

There were very few cars there, but a steady stream passed on the road outside, lighting up the leafless trees in the grounds, and turning the window panes of the hospital into silver squares.

A man came hurrying out, and Percy recognized him as a neighbour from Nidden.

'What you doin' here?' he called.

'Why, Perce, it's you, is it? My boy's broke a leg. Nothin' serious. Blasted motorbike of his. Who you waitin' for?'

Percy told him.

'Young Doreen, eh? Pretty girl, but no better'n she should be, so I hear.'

'You don't want to believe all you hear,' said Percy snappily.

'No, that's right,' agreed the other, sounding somewhat startled. 'Well, I'd best be off. Gettin' chilly again, isn't it?'

Percy did not answer, but watched him get into his Ford car and drive away.

'Everlastin' gossip,' he commented to the unseen animal which was still scrabbling among the laurels. 'Makes you sick.'

And at that moment, Mrs Lilly reappeared and Percy opened the door of the Land Rover for her.

'How is she?' asked Percy when they had joined the stream of traffic outside the hospital.

'Like a little ghost,' replied Gladys. 'Got a drip thing stuck in her. She looks terrible, but the nurse says she's OK.'

'Good. Want a lift up there tomorrow?'

'Oh, I couldn't bother you, Mr Hodge.'

'No trouble. And call me Percy.'

'Well then, thank you, Percy.'

They drew up outside the house, and Percy secretly hoped to be invited into that comfortable kitchen for a drink, but he was to be disappointed.

'I won't keep you now,' said Gladys, as she climbed down to the pavement. 'I've got young Bobby to fetch from my neighbour, but I hope you'll have a bit of supper with me tomorrow.'

'I'll look forward to that,' said Percy heartily. 'See you same time tomorrow then.'

As he trundled home towards Nidden, he felt uncommonly happy. The bonfire awaited tomorrow's lighting on the green, and he remembered how he himself had enjoyed the yearly frolic as a boy. He was glad he had provided the potatoes for tomorrow's celebrations; his father had done so for years, and it was good to keep up the tradition.

What a day! How far, he wondered, had the tramp got on his way towards Banbury in his old gardening boots, and how was poor young Doreen getting on in her hospital bed? You never knew what the day would bring you.

He turned into the farm yard and was greeted by ecstatic barking from Gyp.

'Time we was both fed,' Percy told him, reaching for the dog biscuits with one hand, and the frying-pan with the other.

14. MIXED PROBLEMS

At Barton-on-Sea, Agnes and Dorothy were busy with Christmas cards and parcels bound for friends overseas.

'We really should have sent to Freda Potts in Australia last month,' said Dorothy, studying a pamphlet from the Post Office.

Freda Potts had taught with Dorothy in her first school, and had been a frequent visitor to Thrush Green before making her home abroad.

'So soon?' queried Agnes. 'I should have thought it would have got there far too early.'

'I'm inclined to put a handkerchief in with our Christmas card, and send it air mail,' said Dorothy. 'Really, Christmas seems to get earlier every year; here we are on November the fifth, and still behind time.'

'I wonder how the bonfire will go tonight?' mused Agnes, pen arrested.

'I don't intend to light it,' said Dorothy, 'the leaves are much too wet.'

'I meant at Thrush Green.'

'Ah!' sighed Dorothy. '*That* bonfire! What fun we had with the guy!'

'I wish we were nearer, then we could be there to see it.'

Dorothy looked at Agnes's wistful face. 'We'll bear it in mind for next year,' she promised. 'Perhaps we'll have a day or two up in the Cotswolds, and have a last fling before we hibernate.'

'Lovely!' cried Agnes.

'And I'll ring Isobel tomorrow to hear all about it,' continued Dorothy, reaching for another Christmas card.

'And the rest of the Thrush Green news,' added Agnes. 'It seems a long time since we saw them. Would you like me to do the telephoning?'

'No, no. I can do it when I come back from Teddy's,' replied Dorothy, banging on a stamp energetically.

Teddy, thought Agnes rebelliously, *would* have to come into things! Even a telephone call to dear Thrush Green, it seemed, had to be tailored to fit in with Teddy's requirements.

She banged on a stamp of her own, with some vehemence.

Thrush Green's bonfire was set alight just after six o'clock, and a goodly crowd was there to watch. It was flaming vigorously when Percy made his way towards Mrs Lilly's house. A crowd of people held up his Land Rover for a few moments as they crossed the road from The Two Pheasants. He was hailed by a woman as he waited, and he saw that it was Nelly Piggott.

'Coming over, Percy?' she called, one hand on the van window.

'Can't tonight. Just off to the hospital.'

'Oh dear! Who's bad then?'

'Doreen Lilly.'

He attempted to edge away, not wanting to go into details, but he was obliged to linger as the new schoolmaster, his wife and the two little girls went across towards the bonfire.

'I'm sorry,' said Nelly. 'I hadn't heard.'

At last he got away and Nelly, following the excited Lester children across the grass, had much to think about.

Later, she told Albert of this encounter. 'D'you think he's got his eye on young Doreen, now that Emily Cooke's turned him down?' she enquired.

'Wouldn't be surprised,' grunted Albert. 'Perce is fool enough for anythin', and always had an eye for the girls.'

Mrs Lilly was waiting on the pavement when Percy arrived, and he did not have the opportunity of presenting her with the dozen brown eggs he had brought as a small offering to his hostess.

They made their way to Lulling High Street. The sky on their left was bright with reflection from the bonfire, and Mrs Lilly chattered brightly about the times she had taken Doreen to see it over the years.

'Bobby wanted to go but I promised I'd take him next year. He had a late night yesterday, what with all this upset, and my neighbour Mrs Brown is sitting with him. I got him to bed early tonight. One thing, he's not much bother about going to bed. Doreen was a real handful over that when she was little.'

As before Percy waited while she went in to see her daughter. If anything, it was colder than ever, and a myriad stars sparkled over a world already frosty.

Percy found himself looking forward eagerly to Gladys Lilly's supper, and hoped it would be a cooked one. A chap didn't fancy cold meat and salad on a night like this, and Percy fell to envisaging steak-and-kidney pudding, with good thick gravy oozing out when the knife went in, or perhaps a steaming Lancashire hot-pot like his dear Gertie used to make, with brown potato slices sizzling on top.

The waiting time seemed longer than yesterday's, hungry as he was, and the church clock was striking seven when Gladys came from the door.

'I'm to ring tomorrow morning, and they may let her out after the doctor's done his rounds. She looks more herself today.'

'Want me to fetch her?' asked Percy.

'I don't think you need to trouble,' said Gladys. 'Someone from the hospital car service will bring her, they said. If it's daytime you'll be out on the farm, and you've done more than most would already.'

'Only too pleased to help,' responded Percy. 'Let's leave it that you'll get in touch sometime tomorrow. I'd like to know how she's doin'.'

He left the Land Rover in the street, and followed Mrs Lilly into the house. A delicious smell of cooking greeted them, and Percy realized that he was even more ravenous than he had first thought.

'Now come in, Mr Hodge – I mean, Percy. It's set in the kitchen, and Mrs Brown is having a bite with us.'

Percy felt unduly annoyed at hearing that this was not to be the tête-à-tête he had envisaged. However, it was Gladys's affair, and obviously a nice way of showing appreciation of her neighbour's help during these worrying two days.

Gladys took his jacket and cap, and led him through to the kitchen. Mrs Brown was a small wizened old lady with hair of a startling orange hue. Percy knew her by sight, and remembered that her husband, who was now dead, had been a gamekeeper on one of the Hampshire estates to the south of Lulling.

Introductions were made, Mrs Brown and Percy were invited to sit at the table, and Gladys took the supper from the oven.

It proved to be just the sort of meal that Percy liked best, steak-and-kidney simmered in a casserole with a large dish of potatoes baked in their jackets and another of carrots.

Percy, like most men, enjoyed plenty of meat with brown gravy. When he had married Gertie, an accomplished and imaginative cook, he had stipulated 'no damn stuff in white sauce'.

Gertie soon weaned him by way of cauliflower cheese and fish fillets in white sauce, but he still thought that the predominant colour on a fellow's dinner plate should be brown with a touch of home-grown green – say runner beans, peas or sprouts – on the side.

'Well, this looks wholly good,' he told Gladys. 'I don't get real home-cooking these days.'

'Nothing like it,' agreed Mrs Brown, who seemed to eat at an alarming pace despite the regular clicking of ill-fitting false teeth. 'When I was in service at Marchleaze we had a wonderful cook. Mind you, she was temperamental. Blew hot and cold. One minute all smiles, the next as black as thunder. Being an artist in her own line, you see.'

'Ah!' agreed Percy. Gladys passed him the pepper pot, and was about to speak, but Mrs Brown forestalled her.

'My lady understood her funny little ways,' continued Mrs Brown. 'Never turned a hair when cook sulked. A wonderful woman she was. Heiress in her own right, but would sit down with anyone. Brought up the children the same, but it didn't stop Master John taking to the bottle. And worse! But a lovely boy. Used to have beautiful hair before he went bald. And nice manners too, even when he was half-seas over.'

It soon became apparent to Percy that Mrs Brown was one of those people, all too common, who regaled their listeners with lengthy tales about people who were entirely unknown and, after an hour or so of increasing boredom, thoroughly disliked.

He and Gladys were subjected to a monologue about Mrs Brown's lady, her looks, disposition and extensive wardrobe. The doings of Master John, Miss Adela and the three younger siblings were also described in minutest detail, while Mrs Brown's two companions ate in silence.

The main course was followed by a magnificent trifle, and then by biscuits and a noble hunk of Cheddar cheese. Percy did full justice to everything put before him, and attempted to turn a deaf ear to his neighbour who was now describing the grandeur of her lady's drawing-room.

'And over the mantelpiece there was a great picture of her mother – ever so big – as big as that door there. No! I tell a lie! Perhaps about three-quarters of that door, but with a gold frame that took a bit of dusting, I can tell you. It didn't have no glass over it, it was done in oils, you see, and that could catch the dust too, specially as they liked log fires, and you know what wood ash is if you get a draught. The gardener used to bring in the logs. Why, some of them would be as long as this table here, and as thick as a man's leg. Burn for hours, they would.'

The fireplace and portrait were followed by descriptions of the chairs, cabinets and their contents, the soft furnishing, both for winter and summer, and how the staff set about spring-cleaning when the lady of the house ordered it.

By nine-fifteen Percy was beginning to get restive. He was more than grateful to Gladys for this wonderful meal, but disappointed in having so little opportunity to express his appreciation, or to express anything else, for that matter, with the relentless outpourings of Mrs Brown in full spate.

At last she stopped, looked at her watch, and rose in a flurry.

'So late! I had no idea! I must get back, Gladys. My programme's on, and I want to see if Kevin and Mandy have made it up.'

She waved goodbye to Percy, and Gladys escorted her to the front door, thanking her profusely against Mrs Brown's monologue which still continued.

Gladys returned and smiled at Percy. 'Runs on a bit, doesn't she?'

Percy thought that this was the understatement of the year, but was too polite to comment.

'Have a cup of coffee,' urged Gladys. 'We might have a chat, now she's gone. But this I will say, despite all the gab, her heart's in the right place.'

*

159

It was not long, of course, before the news flew round the neighbourhood that Percy Hodge was now paying his attentions to young Doreen Lilly. Well, hadn't he visited the hospital twice while the girl was there? And hadn't he been seen visiting the house several times since Doreen was home again?

The general opinion was that Percy simply could not keep away from these young girls like Doreen and Emily Cooke, and all foresaw another disappointment in store for the amorous wooer.

But other topics soon crowded out speculation about Percy's adventures. For one thing, the spate of fund-raising continued, and the Fur-and-Feather whist drive, Lulling's Mammoth Nearly-New Sale, and the flutter of raffle books which these activities aroused, turned attention from Percy's plight.

Nelly Piggott had troubles of her own, for one morning Bertha Lovelock had entered The Fuchsia Bush alone, and taken a table dangerously near to the counter where such tempting titbits as home-made shortbread fingers and delicious scones, warm from the oven, gave forth their fragrance.

Nelly, who happened to be in the shop when the lady appeared, was confronted with a number of options to protect the shop's property.

It would look offensive to remove the goods from the counter and to put them out of Bertha's reach. She could, of course, pretend that she wanted to re-arrange them in the kitchen and whisk the lot outside.

She could stand guard over the array, or post one of the girls to stand on duty. She could, at a pinch, telephone Violet Lovelock and tell her that Bertha was at large on her own, and did she know?

All these unpleasant possibilities flashed through Nelly's head, until she came across a more acceptable solution.

She approached Bertha with a smile. 'Good morning, Miss Lovelock. Chilly today, isn't it?'

Bertha inclined her head graciously.

'Can I bring you some coffee?' asked Nelly.

'Yes, please. Nothing to eat.'

Nelly looked around with affected solicitude. 'I think you are going to be in a draught here, Miss Lovelock,' she said anxiously. 'Every time the door opens, you know. Wind's easterly this morning. Let me put you over here. You'll be more comfortable.'

Bertha seemed remarkably obliging, and began to gather gloves, purse, two letters awaiting posting, and an ancient fur stole which she had hung on the back of the chair.

At that moment, however, there was a crash from the kitchen, and Nelly went to see what was the matter, and to order Bertha's coffee.

Her back was turned for approximately twenty seconds, and Bertha was still collecting her belongings when Nelly reached her side. Before long, the old lady was settled by the wall, out of harm's way, and Gloria was approaching with a steaming cup of coffee.

Nelly carried the basket of scones into the kitchen to count them. As she feared, one was missing. One really could not help but admire Bertha's sleight-of-hand manoeuvres, embarrassing though they were, thought Nelly.

Gloria had been left on duty, having been primed beforehand about the action to take should Bertha ever appear alone, and Nelly made a quick decision.

She would do nothing on this occasion; poor old Violet had enough to cope with. But she intended to see that Bertha paid her bill for the coffee, and she would watch to see that she went straight home. Both these things happened, and Nelly was left to wonder if she should mention the matter to Mrs Peters and the girls. Or was it right to turn a blind eye, as she had decided to do?

Being a partner in the firm certainly complicated life, thought Nelly, returning to her domain in the kitchen after she had seen Bertha disappear through her own front door. If Nelly had been a mere assistant, like Rosa or Gloria, she would have reported the matter to Mrs Peters and left it at that. But now she had more important obligations. 'Rank imposes responsibilities' someone had once told her, and Nelly, somewhat ruefully, realized that she must face that fact.

This time no action, she told herself, shaking flour on to a pastry board, but if it happened again she would harden her heart and send for Miss Violet to cope with her sister.

Winnie Bailey was also having private worries. As a doctor's wife for many years, in a small community, she had frequently known of the complaints and conditions of many of her husband's patients. Obviously she had been discreet, and had not interfered in her husband's affairs, but the fact remained that she was often privy to confidences disclosed by Donald's patients almost before she could direct them to his surgery.

The case of Margaret Lester and her family worried her considerably. Her kind heart went out to the man who was doing his best to carry on the sound tradition of good schooling which his predecessors had maintained, whilst instigating some more modern methods of his own.

She was even more concerned about the two little girls. She came across them occasionally, and was impressed by their good manners and friendliness. The children played frequently with John Lovell's two children who were much the same age, and one morning Winnie ventured to broach the painful subject of Margaret's addiction to alcohol with the doctor.

He listened with his usual sympathy. He was devoted to Winnie, recognizing her sterling virtues and unfailing common sense. But on this occasion, he was obliged to be firm.

'There is nothing I can do, Winnie, as you know, until I am approached either by the patient herself or by someone directly responsible for her, like Alan. I am as upset as you are by the problem, and I can only hope that Alan can persuade her to seek help.'

'Have you ever been called to the house?'

'Not for Margaret. I have had occasion to visit the children once or twice, but the migraine attacks about which we hear so much are dealt with by Alan and Margaret herself.'

'But those poor little girls!' cried Winnie. 'What can we do about them?'

'Mighty little, I fear, until we are asked to help. We can only stand by in readiness, and rush to the rescue if necessary.'

'I just dread the possibility of something unpleasant happening in that house,' said Winnie sadly. 'It could so easily.'

How prophetic her words were!

15. FRIENDS AT THRUSH GREEN

November grew gloomier as the days passed. It was not cold, but dark and oppressive. Mist hung in the valleys and the sun was nowhere to be seen. The trees dripped, the hedges were spangled with droplets, and the roads and grass were permanently wet.

Lights were on in the houses, shops and offices from morning until dusk. It was a depressing period for all. Everyone was lethargic, from the young school children to the venerable inhabitants of Rectory Cottages.

Even Betty Bell's exuberance seemed diminished as she went about her duties, first at the school and then at the Shoosmiths' house.

'Fair gets on your wick,' she said, collecting her tin of polish from under the stairs. 'I mean, what's the good of polishing in this weather? "Love's labour's lost", as my mum used to say.'

'Well, perhaps you'd better leave it,' said Isobel. 'The windows could do with a wash instead.'

'No, no. It's polishing today, and that I'll do,' said Betty firmly. 'Can't let the weather have the best of it. By the way, old Dotty – Miss Harmer, I should say – is in bed with a chill. At least, she should be, but she keeps getting out and she's driving Miss Connie up the wall.'

'Oh dear! I'm sorry, I'll ring Connie this morning.'

'It's this weather,' went on Betty, taking up the tin of polish. 'No end of the kids are away from school, and Mrs Lester's taken to her bed again.'

'Dear, dear!'

'And not only to her *bed*,' said Betty ominously, and made her way upstairs, leaving Isobel much disturbed.

Later that day she and Harold roused themselves enough to tackle the task of sweeping up leaves. It was heavy going, for the ground was sticky and the leaves sodden. They wheeled a few barrow loads to the compost heap, and surveyed the hundreds which still adhered obstinately to the lawn.

'I don't know about you,' remarked Harold, 'but I've had enough. It's so damn warm, too. Let's call it a day. We'll tackle this lot when it's dried out.'

'It suits me,' agreed Isobel, who had already shed her coat which lay over the hedge.

'What we want is a good brisk wind,' said Harold. 'Or some frost. Preferably both.'

'Better still,' said Isobel, 'an early cup of tea.'

They went indoors to get it.

It had never been really light all day, but by five o'clock it was truly dark, and the inhabitants of Thrush Green and Lulling were thankful to draw their curtains against the miserable world outside, and turn to indoor pursuits.

Soon after six o'clock the first rumbles of thunder began, and Thrush Green was lit, every so often, by flickering lightning.

Harold, returning from the front porch, was cheerful. 'This should clear the air,' he said. 'No rain yet. I suppose it'll come. Alan Lester's just driven off, by the way.'

'Is Margaret with him?'

'I couldn't see. I just waved, and he hooted. Off to a meeting I expect, poor devil. Thank God, I'm retired and don't have to face meetings any more.'

'What rubbish!' cried Isobel. 'You are often out at committee meetings of the Parish Council and other Church matters, not to mention Scouts and Guides and British Legion and Uncle Tom Cobley and all.'

'I don't count those,' said Harold equably. 'They aren't Business!'

They settled down with their books, while the thunder rumbled. The electric lights flickered ominously, but it was an hour later when there was an almighty crash of thunder overhead and all the lights went out.

'Damn!' said Harold. 'And I've just dropped my glasses.'

'Then don't move your feet,' begged Isobel. 'Where do you think they are?'

'If I knew that,' replied Harold patiently, 'they wouldn't be lost. I'll just grope about. Can you find a torch?'

Isobel felt her way into the hall where a large torch stood permanently. On returning, she picked up the gleam of Harold's spectacles on the hearthrug, and restored them to their owner.

'Good girl! I'll go and light the oil lamp. Hope our neighbours have some auxiliary lighting.'

'Oh, it shouldn't take long,' said Isobel hopefully. 'Don't we get switched to another grid when this happens? Last time it was only a few minutes before the electricity came back.'

She followed Harold into the kitchen and directed the beam of the torch while he lit the ancient oil lamp and carefully replaced the glass and shade.

'It really is a lovely soft light,' commented Isobel when it was installed on the table between their chairs. The fire gave out some light, and a few small logs which Harold added soon leapt into flame.

'It's really quite snug,' went on Isobel. 'Not really bright enough to read. A wonderful excuse to lie back and doze.'

But such hopes were not to be realized, for at that moment the front door bell rang shrilly, and there was a sound of frightened voices. Harold grabbed the torch and went into the dark hall, followed by Isobel.

A flash of lightning illuminated Thrush Green as he opened the door. Huddled together and crying were the two little Lester girls, their shoulders spattered with the rain which was now beginning to fall.

'Come in quickly!' cried Isobel, leading them to the fire. She was shocked to see that they were in their night-clothes –

pyjamas under their dressing-gowns, and their feet were clad only in soft slippers.

'It's Mummy,' said Alison, 'we can't wake her, and I can't reach the candles in the cupboard.'

She was calmer than her younger sister Kate, who was still in tears, but both children were trembling, and not only with the cold, Isobel surmised.

'I found the matches,' went on Alison, 'but I was afraid to go upstairs to find the little paraffin lamp Daddy keeps on the landing. I didn't like the thunder, you see, and the matches kept going out.'

Harold and Isobel exchanged glances.

'I'll take the hurricane lamp and go over,' he said.

'I think I ought to come too,' replied Isobel, much troubled. What on earth would he find? Margaret unconscious? The house in flames?

Harold took command. 'I'll come back for you, if need be. But these two could do with a hot drink. Use the old saucepan. That fire should be good enough to heat some milk.'

Isobel heard the front door bang as Harold departed, and then began to do her best to comfort the children. The thought of matches, candles, and a paraffin lamp in the darkness next door, and the frightened young children's pathetic attempts to find a light amidst the terrors of the storm, made Isobel feel positively sick with horror.

She fetched the milk and set it to heat at the front of the fire, and the two little girls, with a biscuit apiece, sat on the hearthrug and began to calm down.

'Do you know where Daddy is?' she asked, pouring out the milk into two mugs.

'At a meeting,' said Kate.

'Near Oxford,' added Alison. 'At a school with a funny name.'

'An animal,' volunteered Kate. 'A white animal, "White Lion", I think.'

'No, no, it's not,' said Alison firmly. 'It's "White Hart".'

'It's more than that,' maintained Kate defensively, 'like "White Hart Road School".'

At least, thought Isobel, they appeared to be getting back to a more normal sisterly exchange of communication, and there was a slight chance of being able to ring the school where the meeting was taking place.

She was relieved when Harold returned.

'Is Mummy all right?' asked Alison.

'She's fine. Just resting. I told her we'd look after you until your daddy came back.'

He exchanged glances with Isobel, shaking his head slightly.

'I'll try and phone Alan,' he said. 'Any idea of the place?'

'It's a school called "White Something",' said Alison.

'An animal,' added Kate.

Harold found the telephone directory, put it on the table in the light of the oil lamp, and settled his glasses.

'Schools!' he was muttering to himself as he leafed through the pages.

'Ah, here we are! The only "White Something" is "White Rose School".'

'That's it,' said Kate.

'But that's a *flower*,' protested Alison.

'It's a *deer*,' proclaimed Kate fiercely. 'A *rose* deer!'

'That's *roe*, stupid,' shouted Alison, pink with fury.

'Now, now,' said Isobel, 'that's enough! Just be quiet while Harold telephones.'

The children subsided, and Isobel followed Harold into the hall where he was dialling the number by torchlight. She was careful to close the sitting-room door.

'How is she?'

'Flat out, but safe where she is. She's on the bed. I covered her up.'

'Should we get the doctor?'

'That's Alan's job. All I can do is tell him the position. Is that White Rose School? Is Alan Lester there? It's rather urgent.'

'He left about ten minutes ago,' said a deep voice, which Isobel could hear clearly. 'I'm just off myself. I'm the head here, and we've just finished the meeting. Lester should be home in about twenty minutes or so.'

'Have you had a power cut over there? We're groping about in darkness.'

'No. We're still all right, I'm glad to say. Do you want me to get in touch with Lester?'

'No, no. We'll do that. We live next door to the school house. Many thanks, anyway.'

He put down the telephone, and looked at Isobel. 'I think the best thing to do is to put the little girls to bed in their own house, and we'll wait there until Alan gets back. Some home-coming for the poor chap, I'm afraid!'

A quarter of an hour later the children were in bed. The emergency lamp on the landing had been lit, and their bedroom door left ajar.

Isobel crept upstairs to look at them a few minutes later, and was relieved to see that they were asleep.

She opened the door of Margaret's room, heard regular snoring, and closed the door again quietly. If only Alan could get back quickly and take over! She went downstairs, and she and Harold sat in the chilly sitting-room which was lit only by the light of two candles which Harold had discovered in the kitchen cupboard.

How sad this little house seemed now, thought Isobel. In this room, so often, she had gossiped with dear old Agnes and Dorothy about the fun and foibles of Thrush Green parents and their children. Upstairs in Dorothy's old bedroom, which had always been restful and scented with lavender, there now lay poor unhappy Margaret in a room reeking of stale alcohol, while across the landing in Agnes's always-neat bedroom, two defenceless little girls lay in uneasy sleep.

Again Isobel's thoughts reverted to their pathetic efforts to find a light when darkness had suddenly enveloped them. She thought of matches being struck with the little girls' hair hanging dangerously over the flames. She thought of a heavy oil lamp being carried in a child's hands, of spilt paraffin, of leaping flames, of nightdresses on fire, of terror and panic. How easily there could have been a tragedy involving an unconscious mother and her young children! Something would have to be done about Margaret.

She shivered with horror and chill, and thought longingly of the bright fire they had left next door. At that moment a car drew up, the lights of the headlamps sweeping the room, and Harold went to the front door to greet Alan.

'Hello! What's happened? Where are the lights?' Isobel heard Alan say.

She could not hear Harold's reply, just the sound of his voice explaining things.

'My God! I must go upstairs to Margaret,' Alan said, in a shocked voice. 'I'll be down in a second.'

Harold returned, and they sat in silence, listening to the

footsteps in the room above. Within minutes Alan returned, and dropped exhaustedly into a chair, his head in his hands.

'I think,' began Isobel tentatively, 'I should get you a drink, if you can tell me where things are.'

Alan gave a great shuddering sigh, and looked up. 'You are both so kind. I can't begin to thank you.' He stood up. 'I'll take a candle and go and light the Primus. We'll have some coffee.'

'And we'll help you,' said Harold. 'This damn power cut makes you realize how much we depend on switches, doesn't it?'

They all three went into the kitchen, and set about their preparations. It was only ten minutes later, when they had returned to the sitting-room with steaming mugs of instant coffee, that Alan asked for more details.

Harold told him, keeping nothing back. The sudden darkness, the frightened children, the matches, the attempt to light an oil lamp, all were related, while Alan listened with an expression of such horror on his face that Isobel's heart went out to him.

'If you hadn't been there,' he said at last, when the story ended, 'I could have come home to a burnt-out house, and no family! I blame myself. The meeting went on far longer than expected and—'

'It's a way meetings have,' interjected Harold.

'I'd seen that the girls were ready for bed. Margaret was not too bad, but said she would go to bed too as she was tired. As you see, we have no open fires here now, just the night storage heaters, for safety's sake. But of course I never envisaged a power cut, and all it entails.'

'You've got a problem,' said Harold.

'I know that well enough,' said Alan bitterly, 'and this evening has brought it to a head. Tomorrow I shall get Margaret to see John Lovell. We're desperately in need of help, and we must tackle this immediately.'

'Yes, you *must* do that,' said Isobel, 'for everyone's sake.'

Alan sat, turning the empty mug round and round in his hands. At last he broke the silence.

'I'm sure that you both guessed poor Margaret's trouble long ago. After her mishap in Lulling High Street, I don't think anyone had any doubts about things here.'

'I'm afraid people have known for some time,' said Harold, 'but, believe me, the general feeling is of great sympathy. I haven't heard a word of criticism. After all, this is just as much an illness as, say, pneumonia.'

'Not so simply dealt with though,' replied Alan, with a sigh. 'It all began when Margaret had what the medicos call post-natal blues. She never really got over them, and that's when the drinking began.'

'Did you get help then?'

'To some extent. The doctor we had then was very under-standing, and for a time she seemed better. Then I got this job, and she was alone all day, and it began again. It was the main reason for deciding to buy this place, where I felt I could keep an eye on her and she would not feel so lonely. But, as you see, it just hasn't worked out.'

'But why,' asked Isobel gently, 'didn't you get help from the doctor again?'

'Our old doctor has now retired, and frankly Margaret was so ashamed of herself she simply refused to see John Lovell.'

'Well, I'm sure he will be of enormous support to you,' said Harold rising. 'I suspect that he will be mightily relieved to be asked to help. And now we'll be getting back.'

At that moment, the lights came on again, bathing the room in unusually bright light after the mellow illumination from the oil lamp.

'Thank heaven!' cried Isobel. 'Now you will be all right.'

'Not quite "*all right*",' said Alan with a wry smile, 'but better able to cope.'

He put an arm around Harold's shoulders, and thanked him again. To Isobel's surprise he kissed her cheek. He was obviously deeply moved by all that had transpired.

'I shall never be able to thank you adequately,' he said, opening the door, 'but thank heaven for good friends at Thrush Green.'

Two days later Alan arrived at the Shoosmiths' house bearing a magnificent dark red azalea which he presented to Isobel.

'Come in,' cried Harold. 'How are things going?'

'Margaret's coming to see you herself later on. She's with John Lovell at the moment, at the surgery, picking up some tablets.'

'Can he help?'

'Indeed he can. He's been absolutely marvellous, and has fixed up an appointment at a clinic he knows well and thoroughly recommends. With any luck, Margaret will be able to go there within the week.'

'So she is really being co-operative?'

'Absolutely. I know it's early days, and she knows herself it's a long hard road to go, but she was so shattered about events the other night that she said at once we must get the doctor to help.'

'You must let us help too,' said Isobel. 'How long will she be away?'

'Difficult to say, but a few weeks probably.'

'And how will you manage?'

'I rang my mother, and she is coming down to stay for as long as she's needed.'

'She sounds a trump.'

'She certainly is! She's known about this from the start, and helped a lot when we were in the old house. She's lived alone since my father died, and she says she will shut up the house, and come as soon as I ring her.'

'Do the children know?'

'I've simply told them that their mother is ill and needs treatment, and have left it at that. Alison knows what it is, I'm quite sure, but she doesn't speak about it. Kate doesn't seem to have twigged, thank heaven. They both adore my mother, so they'll be happy with her.'

'Well,' said Harold, 'things certainly look more hopeful, and we are so relieved to know that Margaret is getting medical help.'

'It certainly takes some of the burden from my back,' confessed Alan. 'I fear poor Margaret is in for a tough time, but at the moment she is absolutely determined to be cured. She wants to come and thank you herself for all you did.'

'Oh please,' begged Isobel, 'don't let her worry about that. She may find it painful, and she's enough to think about as it is.'

Alan looked grave. 'She wants to do it,' he said soberly, 'and I think it will do her good to tell you about this trouble. Look upon it as one of the first steps towards rehabilitation. That's how I see it, and I think Margaret feels that way too.'

They watched him stride across the green to meet his wife at the surgery.

'I feel desperately sorry for that fellow,' said Harold, as they closed the front door.

'And I feel desperately sorry for the whole family,' replied Isobel. 'It makes you feel that you will never touch alcohol again, doesn't it?'

'Speak for yourself,' said Harold.

16. CHRISTMAS AND AFTER

December had hardly begun before all the frenzy of Christmas began to break out.

At the village school the windows were dotted with blobs of cotton wool representing snow flakes; paper chains hung across the class rooms and frequently collapsed upon the children beneath, much to their delight.

Every time a door opened a powdering of imitation frost, Christmas cards in the making, and pieces of embryo calendars fluttered to the floor, followed by excited children attempting to retrieve their property. The usual pre-Christmas chaos prevailed.

The ladies of Lulling and Thrush Green were busy preparing to raid local hedges and gardens for holly and ivy to decorate St John's and St Andrew's churches, as well as making wreaths for front doors and the graves of those departed and at rest in the churchyards.

The Lulling shops were filled with anxious customers wondering if elderly aunts would appreciate tea-cosies fashioned as sitting hens, or whether it would be better to play safe with yet another bed-jacket.

Husbands were busy buying enormous flasks of fabulously expensive scent, with names such as 'Transport' or 'Vive', destined to end either down the bath drain or as a raffle prize at a future bazaar.

In the electricity showroom, the annual display of a snow-white cooker decked with tinsel stood in front of the window, and the somewhat battered plaster turkey stood on top of it. The inhabitants of Lulling looked with affection upon this old friend. It really would not be Christmas without its reappear-ance, although it was beginning to look uncommonly dark – almost burnt – with advancing age.

At The Fuchsia Bush the results of Nelly's art filled the window: iced cakes clad in gold and scarlet frills, Dundee beauties topped with almonds, and pyramids of mince-pies brought in admiring customers.

In the few days before Christmas, activity rose to fever pitch, and when the ladies of Lulling, having their pre-Christmas shampoo and set, were offered a glass of Cyprus sherry as they sweltered under the driers, it was quite apparent that the festive season, in all its fury, was upon them.

Christmas Day was its usual mild and green self. The children's hopes of heavy snow, tobogganing, making snowmen, and sliding on the ice, were dashed yet again, but their spirits were greatly restored by the plethora of presents, the rich food and the indulgence of their parents.

Out in the country the necessities of work went on un-changed: Percy Hodge attended to his cattle, fed the hens, and moved his small flock of sheep to an adjacent field. As the daylight began to fade he went indoors, followed by the faithful Gyp, fed the dog, made up the stove, and went to his bedroom to change into his best blue serge suit.

Mr Jones, looking out from the window of The Two Pheas-ants, caught a glimpse of Percy's Land Rover as the farmer drove towards Lulling.

'And I wonder what he's got as a present for Doreen,' he commented to Mrs Jones, who was resplendent in a new scarlet cardigan, her husband's Christmas present.

'Might be an engagement ring,' surmised Mrs Jones.

'That wouldn't surprise anyone,' said Mr Jones. 'It's the *wedding* ring that's going to be Percy's problem.'

There was general but nicely-concealed relief when January arrived.

'Good to get back to normal,' said one to the other. 'We had a lovely meal of lamb chops today, and the turkey carcase is simmering for stock.'

'Won't be long before the children are back to school,' the mothers comforted each other.

Dotty Harmer, with her usual forthrightness, summed it up when talking to Betty Bell. 'I love Christmas, always will. But what a lot of fuss! I feel convalescent until mid-January.'

'That's only because you are getting on,' Betty told her, reaching up to unpin Christmas cards from the banisters. She stopped her endeavours to study one of them.

'This is pretty, but I can't make out the message.'

Dotty took it from her. 'It's Latin, dear. "Celebrating the birth of our Saviour", it says. Did you learn Latin at school?'

'What, down the Secondary? Not likely! Us girls was lucky to get a half-hour's Domestic Science as it was called then, and that was only about washing your hands before making pastry, which we all knew anyway from our mums.'

'You really didn't miss much,' observed Dotty. 'It's a tiresome language. How the Romans ever managed to converse I can't imagine. They had the verb at the end of the sentence, you see, Betty.'

'Can't say I do,' puffed Betty, retrieving a drawing pin from the floor.

'For instance, they might say: "Caesar, seeing that the day would be fine and clear, summoned his centurions and their assembled cohorts, with their weapons and a vast array of horses and" – well, what do you think, Betty? "Had breakfast"? "Changed his socks"? "Sang a ditty"? "Faced the enemy"? You see what I mean? *Such suspense* for the listener!'

'I must say,' agreed Betty, 'it seems a bit silly. Perhaps Domestic Science was more my mark after all.'

By this time Margaret Lester was away from the school house, and Alan's mother was in charge. She was a small brisk

Yorkshire woman, and the house was spick and span within twenty-four hours of her arrival.

Margaret had gone to the hospital recommended by John Lovell a few days before Christmas, and she remained there while the festivities were going on, at her own request. So far, Alan told the Shoosmiths, she was making a determined effort to overcome her problem, and the treatment she was getting was excellent.

Alan and his mother did everything possible to ensure that the little girls enjoyed their motherless Christmas. They were invited to several children's parties, including John and Ruth Lovell's and, as is the way with children, did not appear unduly cast down by their mother's absence.

Certainly, Mrs Lester senior was soon welcomed into the world of Thrush Green, and as she was an accomplished bridge player, she spent several happy afternoons at neighbouring houses once the school term started.

Isobel Shoosmith grew very fond of this near neighbour as the weeks passed. She admired her energy, her practical ability and her shrewd appraisal of people. Spotless washing billowed on the school house clothes-line on Monday morning and Thursday morning, and the old-fashioned baking day took place on Fridays when the school house was fragrant with the scent of freshly-baked pies, sausage rolls and jam tarts, as well as such traditional north country delicacies as parkin for the cake tin.

Alison and Kate looked relaxed and cheerful under this new regime. Undoubtedly they had sensed the tension in the household earlier, and were aware of their father's anxiety whenever their mother had immured herself in the bedroom.

They appeared to have forgotten the terrors of that black night which had taken them trembling to the Shoosmiths' door, and everyone tried to make the little girls' path as easy as possible while their mother fought her lone battle away from home.

*

One of the first people to call on Alan's mother was the rector, Charles Henstock. He had heard the rumours of Margaret Lester's trouble as had many other people in Lulling and Thrush Green, and had visited the house as soon as the Lesters had moved there. Now, months later when the news was out, he took to calling at the school house more often, and found a warm ally in Alan's mother, as well as Alan himself.

Alan and his mother seemed glad to discuss Margaret's condition, and the rector seemed remarkably well-acquainted with drink problems, much to Alan's surprise.

'Parsons aren't quite as unworldly as we may appear,' Charles told him, with a smile. 'We get our share of drunkards in country parishes, you know.'

'I haven't noticed a great many reeling out of The Two Pheasants,' commented Alan.

'Jones keeps a respectable house,' responded Charles. 'And so do most of the Lulling publicans. I'm afraid the trouble occurs when too much is taken in the home, as was case with your poor wife. At least she was never violent with it. I know at least four cases in my parishes where the men absolutely terrify their families.'

'What do you do?'

'Remonstrate, of course. Usually to little effect. Then I try to get them to Alcoholics Anonymous who do wonders. My good friend Anthony Bull told me about them. He gets far more problems in his town living, and is far better at coping with them than I am, I fear. But I do try to comfort the families.'

'And that,' Alan assured him, 'you do superbly.'

'I agree,' said his mother. 'Now I'm going to mash the tea, and you must try some of my Grasmere gingerbread.'

News of Margaret Lester's absence from Thrush Green had reached as far as Barton-on-Sea, for Isobel and Agnes had kept in touch by telephone ever since the two schoolteachers had retired.

Dorothy and Agnes discussed the situation as they sat by

the fire one grey January afternoon. Dorothy's attitude was inclined to be censorious. Agnes, less worldly, was more sympathetic.

'It must make a difference to the school,' commented Dorothy, lowering the crossword to her lap. 'I'm sure the parents must be unhappy at the thought of all that going on behind the scenes.'

'Isobel says that she has only heard sympathy for the poor man,' said Agnes. She was nursing Tim, fondling his ears which he particularly enjoyed.

'But it must mean that he is unable to give complete attention to the running of the school, Agnes. And as you well know, that is a *full-time* job.'

'He seems to be doing very well.'

'I'm not sure,' said Dorothy meditatively, 'that he shouldn't consider giving up the post in the circumstances. What an example to the children!'

Agnes ceased stroking Tim's ears. 'But surely, he's setting a very *good* example to the children! He's behaving bravely, carrying on his job, caring for his poor wife and children—'

At this moment Timmy, offended by the neglect of his ears, leapt to the floor, in a state of umbrage. Agnes bent to apologize.

'It doesn't alter the fact,' said Dorothy severely, 'that he has rather more to cope with than a normal headmaster should. I was never too sure that he was the right man to take over from me. It now seems my forebodings were justified.'

Agnes knew better than to argue when Dorothy was in this trenchant mood. Silently she attempted to lift the cat back to her lap. But Tim was not to be mollified, and stalked to the door.

'That cat,' remarked Dorothy, 'is getting too big for its boots. Teddy says he thinks we overfeed it.'

Sometimes, thought poor Agnes, I should like to scream when Teddy's name is mentioned, which seems to be every ten minutes.

'I don't think that Teddy knows very much about cats,' she ventured.

'He's never had one,' conceded Dorothy, 'but he really is most knowledgeable about *dogs*. In his time he has had two corgis, three cocker spaniels, and a Norfolk terrier. All devoted to him, of course.'

'Eileen told me that he doesn't seem to like her dog.'

'Well, naturally. You know how badly-behaved it is. Eileen is quite incapable of training anything. Far too indulgent. All young things need a little discipline now and again. Teddy says that he and his brothers were very strictly brought up, and you see how well it has stood him in good stead in his affliction. Never a complaint passes his lips. An example to us all.'

The maudlin expression on Dorothy's face as she pronounced this eulogy was almost more than Agnes could bear. She rose to let the ungrateful cat make his exit, then returned to her armchair.

'How's the crossword?' she said brightly, intent on diverting the subject from Teddy.

Dorothy rose to the bait. 'Well, I really can't see what DAIRY CATS have to do with architecture, but according to the clue, which may be erroneous of course, there is some connection.'

'CARYATIDS,' pronounced Agnes, and took up her knitting.

January grew steadily colder as the month progressed. The newspapers displayed chilling photographs of Scottish shepherds on skis searching for their flocks, and trains marooned in snowy wastes awaiting help from helicopters.

Further south, rescuers and rescued were shown taking shelter in the Izaak Walton Hotel at Dovedale in Derbyshire, and intrepid skaters at Cambridge were depicted attempting to reach Ely on the ice.

Even as far south as Barton-on-Sea the snow fell, and freezing fog and icy roads kept Agnes and Dorothy indoors for several days.

Dorothy began to get restive one Friday afternoon. 'I really think I should make the effort to call on Teddy. He so enjoys my reading to him, and I'm sure he must find this weather as depressing as we do.'

But within five minutes, while she was still resisting Agnes's attempts to dissuade her, the telephone rang and Eileen was in conversation.

'I really don't think you should venture out, Dorothy,' Agnes heard her say. 'It's not just that the roads are so slippery, but Teddy has an appalling cold, and I've forbidden him to move from the fire.'

'In that case,' said Dorothy who had become rather pink in the face, much to Agnes's alarm, 'I feel I should come and see him.'

'He says he would rather you didn't.'

'Oh, really?'

'He's so anxious that you might pick up the infection. You see you haven't had any flu jabs. I'm so glad I did, it gives me much more confidence in a case like this. No *please*, Dorothy, put off your visit until I let you know how my patient is.'

'Very well,' said Dorothy, in a tone as icy as the outside world. 'Give him our love, and I hope he will soon be better.'

She put down the receiver with unnecessary force, and turned to Agnes. 'I expect you heard all that – Eileen's voice is exceptionally loud. Obviously, I am not wanted there at the moment.'

'Perhaps it's as well,' said Agnes.

'What I *cannot abide*,' said Dorothy ferociously, 'is the perfectly dreadful proprietorial attitude that Eileen takes over Teddy! Anyone would think she *owns* the man! He will have to put her in her place one day. Her behaviour is outrageous!'

Agnes remained silent.

The cold spell was particularly severe in the Cotswolds: the stone houses crouched like sheep in the snow drifts, and many of the dry stone walls had vanished completely beneath the blanket of snow. The birds, fluffed out with the cold, sat motionless in the black hedges or lined the rafters in barns and out-houses, seeking what shelter they could from the bitter weather. The smallest birds, such as the wrens and tits, sought comfort in garden nesting-boxes, and huddled together for warmth.

Flocks of rooks swept the sky, searching the inhospitable fields beneath them for food and cawing mournfully. The farmers had rounded up their cattle and brought them down to fields and yards nearer the farm. Water was a problem: field pumps had frozen, water pipes burst and everyday living was a constant battle in these cruel surroundings.

People struggled on foot to the shops for such essentials as meat and bread, and one enterprising baker drew a sledge through the streets of Lulling to deliver his loaves.

Cars had been abandoned on many of the more exposed hills, and at one stage it was only possible to get through the lanes around Thrush Green in high vehicles such as Land Rovers.

The sky remained grey and fresh snow fell frequently,

smoothing over the black ribbons made by tyres and the inky footsteps of each day's activity. Old people and young children were kept indoors, all longing for a return of sun and freedom.

At the village school the numbers were almost halved, for children living at any distance could not make the journey, and coughs and colds kept others in their beds. Simply keeping warm was as much as most people could undertake.

It was in this inhospitable period that Margaret Lester was driven home in an ambulance, the only safe vehicle to manage the main roads from the clinic to her house. She emerged, looking like a ghost, pale and dark-eyed, to be enveloped by her husband's arms and the happy greetings of her family.

The door closed behind her. The ambulance started on its return journey, and Margaret was left to continue on the long hard road to recovery.

17. CHANGES FOR THE BETTER

The thaw came at the beginning of February. It brought with it fog, filthy roads and influenza. The last remnants of snow lay along the roadside in dwindling heaps, discoloured by dirt thrown up by the passing traffic.

Under the hedges, beneath the dripping leaves, more snow lingered, fretted with the claw marks of innumerable foraging small birds. Mist floated in the valleys with no wind to disturb it, and the River Pleshey moved sluggishly between the bleached dead grass of its banks.

It was a dispiriting time, and the only comfort was that life could begin again, in a torpid manner, as the icy roads cleared and people began to move about their daily business.

It was a great pleasure to Nelly Piggott when the Bingo sessions began again. The hall had been shut through the worst of the weather, for few people left their firesides after dark, and the practical difficulties of keeping the large hall heated and cleaned proved impossible.

Mrs Jenner called for Nelly and the two women made their way down the hill to their evening's amusement. Gladys Lilly did not appear.

'She may well be down with this flu,' surmised Mrs Jenner. 'I know Doreen's been off work this week with it.'

Nelly, who had been consumed with curiosity for months about the possible romance between Mrs Jenner's brother Percy and the young girl, felt that she could do a little circumspect investigation.

'A nice girl. Your Jane thinks the world of her. Your brother was very good to her too, when she was took bad that day. Does he still keep in touch?'

Mrs Jenner, who was no fool, realized that Nelly was avid for information. Normally she would have been somewhat terse in reply for she disliked gossip and, as a nurse, had been trained to be discreet. But she was fond of Nelly, and would not wish to snub her.

'To tell the truth, I don't take much interest in Percy's affairs. He's never been the same since his Gertie died, and made a fool of himself over a lot of silly young things, as everyone knows.'

'It's understandable,' said Nelly tolerantly, 'men being what they are. Poor tools really, compared with us.'

'Exactly!' agreed Mrs Jenner. 'But I know no more than you do, Nelly, about Percy and Doreen. I did have a quiet word with Jane, but she says the girl hardly ever says very much, and in any case she'd be extra careful when speaking to Jane, her being Percy's niece, you see.'

'Well, who knows?' said Nelly cheerfully. 'It might turn out very nicely. Gladys has brought her up proper, good at cleaning and cooking, and that little Bobby is as nice a child as you could meet in a month of Sundays. Percy could do a lot worse, I reckon.'

By this time they had reached the hall. It was noisier than usual, as people greeted each other after their enforced absence and compared notes on burst pipes, leaking roofs, coughs, colds and all the other ills of a hard winter.

'Good to have a bit of company,' cried Nelly to her friend, as they settled down to a convivial evening. To be sure, she had not learned anything about the Percy–Doreen affair from Mrs Jenner, but no doubt time would tell.

At Thrush Green, Margaret Lester was slowly coming to terms with life. The spring term was now in its stride, and with the worst of the weather over, attendances became more normal.

Alan Lester watched his wife with acute anxiety. She was still as adamant as she was on her return that no alcohol should be allowed into the house. Some medical men, she told Alan, were of the opinion that a tiny amount now and again could do no harm to those trying to break the habit, but Margaret, in her zealous mood, would have none of it, and Alan thought that she was right.

He thought that it was right too that she talked freely about the dangers to their children. She could not forgive herself for what might have happened on the night of the power cut, and was filled with such horror and remorse that Alan sometimes wondered if this bitter self-torture might be holding back her full recovery.

His tough old mother was more realistic. 'She's working things out in her own way, and in her own time,' she told him when Margaret was out of the room. 'It is one way of keeping her off the bottle, which is the main thing, and she is getting it out of her system with this suffering. I know it's distressing for you to watch, when you've been laid open to all these wishy-washy ideas that things should be easy for everybody, but I was brought up to fight the good fight, and to recognize the devil as well as the angels. And it's fighting that's going to be poor Margaret's salvation.'

Old Mrs Lester certainly was a tower of strength to the family during these first weeks of Margaret's return. It was planned that the whole family would go to Yorkshire at half-term, to take Alan's mother back and to give them all a change of scene.

Meanwhile, Isobel and Harold, in company with other friends nearby, gave as much attention as they could to the family. The little girls were invited out frequently. The Shoosmiths took Margaret out with them on their afternoon strolls. Winnie Bailey and Ella Bembridge had pleasant hen-parties which included both Mrs Lesters. There was no doubt about it; what with her own determination, fears of what-might-have-been, and the support of family and friends, it was apparent that Margaret had every hope of winning her battle.

When the first pale rays of spring sunshine emerged, life started to look more hopeful. The snowdrops, aconites and crocuses began to bring colour to the gardens, and along the road to Nidden yellow tassels of catkins waved from the hazel bushes.

Seed catalogues were studied, and orders sent for stocking the kitchen and flower gardens. Travel brochures, adorned with sun-bronzed men and maidens with enviable teeth, hair and figures, were browsed over in the homes at Thrush Green and Lulling. Should it be Greece this year? Or Spain perhaps, or even Turkey? What about taking some savings out of the Lulling Building Society and having a real splash somewhere in the Bahamas?

Most of these day-dreams were shattered by programmes on the television of fractious infants, exhausted mothers and bad-tempered fathers, jammed together in airport lounges for hours on end, awaiting flights which failed to materialize.

The brochures were thrown away. What was wrong with dear old Ilfracombe anyway?

Hardy souls such as Ella Bembridge took their first long walks of the year, striding along enjoying the exercise and the heady smell of spring in the air.

Those who were just over bouts of the widespread influenza tottered out for a few turns in the lanes, well-muffled up against any chill in the air, and felt greatly relieved to get back to the comfort of their armchairs after ten minutes or so.

Among this last category came Doreen Lilly and Gladys, each holding the hand of young Bobby. They came slowly up the hill and stopped to speak to Albert Piggott who was picking up litter by the church gate and depositing it in his bucket. Most of it came from careless customers at The Two Pheasants, for although Mr Jones provided a conspicuous litter-bin, there were always a few untidy consumers who preferred to fling their litter to the ground.

When the wind was from the west, a certain amount ended up by the churchyard, much to Albert's fury.

He was glad, as always, to stop work.

'Say "Good morning" to Mr Piggott,' prompted Gladys.

'I've 'ad the flu,' said Bobby with pride.

'Oh-ah!' said Albert.

'*And* my mummy. She 'ad the flu.'

'Oh-ah!' said Albert again, looking at Doreen. She smiled but said nothing.

'But my Granny never,' continued the child.

'I was the lucky one,' said Gladys briskly. 'We thought a little fresh air would do us good.'

'We're goin' to Uncle Percy's to see the lambs,' volunteered Bobby.

Albert became more alert. 'Better watch they don't bite you,' he said.

The child looked at his mother with alarm, but she remained silent.

It was Gladys who answered. 'Mr Piggott's making a joke,' she explained. 'Lambs don't bite. Now, come along or we'll be late.'

They nodded farewell and continued their journey towards the farm.

Albert crossed the road to The Two Pheasants.

'That girl don't say much, do she?' he said to Mr Jones. 'Cat had her tongue, I shouldn't wonder.'

'I like a quiet woman myself,' said Mr Jones diplomatically. 'Maybe she's shy.'

'Not shy enough, to my way of thinking,' commented Albert censoriously. 'Anyway, old Perce is "*Uncle* Percy" now. I suppose he'll be "*Daddy* Percy" before long.'

'I shouldn't count on it,' advised the landlord. 'Not with Percy's record.'

It was on one of these early spring mornings that an extraordinary event took place in the house of the three Misses Lovelock.

It was the custom each morning for Violet to make a pot of Earl Grey tea in her bedroom, and to take a cup to each of her sisters.

Years before, of course, there had been a resident maid who would mount the stairs with a jingling tray and distribute the tea. She would also pull back the curtains, and comment on the weather in Lulling High Street.

Those days had disappeared long ago, and Violet, with great initiative, had bought herself a tea-making machine which she installed in her bedroom and learnt to manipulate with commendable speed.

She quite enjoyed the early morning ritual, and Ada and Bertha were grateful for her service. Each sister kept a tin of biscuits in her room. Violet favoured Gingernuts, Ada Rich Tea, and Bertha stuck to Digestive. Sometimes the cup of tea, with a dip into the biscuit tin, was all that was required by way of breakfast as the ladies grew older and frailer.

On this particular morning, Violet carried in Bertha's cup and found her sister sitting bolt upright and looking rather flushed. She nodded her thanks as Violet deposited the steaming cup on the bedside table, and patted the bed, inviting her sister to sit.

'What is it, dear?' asked Violet.

'Spring-cleaning,' said Bertha.

'It's rather early to be thinking of that,' countered Violet.

'We'll start in here,' announced Bertha. 'This room has become most frightfully cluttered. Why have you brought up so much rubbish from downstairs?'

'You brought it up yourself, Bertha.'

'Nonsense! Why should I want all the silver and some of the furniture too! It *hampers* me. It must be cleared away.'

By now, Bertha was becoming much agitated, and Violet decided to humour her.

'Well, we must make some plans, dear. Meanwhile, drink your tea while it's hot, and I'll come in again when I'm dressed.'

By that time, Violet surmised, her sister would have forgotten all about it, and the day would proceed in its usual way.

But she was wrong.

When, some half an hour later, she opened Bertha's door, it was to discover a scene of complete chaos. Wardrobe doors stood open. Every drawer gaped, and the unmade bed was piled with an assorted jumble of silverware, porcelain, photoframes and bric-à-brac of every variety.

'Bertha!' cried Violet aghast. 'What on *earth* are you doing? I've never seen such a mess!'

'Must make a start,' puffed Bertha, now scarlet in the face. She threw a silver tankard, presented years before to their father, on to the bed, dislodging a heap of smaller articles which cascaded to the floor.

Violet took charge. She forcibly pushed Bertha into a wicker chair, and stood over her.

'You will give yourself a stroke, rushing about like this, and then where shall we be? Just leave everything alone, get dressed, and Ada and I will help you to put everything away later this morning.'

Bertha seemed to see reason and shrugged her shoulders. 'Very well,' she replied, with immense dignity. 'We'll spring-clean later on.'

Without speaking, Violet collected Bertha's underwear from beneath a pile of assorted objects, and put the articles by her.

'I'll be back,' she said at last, and went to apprise Ada of this latest domestic upheaval.

Later she returned, meeting Bertha on the stairs. Her sister was carrying a large silver tray piled precariously with small objects.

Violet took it from her and preceded her to the drawing-room, where she deposited the tray on a sofa.

'Now sit down, Bertha, and we may as well sort out this pile now.'

'Such an odd collection,' replied Bertha, who seemed quite calm. 'Do you know, I'm sure we have a silver coaster that is Charles Henstock's. And a pair of sugar tongs that I distinctly remember seeing at Ella's. Why on earth did they give them to us?'

Violet, who knew very well the acquisitive nature of her sister and indeed had been equally guilty on occasions, decided to ignore the question.

The two articles mentioned were on the tray, and she quietly put them aside. She also returned a pair of silver vases, three photoframes and a pair of candlesticks to the mantelpiece.

'It looks better at once,' said Bertha approvingly. 'It was a very silly idea of yours to lumber up to my bedroom with all this stuff. And some of it, you see, not even belonging to us. It looks so dishonest.'

'It does. Shall we go upstairs and fetch some more?'

After an hour or two of sorting out, all three ladies were exhausted and decided to have lunch, which could only be biscuits and cheese with tinned pears to follow, then their usual short rest, before continuing with their labours.

What was really peculiar, thought Violet, as she lay on her bed after lunch resting her aching bones, was the way in which Bertha had put aside all those pretty pieces which had been begged, permanently borrowed, or simply purloined over the years, and those which were legitimate Lovelock property. Could there be some deep-seated guilt which had been suppressed all these years? Was this frenzy of activity a form of remorse? Or was Bertha simply suffering from another mental breakdown, and would she be her usual inconsequent and kleptomaniac self by morning?

It seemed best, thought Violet, to go along with this spring-cleaning urge. At least, it restored Bertha's hoard to their rightful places in the house, and a lot of prized objects to their rightful owners. It was not going to be simple, thought Violet uneasily, explaining the return of such valuables as Ella's tongs and Charles's coaster, but it would just have to be done. Bertha's eccentricity would be a good excuse.

Wearily, she clambered from her resting place and went into Bertha's still cluttered bedroom.

The clearing of the room, and its return to comparative normality, took the three sisters the best part of a week to complete.

Bertha still maintained her air of perplexity about the amount of things collected in her room, and it was apparent to Violet that nothing much could be done about it. Was Bertha genuinely confused, or was she deliberately blaming others for her own behaviour? Violet guessed rightly that no one would ever know.

The only practical thing to be done was to return other people's property, and this unwelcome duty she undertook.

It was humbling to find how kindly friends responded to her apologies. In truth, the Misses Lovelocks' ways were such common knowledge in Lulling and its surroundings, that it was quite a pleasant surprise to see their property again.

'I must admit I had wondered where that coaster had hidden itself,' said Charles. 'It was one of a pair that Anthony Bull gave us one Christmas, with two bottles of exquisite Claret. I am delighted to know it is safe.'

Ella was equally understanding about her purloined Victorian sugar tongs. The Shoosmiths welcomed back a bonbon dish, and also collected a cigarette box which had been Miss Watson's. The Youngs were glad to see an Edwardian dolls' tea-set again, and John Lovell was delighted to receive a silver ash tray which he had never missed.

All in all, Violet had an easier time than she had envisaged as she returned these long-held objects, and was grateful that no recriminations were forthcoming. It was, she felt, really more than she deserved, and said much for the generous spirit of their old friends.

As the days lengthened people's spirits rose. It was good to get out and about again in the light, and to go and come back from an afternoon tea-party without having to remember a torch.

The sun appeared almost every day, and gardeners were already busy. So were the birds, flying with grass and feathers trailing from their beaks, as they set about nest-building. Prudent housewives were already planning dates for the chimney sweep, the window-cleaner and painters and decorators.

The January sales were far behind, and Lulling shops already displayed summer hats and frocks, and even swimsuits for those who had been bold enough to book a holiday abroad.

It was a heady time, and at Barton-on-Sea Dorothy broached the subject of a few days away.

'We both need a change,' she declared. 'You've looked quite peaky ever since that last cold, and my hip is definitely getting arthritic. Somewhere fairly flat, I think, don't you? What about East Anglia? I had a wonderful cycling holiday there as a girl.

Hardly ever needed to get off, you know, the slopes were so gentle.'

'There are some splendid churches,' said Agnes. 'We could go on day-trips by bus perhaps, if we found somewhere central.'

'We should have the car for that,' said Dorothy. 'I'm not so arthritic that I can't drive.'

Agnes fetched the engagement calendar, and the two ladies studied it.

'Very little on in the next few weeks,' commented Dorothy. 'I can swap church flower duties with someone, and we can cancel that Conservative lunch.'

'Good! I was already wondering what to wear. My best suit needs cleaning.'

'There's just Teddy, of course,' mused Dorothy, tapping the calendar with her pencil. 'Still, I should think Eileen could read the newspaper to him quite as well as I do.'

'Not *as well*,' said Agnes, 'but *adequately*, I expect, for such a short time.'

At the end of the month the schools of Lulling and Thrush Green broke up for half-term.

The weather continued to be mild, and the Lesters were ready packed to get off early on the Saturday morning. Alan's mother had said her farewells, and promised to return to the village in the summer.

'Or earlier if I'm needed,' she confided to Isobel, 'but I pray it won't be necessary. So far, so good. I can't tell you how I admire Margaret over this affair. She's doing splendidly.'

'She had your help,' pointed out Isobel, 'and the support of the family.'

'That was very little really. She knew it was a case of self-help, and she's stuck to it.'

Later, Alan came round to leave the key and the Yorkshire telephone number. 'I think I've switched off everything possible,' he told Harold, 'but no doubt I shall remember something vital when we're halfway up the Ml.'

'Then ring us,' smiled Harold. 'Go and enjoy yourselves. See you next week.'

Ten minutes later they saw the Lesters drive away, a bevy of hands fluttering their goodbyes.

18. The Birthday Party

Miss Bertha Lovelock had been born on February the twenty-eighth in a Leap Year. Her mother had often told her how narrowly she had missed being born on the last day of February in a Leap Year, and the horror of having only one true birthday every four years.

This particular year was Bertha's eightieth birthday, and Violet intended that the occasion should be marked by a party. It would only be a *small* one, all the sisters agreed, just for a few old friends, and after considerable thought and discussion it was decided to have a modest tea party at the house.

Consequently, Violet went next door one morning to The Fuchsia Bush to order a birthday cake, two dozen scones and other small cakes for the celebration.

Mrs Peters attended to her, and was extremely helpful. She was fond of her eccentric neighbours and Bertha's pilfering was now, everyone hoped, a thing of the past.

'Not too rich a mixture,' said Violet. 'We shall all be elderly, and not able to digest anything too heavy.'

'None of our produce is *heavy*,' protested Mrs Peters, stung by this criticism of her wares, 'but I do understand. Would you prefer a madeira cake, suitably iced, of course?'

Violet pondered awhile. 'No. I think a fruit mixture, but without brandy perhaps. I will leave the recipe to you and Mrs Piggott. I feel sure it will be delicious.'

'I wonder,' said Mrs Peters diffidently, 'If you would like one of my girls to come in and wait on you? It is early closing in the town on that day and we are never busy then. I could spare Rosa or Gloria for two or three hours if it would help.'

'That is most kind,' said Violet sincerely. 'We shall be about ten or twelve altogether, and should be glad to have one of the girls.'

So it was left, and Mrs Peters also made a note to order a small bouquet to be taken in as a tribute from all at The Fuchsia Bush. It was a great relief to have things on an even keel again. Keeping the boat upright, she thought, as she bustled about her duties, was a tricky job anywhere. Next door to the dear old Lovelocks, it was doubly so.

The great day was blessedly mild and sunny.

Violet took a suitably celebratory breakfast, the brownest boiled egg, boiled lightly, to her sister, and she and Ada sat sipping their tea as Bertha unwrapped their presents.

Ada had given her a silk scarf which all three recognized as a Christmas present to Ada from a distant cousin. Naturally nothing was said about this, but the three frugal sisters secretly approved.

Violet's gift was a box of Floris soap, and this she had actually bought at the local chemist's. It was much appreciated.

'Now you must take things gently today,' said Violet. 'Ada and I are going to cut a few sandwiches after we've had our afternoon rest, and then we shall dress in readiness for our friends.'

'Are they all coming?'

'Well, no, dear. I think I told you yesterday that the Bulls are abroad, and Ella is staying with a school-friend in Scotland.'

'So who are we expecting?'

'The Henstocks, the Venables, and Winnie Bailey. There's just a chance that Dotty Harmer will come, but she was expecting some wire netting to be delivered, and particularly wanted to see the man as the last lot started disintegrating far too soon, according to Dotty.'

'Oh dear! I wonder how long she had had it?'

'Since Coronation Year, I gather, but Dotty thinks it should have gone on for another ten years or so.'

'Well, we must just hope that we will see her,' said Bertha, putting aside the breakfast tray. 'Anyway, it is going to be a lovely day for me. I suppose *eighty* really is a great age?'

Her sisters assured her that it was indeed an achievement.

It had been decided, when plans for the party had been drawn up, that only the Lovelocks' contemporaries would be invited. Anthony Bull and his wife were the exceptions.

Justin Venables – known locally as 'Young Mr Venables' to distinguish him from his father, now long-dead, and his wife, had grown up with the Lovelocks. They had attended the same dancing classes in Lulling, fox-trotting to 'Tea For Two' and 'She's My Lovely', in the far-off twenties and thirties.

They had shared picnics in ancient open cars, made up parties for the local Hunt Ball, and attended private dances at some of the large houses in the surrounding countryside. They had organized innumerable projects for charity, and had seen Lulling change from a sleepy little Cotswold market town to a busy community in which strangers thronged the streets, and far too much traffic struggled to pass through.

It was an altered world, but their memories of the past held them together with ties which endured.

Dimity and Ella, though a little younger, had also played a close part in the sisters' lives, and Dotty Harmer, who was almost exactly the same age as Bertha, was another friend who had shared in the early Lulling activities. The fact that her father had been a much respected (perhaps 'feared' would be more truthful) headmaster of the local grammar school for many years, strengthened Dotty's position as a pillar of society in the town.

Charles Henstock had appeared in Lulling some time after the war, and although he knew little of the Lovelocks and Venables in their youth, was welcomed as a man of the cloth and, later, as Dimity's husband.

It was the absence of Anthony Bull which caused Bertha the greatest regret. Her admiration for this handsome priest was absolute, and his was the first name she had put on her list.

However, it had to be faced. Anthony and his wife had promised to go to Italy with another couple, and the hotel and flight had been booked for months. Bertha had to be content with a congratulatory cable, and an arrangement of spring flowers from Interflora from the absent Bulls.

By half-past three the ladies were in a flutter of anticipation: Bertha was resplendent in navy silk, Ada in pearl-grey, and Violet, as the youngest, quite dashing in coral-pink.

True to her word, Mrs Peters had sent in Rosa complete with a sheaf of daffodils and irises, and a card saying:

'From all at The Fuchsia Bush
Congratulations and Best Wishes'

Bertha was much touched. Violet, watching her, wondered if any trace of guilt added to her sister's high colour, but dismissed the thought as unworthy of this occasion.

Justin and his wife arrived first, bearing a large box of Bendick's mints which they knew Bertha loved. The Henstocks came a few minutes later with a bottle of Bertha's favourite eau-de-cologne, and Winnie arrived with a box of exquisite linen and lace handkerchiefs.

The birthday cake stood on a side-table, and everyone agreed that The Fuchsia Bush had excelled itself. Ada and Violet's sandwiches were sampled, the buttered scones were passed round by Rosa, who was seemingly awed by her surroundings and the venerability of the guests, and all went swimmingly.

The conversation, rather naturally, was of the past.

'And Justin was a demon on the tennis court,' Bertha told Charles. 'A terrible smashing service he had, I remember.'

'So did Winnie,' Violet reminded her. 'She was one of the first Lulling ladies to serve over-arm. We were all greatly impressed.'

'And do you remember your first car, Justin?'

'Only too well. It let me down on Porlock hill which wasn't too awful, but when it practically exploded in Lulling High Street, my father said it was a disgrace to the firm and that clients would be taking their affairs elsewhere.'

Back and forth the reminiscences flowed as Rosa cleared the tea things away. The cake was to be cut a little later, and taken with a glass of champagne. This was Violet's idea, and she had kept the champagne a secret, knowing full well that she would have been chided for gross extravagance if she had told Bertha earlier.

The sun was still shining, and the company took a turn about the garden to admire the crocuses and the budding daffodils. Secretly, Justin grieved over the neglected state it was in. In their young days, a full-time gardener had been employed, and the kitchen garden had produced all that was needed to supply the Lovelock family and staff. Now a young man came once a fortnight to cut the shabby lawns and the weeds in the borders were strangling the perennial pinks and peonies and roses which had once been the pride of the family.

The outside paintwork, he noticed, was also neglected and flaking. Some of the Cotswold roof tiles had slipped, and one or two were missing. It was sad to see such a noble property in disrepair, but he knew that the Lovelocks' parsimony would never let them spend even the smallest amount on repairs, and this project would certainly need several thousands to put it back into its former state.

Well, he thought, as they followed their aged hostesses indoors, maybe it will last the old ladies' time, and then let's hope someone with money, and love, will take it over. On their return to the house, they were met by an untidy figure, who was being divested of her coat by Rosa.

Dotty Harmer had arrived.

'Well, what a lovely surprise!' cried Bertha. They pressed their wrinkled cheeks together. 'We had quite given you up. Tea, Dotty?'

'No, thanks. I've just had a cup with the wire-netting fellow.'

'Then you are in time for a slice of my cake. Do sit down.'

There were general greetings as Dotty handed a small parcel to Bertha who began to unwrap a square jeweller's box with some trepidation. One could never be quite sure of Dotty's offerings; it might well be some rare beetle found in her garden, or a fossil from her father's collection.

Fortunately, the little box contained a brooch, a circle of seed pearls surrounding the letter B in gold.

'But, Dotty,' protested Bertha, suitably touched, 'this is much too valuable to give away. Am I right in thinking it was your mother's?'

'Quite right, Bertha. She was "Beatrix", you know, and I thought it was only right that you should have it.'

'Then thank you *very* much. I shall treasure it.'

She began to pin it on the lapel of the navy silk frock, amidst general admiration.

Rosa now opened the champagne with a suitably celebratory pop and the glasses were filled while Bertha began to cut the cake amid polite cheers. When they were settled, Charles stood up, raised his glass and asked everyone to drink to the health of their good friend Bertha.

'Well,' said that lady when this had been done, 'I suppose I ought to say something.'

'Indeed you should,' said Justin.

'What shall I say? Just how delightful it is to have so many old friends here today. I only wish dear Anthony could have been here, too.'

'We all wish that,' said Charles.

'Why *Italy*?' enquired Dotty waving her glass, and splashing Dimity's best dress. 'The food is so indigestible, and the meat so scarce, and really the way they treat their animals is quite appalling. I read only the other day—'

'Dotty, dear!' said Dimity reprovingly, and Dotty subsided.

'I was going to say,' said Bertha, with some hauteur, 'that I particularly wanted Anthony here today as I have a little project of mine to tell you about.'

'About animals?' asked Dotty animatedly.

Charles Henstock began to look alarmed. What on earth was Bertha about to disclose?

'I think we ought to have a proper memorial in the church to celebrate Anthony's ministry here,' announced Bertha.

'His name has been added to the list of vicars on the chancel wall,' interposed Charles gently.

'That's as maybe,' rapped Bertha, who was now trembling with excitement. Two red spots had appeared on her cheeks, and her eyes flashed. Could the champagne have something to do with it, wondered Rosa?

'I intend to leave all my money to St John's, as some of you may know, with directions about the sort of thing I have in mind as a public tribute to dear Anthony.'

'But, Bertha . . .' protested Justin. He was ignored.

'Something worthy of the man. No piffling little plaque or a pedestal for flowers. I had in mind something in the way of a large stained-glass window, or perhaps a new Organ. The present one wheezes dreadfully at times. Most irreligious.'

'Anthony wouldn't want that,' said Dotty. 'He hated any sort of ostentation. You think again, Bertha dear. Give a nice dollop to some charity he suggests. He was always very generous to the RSPB, I recall.'

This unusually sensible suggestion of Dotty's was met with a murmur of approval from the company. Most of those present were acutely dismayed by Bertha's proposals; Justin, as her solicitor, was frankly appalled, and her two sisters were becoming increasingly distressed as Bertha's agitation grew.

'I shall do exactly as I like,' shouted Bertha, 'with my own money! No one, not even my own sisters, has really appreciated all that Anthony Bull did for Lulling. I am absolutely adamant that he should be remembered!' She pointed a shaking finger at Justin. 'I shall be in your office tomorrow to alter my will, Justin. If it's the last thing I do, I shall honour dear Anthony with some fitting memorial in the church he served so well.'

She pulled a handkerchief from her pocket, and began to dab at the tears which now coursed down her papery old cheeks.

'So *nobly*,' she added, sniffing. 'With such *distinction*! With such *inspiration*!'

'There, there!' said Dimity, putting an arm round Bertha's shaking shoulders. 'You are over-tired. It has been a wonderful party, but I feel we should go now.'

Bertha looked about her in a bewildered manner. 'Please do. I can't think why you are all here anyway. Some idea of Violet's, I suppose.'

'Bertha, *please!*' protested Violet and Ada in unison.

'Now what have I said?' demanded Bertha fiercely. 'All I've done is to tell you what I propose to do. Charles knows all about it anyway. I can't understand why you are all so silly. And why have we got this sticky cake for tea? You know I much prefer madeira or seed, Violet. So extravagant!'

By this time, the Venables and Henstocks had risen, and were making their farewells. Ada and Violet, almost in tears themselves, saw them to the door.

'She's simply over-excited,' said Charles to the two agitated sisters. 'Don't worry about it. We've thoroughly enjoyed the party and if I were you I should see that she goes upstairs to rest.'

'You are so understanding,' quavered Ada. 'Do you think she really will buy a stained-glass window, or a new organ?'

'No, I don't,' said Charles. 'Don't think any more about it.' The last thing the departing guests heard as they descended the steps to Lulling High Street was Dotty's voice advising Bertha.

'You'll have the devil of a job getting anything done in the church, Bertha. Consistory courts, ecclesiastical faculties and I don't know what. You spend it on the animals. I can give you the address—'

The closing of the front door terminated Dotty's harangue.

The four old friends were in a state of shock as they walked together to their homes.

The two women were ahead, and discussing anxiously not only Bertha's extraordinary proposal, but also the possibility of a mental breakdown.

Justin and Charles were having their own less feverish conversation.

'An unhappy end to a jolly party,' said Charles.

'As you say,' agreed Justin.

'Is it possible for her to change her will?'

'It's possible,' said Justin, 'but highly unlikely. As you can see, she is quite unstable.'

'I feel so sorry for the other two.'

They kept step with each other, their breath now showing in the chill of evening.

'Did you really know anything about this crazy idea?' asked Justin at length.

'She mentioned it some weeks ago,' said Charles uneasily, 'but I thought it was just a passing whim.'

'I think it is. I don't propose to do anything about it, and I am quite sure she will not turn up at my office. Ada and Violet will see to that, though it's my belief Bertha will have forgotten all about the business by morning. In any case, I can handle all this.'

'Thank heaven for that,' sighed Charles. 'I only hope that Anthony doesn't come to hear of it. The very idea would horrify him. I tremble to think how he might react.'

By now they had reached the Venables' gate and caught up with their ladies.

'You need never tremble on Anthony Bull's behalf,' laughed Justin. 'He can cope with any situation in the world, which is why Bertha admires him so much.'

And on this cheering note, they parted.

19. SEVERAL SHOCKS

The Lesters returned from Yorkshire looking all the better for their break, but within a week of taking up his teaching duties Alan Lester had been smitten with influenza. Dr Lovell was called to the school house three days later when it was obvious that something more severe than the usual influenza was involved.

'He won't eat or drink,' Margaret told him agitatedly.

John Lovell surveyed his prostrate patient and felt his stomach. 'It's gastro-enteritis as well as the common bug that's been plaguing us all.'

He left two pills, a prescription, and a stern order 'to keep drinking'. 'And see that he does,' he told Margaret as they went downstairs. 'Don't worry, he's going to be all right in a day or two. I'll be in again tomorrow.'

It was certainly a vicious viral attack, and Alan Lester was too weak at the end of five days to return to work. A supply-teacher, well-known in the district, came to hold the fort until he was fit to resume his duties.

Margaret nursed him diligently, administering pills at the appointed times, making up jugs of lemon barley water, washing and ironing innumerable pairs of pyjamas, and changing the bed linen.

'I'm afraid she will exhaust herself,' Isobel said to John Lovell when she enquired about his patient. 'She's not a hundred per cent fit herself.'

John Lovell smiled. 'It may be tough luck on Alan,' he said, 'but it's the best possible luck for Margaret at the moment.

Concentrating on someone else's trouble is a sure way of forgetting your own.'

In her weekly telephone call to Barton-on-Sea, Isobel told the ladies about the stricken headmaster and Mrs Hill who had come to take his place.

Dorothy Watson was far from pleased when she heard this, and said so to Agnes. 'Well, I only hope she doesn't have too much to do with teaching reading to the younger children. You know how pig-headed she was about the "Look-and-Say" method. That, and that alone! The arguments I had with that woman about the need for using *all* methods! I told her, time and time again, that the children knew the red card said "Stand up" and the blue one said "Go to the door", and the one with the corner off said "Hands on heads", so that the children didn't really *read* them at all. I proved it to her one day, as you may remember.'

'Very well indeed,' said Agnes hoping to stem the flood of outraged memories, but in vain.

'I put the same sentences on the blackboard,' Dorothy continued remorselessly, 'and could those children read them?'

'No, they couldn't,' said Agnes dutifully. 'You certainly proved your point there.'

'I only hope that poor fellow gets back to school before she does *irreparable* harm,' said Dorothy. It was plain that she was still very much The Teacher.

'Would you like me to ring that hotel in Bury St Edmunds? It sounded very pleasant, didn't it?' asked Agnes, changing the subject.

'Yes, that would be kind of you. And if they can't have us, I will try Lavenham tonight.'

Having successfully dislodged Dorothy from her hobby-horse, Agnes went to the telephone. Really, one trembled for dear Dorothy's blood-pressure at times like this!

*

It was at about this time that Doreen Lilly was observed in the company of a handsome young man.

Only close neighbours of Gladys and Doreen first noticed him, and he was dismissed as a family friend, a cousin perhaps, or someone breaking his journey from London to the west. As it happened, the last guess was nearest the mark, for the young man was the window cleaner with a mother in Cirencester. He had befriended Doreen in London, where he worked, and had returned her to her mother, with young Bobby, months before. He had called once or twice since then, usually after dark, so that his visits had gone unobserved. Now, it seemed, he was paying the daughter more regular attention.

It was soon common knowledge in Thrush Green, and Jane Cartwright mentioned it to her mother one day.

'Not that Doreen says anything. I never get a squeak out of her, though she is always polite and a very good worker. If anything does come of this, I shall really miss her.'

'I've heard nothing,' said Mrs Jenner, 'but if Gladys Lilly says anything about it, I will let you know.'

'What about Uncle Percy? Do you think he's heard the rumours?'

'I really don't know. Percy's quite old enough to run his own life, and if he's silly enough to imagine a young girl is going to make him a wife, then he should know better. Heaven knows he's been jilted often enough! Look at Emily Cooke! Surely he's learnt his lesson from that affair.'

'I don't think Uncle Percy will ever learn,' said his niece sadly. 'All I know is I'd like to see him settled. He really needs a good wife.'

'Well, that's his problem,' said Mrs Jenner, and the conversation turned to other matters.

The general opinion was that poor old Perce was going to come another cropper, and the situation was observed with some amusement and very little sympathy. Not surprisingly, among the most unfeeling was Albert Piggott. He took it upon himself to find out Percy's reactions to this delicate matter one cold March morning.

The grass of Thrush Green was shivering in an easterly wind, and the rooks above the fields behind The Two Pheasants were being blown about the sky, cawing raucously.

Albert was sipping his half-pint when Percy arrived. The newcomer blew on his fingers and made for the fire.

'Coldest we've had all winter,' he remarked.

Albert nodded. 'Bad weather for lambin',' he rejoined. 'Well, bad for all young things.'

Percy did not respond to this remark, simply ordering a pint from Mr Jones and turning his back to the comfort of the fire.

'I said it was bad weather for *all young things*,' repeated Albert loudly, intent on leading up to the matter he had in mind.

' 'Tis that,' agreed Percy, collecting his tankard. 'There's a new baby at the Cookes', they say.'

'What *another*? Not your Emily's, I hope?'

Percy began to look irritated, just as Albert intended.

'She's not my Emily, as you well know. And no, it ain't her baby. It's the young sister's, if you must know. And they're both pretty poorly, so I gather.'

'That's bad,' commented Mr Jones, a kindly man.

'I expect she asked for it,' said Albert. 'These young girls are all kittle-cattle. They take up with whoever comes along. Look at Doreen Lilly now.'

This did cause some reaction from Percy, who put his tankard down, and turned towards Albert.

'What about Doreen?'

'Got some new young man hangin' round her, they say.'

'Who says?'

'Well, most everybody. Some chap from London she met when she was workin' up there. Nice-lookin' bloke. Quite the film star.'

'She's a pretty girl herself,' said Percy equably. 'You can't wonder she gets a follower or two.'

He drained his glass, wiped his mouth on the back of his hand, and nodded to the landlord.

'Must be off. Got some sheep dip to pick up. Be seein' you, Albert.'

The door slammed behind him, and a gust of chilly air swirled about the room.

'You didn't get much change out of him,' observed Mr Jones, putting another log on the fire. 'And serve you right, Albert Piggott, trying to stir up trouble.'

'Silly old fool asks for it,' growled Albert, but he had the grace to look discomfited.

Meanwhile, at the Lovelocks' house things continued their erratic course.

On the morning after the disastrous birthday party, Violet went into Bertha's bedroom bearing the usual cup of tea. She had had a poor night herself, tortured with remembrances of the humiliating end to the party. The question of the will hung over her. Would Bertha go ahead with this deeply embarrassing plan? Would Justin be able to cope with it? Could Bertha really put in hand such a preposterous plan as the ordering of a stained-glass window, or an organ? Come to that, would Bertha decide on something even more extravagant: a side chapel, say, or a complete reorganization of the interior seating? Really, there was no end to the list of follies which her poor sister might decide to undertake. And would she be stopped? And if so, by whom?

She found Bertha sitting peacefully in bed, brushing her sparse locks with a silver-backed hairbrush. She smiled at Violet.

'Oh, lovely! How I do look forward to this first cup of tea! So sweet of you, dear, to provide it.'

'And how did you sleep?' enquired Violet, remembering her own disturbed night.

'Like a top, dear, after that lovely party. It all went so well, didn't it? I am so grateful to you and Ada for making it such a perfect day.'

Violet stood in silence, looking out of the window at Lulling High Street which was already busy with traffic. It was quite apparent that Bertha was not going to admit to any of the unpleasantness that had occurred. Was this intentional, or did she really forget anything disturbing?

She left Bertha sipping her tea, and returned to her own bedroom. She had come to a conclusion which was to support her throughout the years to come. She must simply take Bertha as she found her, day by day. It had to be faced. Bertha was slightly mad. She was senile, and quite erratic. In the future, she must be cared for as one would care for any patient with mental trouble. It would involve constant supervision, hopefully at home in the house they had shared all their lives, but if need be, in some suitable institution.

Meanwhile, she knew she had the support of John Lovell, Justin Venables, and dear Charles Henstock. With such a powerful trio behind her, Violet felt that she could cope with all that life with Bertha might bring.

After a fortnight away from school, Alan Lester tottered back to his classroom. He felt ten years older, and looked it too. Why was it taking so long to recover, he asked the doctor querulously.

'Because you were thoroughly run down when this hit you,' John told him. 'You've been under appalling strain for years now. I have a theory that those days in bed are nature's way of making you let up.'

'But it's absolutely absurd,' protested Alan. 'I walk across to the school and have to sit down to get over it. Then I try to write on the blackboard, and I can scarcely get my arm up. Can't you give me something to put some spunk into me? I'm a walking zombie.'

'I'll give you a tonic,' promised John. 'Just take things gently, and you'll be yourself again in a few days.'

The doctor was not the only one to supply jollop. When Betty Bell related the fact of Alan Lester's prolonged convalescence to Dotty, that resourceful lady produced a large bottle filled with a murky liquid which had already corroded its metal cap.

'Now, this is just the thing,' Dotty told her. 'You take this to the school house, Betty, and tell the poor fellow to take a tablespoonful three times a day. It's a wonderful pick-me-up. One of my old aunt's recipes. It has rose-hip syrup and black treacle in it.'

'What else?' asked Betty suspiciously.

Dotty looked flummoxed. 'Now what was it? Certainly horehound and a bunch of garlic, so good for the chest. And I am sure there were half a dozen other things, all wholesome of course, I will look at the recipe if you like.'

Betty said she was not to bother, accepted the bottle, and privately determined to warn the patient to leave it sealed. She confided her decision to Harold Shoosmith some days later, and he heartily approved.

'Well, I was afraid it might explode in his face,' said Betty. 'It looked dangerous to me. Do you reckon it might have been any good?'

'As paint-stripper maybe,' replied Harold.

Isobel was able to tell her Barton friends that the headmaster had returned to his duties, and that Mrs Hill had now departed to brush up her 'Look-and-Say' method of reading for her next session as supply-teacher in the district.

Dorothy sounded greatly relieved. 'And I will ring next week, Isobel, for we're setting off in a day or two for our little break. We shall be at The Swan at Lavenham. Such a good centre, and we were very well looked after there last time.'

Isobel sent her best wishes for the jaunt, and asked about Timmy.

'Oh, Eileen is looking after him. And Teddy too,' was the reply.

I wonder, thought Isobel, as she put back the receiver, who will worry most? Agnes about Timmy, or Dorothy about Teddy?

The day before the ladies were due to depart from Barton, they suffered an appalling shock.

The packing was half done, and last-minute duties attended to: the newspapers had been cancelled, the milkman instructed to leave only half a pint each time for Timmy's use, and the spare keys deposited with Eileen. The maps were ready on the hall table, the coffee flask waiting in the kitchen and Agnes had already put out the clothes she intended to wear on the journey.

They were having their after-lunch rest when the telephone rang, and Agnes answered it. Dorothy sat up, alert. It was Eileen's voice at the other end, and it sounded strained.

'Such a dreadful cold. I was coming up to tell you the news, but frankly it wouldn't be fair to you, just as you are going off.'

'What news?' enquired Agnes.

'Well, dear, we both wanted you and Dorothy to be the first to hear – Teddy has asked me to marry him.'

There was a little cry, hastily checked, from Dorothy. Agnes found herself trembling, but kept her voice steady.

'But that is wonderful!' she said. 'Congratulations!'

'It won't be for some time, but no point in waiting about at our age. I only wish I hadn't developed this appalling cold. I think I must have caught it from Teddy.'

There was another choking sound from Dorothy, who now hurried to the bathroom. Agnes heard the bolt slam home. Her heart sank.

'This won't make any difference,' Eileen was saying, 'to my looking after Timmy. I shall be quite fit enough to pop along tomorrow when you have gone. Is Dorothy there? I should like to tell her our news.'

'She's not at the moment,' said Agnes truthfully, 'but I shall pass on the message. I know she'll be as delighted as I am.'

'Teddy asked me to give you the news. He said women are so much better at these things.'

The great coward, thought Agnes indignantly!

'Well, our love and congratulations to you both,' said Agnes. 'We'll ring before we go, and if you are not up to it, I will ask Mrs Berry to see to Timmy, so don't worry about that.'

She hurried to the bathroom door.

'Are you all right, Dorothy? I expect you heard?'

'I heard,' said a muffled voice, 'and I'm quite all right.'

Reluctantly, Agnes returned to her chair. Her heart was thumping in an alarming way, and her hands trembled as she picked up her knitting. Poor, poor Dorothy!

She seemed to be a very long time in the bathroom, and Agnes's anxiety grew. Was she prostrate with grief? Had she collapsed on the floor, perhaps striking her head on the wash-basin and now lying stunned? Could she – dreadful thought! – be contemplating *suicide*?

The bathroom cupboard certainly held medicine, but nothing much more toxic than aspirin, TCP and calamine lotion. To be sure, there was a bottle of disinfectant for the lavatory. And prisoners in cells sometimes *hanged* themselves, but apart from the belt of the bath-robe there was really nothing to hand in the bathroom in that line. In any case, Agnes thought wildly, that hook on the door would scarcely stand the weight.

It was really devastating, decided Agnes, knitting furiously, how one's mind encompassed a hundred horrors in the space of a minute. If she did not pull herself together she would be mentally choosing the hymns for Dorothy's funeral, and wondering if the Distressed Gentlefolks Aid Association could do with her clothes.

At that moment, Dorothy returned from the bathroom and

stood with her back to Agnes, gazing out into the garden. Her hand clutched the wet ball of her handkerchief, which she was turning round and round.

Agnes dared not speak, and waited with a pounding heart for Dorothy's first words.

'Thank you for coping with that, my dear. I couldn't have spoken. I simply couldn't.'

'I understand. It's been a shock to us both.'

Dorothy went back to her armchair. Her face was blotchy, but the tears had gone. 'I've been a fool, Agnes.'

'That happens to us all,' said Agnes gently. 'It doesn't really matter, you know. Just don't upset yourself. I think Eileen will make Teddy a good wife. After all, they've known each other for many years.'

'Well, I'm not forecasting anything,' said Dorothy with a slight return to normality. 'It's their affair. I shall ring Eileen, and Teddy too, this evening, to congratulate them.'

'That's right,' said Agnes approvingly. 'We must leave things comfortably here before we set off tomorrow. It's a very good thing we are having this break. It will do us both good, and we shall be able to come back and face their wedding.'

'Do you think we'll be invited?' asked Dorothy in alarm. 'I don't think I could face it.'

Agnes was silent for a moment, gazing in dismay at her knitting. 'I've done at least two inches of *moss-stitch* when it should be *rib*,' she cried. 'I shall have to unpick it.'

Dorothy rose. 'I shall make us some tea,' she announced. 'I don't care if it is only three o'clock. We both need it.'

Agnes heard her in the kitchen, filling the kettle for that never-failing help in times of trouble.

To her surprise, Dorothy reappeared within a minute. 'What I cannot *stomach*,' she told Agnes fiercely, 'is the way *Teddy* asked *Eileen* to break the news. So like a man!'

'Just what I felt,' cried Agnes. 'Men are such *cowards*!'

Neither of the ladies slept well that night. Dorothy, though proud of her good behaviour on the telephone that evening to Eileen and the perfidious Teddy, still smarted from self-recrimination over her conduct during the last months. It was hard to accept the fact that one had been foolish and invited ridicule. She thought of Agnes's kind remark about everyone being foolish at some time. It gave her some slight comfort.

In the adjoining bedroom, Agnes's thoughts were more anguished, mainly on her friend's behalf. Certainly Dorothy had appeared calmer as the evening had progressed, and her congratulatory messages to Eileen and Teddy had been done most graciously. Agnes, knowing how much she was suffering, was immensely proud of her. But was it a good thing to suppress her feelings, wondered Agnes, as she lay worrying in the small hours, still unable to sleep.

Those dreadful moments considering Dorothy's possible suicide in the bathroom came back to torment her. Was Dorothy *really* over it? Or would she do something senseless within the next day or two, suddenly distraught? Agnes recalled reading about some unhappy person who had driven deliberately straight into a lamp-post after being crossed in love. And only last week she had read about another poor fellow driving over a precipice to his death.

Well, thought Agnes, trying to find some crumb of comfort,

there were not any precipices between Barton-on-Sea and Lavenham.

And on that somewhat unsatisfactory thought, she fell into an uneasy sleep.

20. WEDDINGS

As if to compensate for the wretched winter, March grew more balmy as the days passed.

At Thrush Green, the sticky buds on the chestnut trees were beginning to sprout tiny green fans, and the stark hedges were softening with young leaves. Daffodils and early tulips brightened the gardens, and at the edge of Lulling Woods the banks were starred with primroses. Beneath the hedges, hidden in dead silky grass, blue and white violets lurked.

Chaffinches, tits and other little garden birds foraged ceaselessly to feed their nestlings, and Percy Hodge's lambs skittered about their field, bleating with the excitement of youth and fair weather.

Altogether it was a heartening time, and people were glad to get outdoors and greet each other without shivering in the wicked east wind which had cut short many a neighbourly conversation earlier.

Alan Lester recovered his strength, and the fact that the schoolchildren could spend their playtimes out of doors, running off their high spirits, greatly helped him through his convalescence.

As John Lovell had predicted, Margaret had thrived on the nursing she had been obliged to undertake. She was now taking a much more active part in the affairs of Thrush Green, and Ella Bembridge and Muriel Fuller were largely responsible for this.

Now that their part in preparing the new room at Rectory Cottages was finished, the two needlewomen were at a loose

end, and fairly jumped at Charles Henstock's diffident suggestion that St Andrew's could do with some new hassocks.

With considerable energy, not to say bullying, they had roped
in half a dozen helpers, including Margaret Lester, who was an
accomplished needle-woman; the choosing of designs, colours
and types of wool and canvas engaged all the ladies as spring
fever inspired them. This led to other activities, especially for
Margaret, who found herself, before the month had ended, not
only secretary to the Women's Institute, vice-president of Lulling Brownies and the Red Cross, but also a part-time assistant
at the Sue Ryder Charity shop. Alan's relief in her rehabilitation
knew no bounds, and Thrush Green rejoiced with him.

Dotty Harmer too was imbued with this spring fever, and
decided to supply the ducks with a sloping ramp to ease their
access to the pond. She had asked Albert's advice on the
project, and he had weaned her from the ambitious plan of a
concrete structure to one involving less work for himself. A nice
wooden plank, he told her, would be just the thing, and could
be lifted out for a good scrub if it grew too slimy.

Dotty saw the sense of this, and once it was installed she had
the delight of watching her tiny yellow ducklings waddling up
and down the slope. Even Albert's flinty heart was softened
by this domestic scene, and felt pride in the result of his suggestion for the ducks' convenience. He told Nelly about it when
she returned one evening from The Fuchsia Bush.

But Nelly had news of her own. 'That young chap who's
courting Doreen came in today. She was with him, and little
Bobby. I bet there's a wedding there before the summer's out.
Gladys will be glad, I should think. There's not much room in
that place of hers with Doreen and the boy.'

'Maybe they'll all go and live there,' suggested Albert,
looking, as usual, on the gloomy side.

'Rubbish!' snorted Nelly, whisking away his empty plate.
'Gladys will see that doesn't happen. She won't want a great
useless man under her feet any more than I do.'

Albert took the hint, and made his way over to The Two Pheasants.

The mild weather was widespread, and Agnes and Dorothy enjoyed their change of scene.

Isobel had a call from them in the middle of the week, to say that they had decided to make a detour on their way home and would call to see them if it was convenient.

'Of course!' cried Isobel. 'What a lovely surprise.'

'And we want you to have lunch with us,' continued Dorothy, 'at The Two Pheasants, if you will be kind enough to book a table. Better say one o'clock, or a little after. We intend to make an early start, but it's impossible to guess what hold-ups there will be these days. Even *here*, in *Suffolk*, there is an amazing amount of traffic.'

She spoke as though East Anglia should be in the horse-and-cart stage, and seemed to resent the fact that it was as congested as the rest of England.

Isobel commiserated, thanked her for the lunch invitation, and promised to do as she asked.

She went to tell Harold the news. 'So nice of them,' she commented. 'They really have made themselves a peaceful pleasant life since they moved to Barton. They don't seem to have a care in the world.'

Needless to say, she knew nothing as yet about poor Dorothy's damaged feelings, and Agnes's concern for her companion.

Harold Shoosmith, on his walk to The Two Pheasants to book a table for four, met Mrs Jenner who was on her way to visit her daughter at Rectory Cottages. They agreed that it was good to see the sun, that it made one feel ten years younger, that it was about time they had a decent spell of weather, and after these necessary civilities they parted.

Jane Cartwright was in her little office filling in forms. She rose to greet her mother.

'Doreen's just been in. She's definitely engaged to that young man and, of course, I'm glad for her sake but we'll all miss her.'

'Why? Is she likely to move from Lulling? Can't he get a job here? I could do with a good window cleaner myself.'

'He's evidently got a lucrative round in London, hotels and shops, that sort of thing. And he's got a flat too, so of course they'll set up home there.'

'Gladys will be relieved anyway,' surmised Mrs Jenner. 'Maybe I'll hear more about it tonight at Bingo.'

Gladys Lilly seemed only too pleased to enlarge on the news of Doreen's future as she, Nelly and Mrs Jenner dallied over their coffee during the Bingo interval.

'He's a good fellow,' she enthused, 'and Bobby likes him. It's time that child had a man to deal with him now and again. Our Doreen's too soft with him. Looking back, I can see it was a blessing in disguise when that second little stranger came to nought.'

Her companions sighed, and nodded sadly in agreement.

'One's one thing,' went on Gladys, 'but a chap's going to think twice before taking on two.'

'That's right,' agreed Nelly.

'So when is the wedding?' enquired Mrs Jenner.

'Next month. Just down the registry, and then a quiet buffet lunch at my place.'

'Very suitable,' approved Mrs Jenner.

Gladys Lilly began to fidget with her gloves, and looked unusually coy.

'And that's not all,' she went on. 'I'm thinking of getting married myself.'

'No!' gasped Nelly.

'I'm glad to hear it,' said Mrs Jenner warmly.

Gladys became even more agitated. 'Well, I hope you'll still be glad when I tell you who it is. You see, it's your brother Percy who's asked me.'

'Well, I'm blowed!' cried Nelly. 'And we all thought—'

Mrs Jenner cut in before the sentence could finish. She leant across the table, and kissed Gladys's flushed cheek.

'Of course I'm glad! It's the best day's work Percy ever did, and I couldn't wish for a nicer sister-in-law.'

Nelly imparted the great news to Albert that night when he returned from The Two Pheasants at closing time.

It was gratifying to see his stunned expression.

'Never thought old Perce would have so much sense,' was his comment eventually.

'Mind you,' said Nelly, 'she's getting the worst of the deal, if you ask me. That place of his will want cleaning from top to bottom, and Percy don't like parting with money, like some others I know of not a hundred miles from here.'

Albert ignored this side-swipe, still bemused by Percy's good fortune.

'They say she's a good cook too,' he was muttering to himself. 'D'you reckon she's throwing herself away on old Perce? I mean, he's no great catch, is he?'

'Very true,' agreed Nelly, setting the kitchen table for breakfast with her usual rapidity. 'But then what man is?'

She stopped suddenly, clutching a handful of cutlery to her well-filled cardigan.

'You see, it's *love*,' she told Albert. 'That's what makes people do these silly things. *Percy's* a lucky chap, but I only hope poor *Gladys* don't live to regret the day!'

Such exciting news soon spread like a bush fire through Thrush Green and Lulling; it was generally agreed that this was a most suitable marriage, and that Percy was an extremely lucky fellow. No one, said the gossips, could be more capable of coping with that neglected house and poor lonely Percy than Gladys Lilly, who had always been much respected in the neighbourhood. Why, she might even get Percy to attend chapel, and that would be a real advance!

Charles Henstock told Dimity that he was delighted on Percy's behalf, and had always thought that a marriage made later in life was usually successful. Why, look at his own! It would have been nice if he could have officiated at the wedding ceremony, but he supposed that Gladys would wish to have it at the chapel, or perhaps they would simply have the civil ceremony at the registrar's office.

Dotty Harmer told Albert, when he came to inspect the duck ramp for signs of wear, that Gladys Lilly was one of the most sensible women she knew, and always kept a pot of goose-grease to rub on chests suffering from winter coughs and congestion.

Winnie Bailey and Jenny greeted the news with relief: at last Percy would stop pestering Jenny and all the other young girls who had excited Percy's amorous inclinations in the past.

Mrs Jenner and Jane were much in favour of the union, and the thought of her old home being restored to its former cheerful state gave the older woman great happiness. The neglected garden too, she guessed, would soon be put into good order, and her brother's disreputable appearance would change for the better with Gladys to feed him properly, mend his clothes, and send him regularly to the barber's.

Percy himself went about in a daze of happiness. He had to stand a good deal of banter, but was so pleased and proud that he accepted all the jibes with a smiling countenance, and even stood a round to his cronies at the pub.

Doreen Lilly's forthcoming marriage did not promote quite so much interest. After all, she was young and pretty, bound to marry sometime, and in any case, the chap was a foreigner, wasn't he? Nevertheless, Charles Henstock felt that Anthony Bull should know what was happening to Doreen and her mother, and rang him one evening.

'Splendid news!' said Anthony heartily. 'She was such a pathetic little waif when I saw her last. I hope you'll let me know her address when they come to London eventually. I should like to keep in touch. And as for Gladys, I remember her so well, and her first husband's lardy cakes. Give them all my congratulations.'

The day of Dorothy and Agnes's visit dawned fair and cloudless, and the ladies arrived a little before one o'clock, happy with their successful negotiation of a new route.

'Really no bother!' cried Dorothy. 'Agnes is a first-class navigator. We did find that Milton Keynes kept getting in the way, I must confess, but once we left that behind it was plain sailing.'

They had a celebratory glass of sherry while they exchanged news, and then walked across the grass to The Two Pheasants.

The children were still at play before afternoon school, and Alan Lester, who was on duty, hurried to greet the two teachers.

'Do come in. We'd all love to see you. You haven't met my wife yet, and she would be so pleased.'

But the ladies explained that they had to be off soon after lunch.

'Then next time! I'm sure there will be a next time,' said Alan, looking enquiringly at the Shoosmiths.

'Indeed there will,' cried Isobel. 'We hope they will be here again very soon.'

A Land Rover was parked outside The Two Pheasants, and a black and white collie had its head out of the driver's window.

'Why, it's Percy Hodge's dog,' exclaimed Dorothy, stroking the silky head. 'It's so good to see that it hasn't suffered from that wretched accident.'

'No harm done,' said Percy, who had just emerged from the pub looking unusually spruce, and in the company of a middle-aged lady.

Dorothy was surprised and relieved at Percy's affability. He had remained somewhat surly after she had slightly injured Gyp, and their subsequent encounters had been definitely frosty.

Yet here he was, positively beaming at them!

'This is my wife-to-be,' he announced with pride, and all was revealed to the bemused ladies. There were congratulations all round, and Dorothy patted Gyp with renewed affection before the couple drove off, and the Shoosmiths ushered their visitors into the bar where they were welcomed warmly by Mr Jones and his wife.

They returned to the Shoosmiths after lunch, and Dorothy was taken down the garden by Harold to collect a cutting of winter jasmine which he had kept for her.

It gave Isobel and Agnes a chance to exchange confidences.

'And is Dorothy still attentive to Teddy's needs?' asked Isobel.

The flood-gates opened, and Agnes described the dreadful consequences of Eileen's telephone call, remembering how sympathetic Isobel had been when the matter of Teddy had cropped up earlier when she was staying there.

'She has been so brave,' Agnes said. 'After the first awful shock she pulled herself together, and I hope this little break has given her time to come to terms with things.'

'Poor Dorothy!'

'I just dread meeting Eileen and Teddy face to face. It might well open up the wound for Dorothy, and I really don't think I could bear to see her suffer so again.'

'Dorothy will cope,' said Isobel. 'You see, things will be easier than you imagine. I'm sure that the future will be much as you both planned it when you went to Barton-on-Sea.'

Dorothy returned, farewells were said, and the ladies set off homeward.

Agnes dozed part of the way, and woke with a start to find that they were within a few miles of home. Her fears came flocking back like menacing birds. How would Dorothy react to this return to familiar things? Would she be able to keep up this brave front of calm? Would she be able to face Teddy and Eileen in their new role of those about to be married?

These thoughts, as well as the hope that their house would be free from flood, fire and burglars, kept Agnes in a state of severe agitation.

Dorothy turned the car into their lane. They passed Teddy's house and Eileen's opposite it. All was calm and deserted.

'Two weddings at Thrush Green,' said Dorothy, 'and another to look forward to here.'

And Agnes saw, to her intense relief, that her friend was smiling.

EARLY DAYS
A Childhood Memoir

* * *

Miss Read

From the author of the bestselling
FAIRACRE *and* THRUSH GREEN *series*

'The larks were in joyous frenzy above. The sky was blue, the now distant wood misty with early buds, and the air was heady to a London child. A great surge of happiness engulfed me. This is where I was going to live. I should learn all about birds and trees and flowers. This is where I belonged . . . This was the country, and I was at home there.'

Early Days is alive with vibrant childhood memories of an extended family of grandmas, uncles, aunts and cousins, and their houses – full of mystery and adventure – where Miss Read lived in the shadow of the First World War.

At the age of seven, Miss Read moved to a small village in Kent, into a magical new world where her love of the English countryside grew – a passion that would be found in her much-loved novels. Her evocative descriptions of the village school, the joys of exploring the woods and lanes, toffee-making and riding on the corn-chandler's cart, vividly convey this time as one of the happiest of her life.

Full of unforgettable characters, tender memories and the colourful intrigues of everyday life, *Early Days* is a charming and affectionate insight into the childhood of a bestselling author, and a bygone era.

ISBN: 978 0 7528 8220 8
UK £7.99